DIAMOND REEF

A CHASE GORDON TROPICAL THRILLER

DOUGLAS PRATT

MANTA
PRESS

For Ashlee

1

The clanging of the halyard against the mast finally got through to me in my sleep. I lifted my head that had been buried into a pillow. The ports were covered, blocking out the majority of the light; the cabin was stuffy and humid, and the smell coming off me was equally offensive. My sheets were damp with sweat, and my hand wiped my sweat-drenched hair back. The locks were hanging past my ears after four months without a barber in sight.

Reaching over my head, my fingers twisted the knobs to open the hatch. Usually, I would switch the little air conditioning unit on when I'm connected to shore power and the hatches are closed. I was lucky to get into the slip before the storm hit last night, and I was too tired to really care. So, now I was covered in sweat, and my aroma was close to week-old-gym-sock level. Making matters worse, I hadn't seen a shower in several days. The whole boat probably smelled like that. The rear hatch was still closed because of the rain, I realized, limiting the breeze.

The sun had already set, and the last bits of daylight

were quickly dissipating as I got into the marina. After pounding my way across the Gulf Stream for most of the day, I ended it with a race against a lovely squall that shifted direction into my path. I had been cruising and gunk-holing my way around the Bahamas for the last four months in my sailboat, a Tartan 40 named *Carina*. After securing the last lines as the rain pounded down, I wasted no time in shedding the rain suit and soaking wet clothes and falling into my berth naked and exhausted.

Unless the weather is storming, like last night, all the hatches remain open. The sea breeze flows through the cabin and keeps the temperature tolerable, especially at anchor. If the boat is in a marina, often the sea walls and other structures block the wind meaning that hatches don't get enough air movement, and the cabin turns into a sweatbox. That's a good reason for staying out of the marinas.

Personally, that's an easy feat. I enjoy the secluded islands and empty coves that offer unlimited fishing and snorkeling.

Pumping the handle on the faucet in the galley, I filled the coffee pot with water. The water gurgled a bit from the spout. My tanks were getting low on water, and my coffee stores were also getting pretty low. Actually, most of my food and staples were running low. That's part of the reason I was back in Florida. I needed to restock the lockers and refill my kitty before cruising farther south. My plans are generally fluid, dependent on my bank account and desires. Long term, my plan is an extended cruise through Cuba and down to Panama. Short term involves a shower, some breakfast, and a few weeks of bar shifts.

When I'm ashore, I work about two hundred yards from my slip at the Manta Club. Bartending is great for filling the coffers without the stress of a full-time job. The Manta Club is situated in the Tilly Inn, and the owner and I have an arrangement, one that seems overly beneficial to me. I get to use one of the transient slips for boats that are only staying less than two weeks in the marina attached to the hotel. Besides bartending, she wants me to be a deterrent to any problems that some weekend boaters might cause. Mostly that involves me telling guys to quiet down after eleven at night, and one time I stopped a guy who'd had too much liquor courage from pummeling the dockmaster, Randy.

When I opened the rear hatch and companionway, the interior of *Carina* cooled rapidly as the air flowed through. Not being dressed yet, I stuck just my head out of the companionway. The docks appeared quiet. The sun was already posting up at the mid-morning position. I loved the breezy Atlantic air, but I'd crank the air on when I left. Florida has a nasty way of popping up dark clouds filled with rain. With open hatches, my bed would be soaked in just minutes.

I pulled on some shorts before taking a cup of coffee up to the cockpit. I sat back and sipped while the gulls squawked above my head.

"Back in port, eh?" a voice said behind me. I glanced over my port shoulder to see Randy walking along the dock toward *Carina.* His short legs and fast gait made him look to be wobbling along, trying to keep his balance.

"Yeah," I said. Standing up, I grabbed his hand as he extended it. His rough hand gripped mine tightly, and his teeth flashed through the grizzled beard. "I pulled in last night at dusk."

"You beat that squall?" he asked.

"Barely. I was tying off the boat when the storm hit. Got soaked to the bone." I lifted my cup of coffee. "You want a cup?"

"Sure, I never turn down a cup." He said the same thing every time I offered him a cup of coffee. Randy never turned down a chance to talk to anyone.

Grabbing both sides of the opening, I jumped down the companionway over the steps. My only other coffee cup hung from a hook in the galley. I didn't add cream or sugar. The cupboard was bare, so Randy could take it black or not at all. I climbed back up the steps to find Randy already situated on the other bench as if his workday had already ended.

Handing him the warm mug, I asked, "Anything exciting going on in the last few months?"

"Eh, not much. Had to fish two dead manatees out of a couple of slips last week."

I groaned, "That's lovely."

"Yeah, the health department and some day workers for the state came and carried them off. One of the women lost it when the bloated one oozed on her. Think it might have been her first day on the job." He took a swallow of coffee while discussing bloated manatee corpses like it was baseball.

"Come see the clean, fresh waters of South Florida," I said.

"I'll say this, we never found bloated bears in Lake Winnipeg when I was a kid," Randy said.

"Maybe," I responded, "but in Winnipeg, the girls didn't wear bikinis year-round either."

Randy laughed, "No, I'll take the rotting manatee corpses and bikinis over the cold."

"Just don't drink the water," I replied, draining my cup.

Randy worked on his cup for a few more minutes. "Guess I better get back to work before the boss shows up."

"Hell, you don't work half the time," I retorted.

"Nope, but it's all about looking like I'm working." Randy stood up and handed me the mug. "By the way, the boss said to send you up when you got back."

"Of course," I answered. "As if I wasn't going to show up."

Randy shrugged. "Thanks for the coffee." He stepped over the gunwale and onto the dock.

"Anytime," I said. "Showers busy today?"

"Nah, most of the transients are already out or still sleeping in." Randy turned and trudged up the dock.

Luckily, the Tilly Marina has a shower. *Carina* is outfitted with a decent sized shower in the head, but the water pressure leaves a lot to be desired. Unless I'm able to connect to the water supply at a marina, I don't take a lot of showers on board. Water reserves are pretty valuable in the islands. Even those few showers are quick and cold, to preserve water.

I dropped back through the companionway with the mugs in my hand. I washed and rinsed Randy's cup. I filled mine up one more time. I reached into the hanging locker next to the v-berth. Laundry was going to be a priority this afternoon. I was able to scrounge some clean clothes and a towel. With my towel over my shoulder, my clothes and bag of toiletries in one hand and my coffee in the other, I climbed off *Carina*. I took an extra few minutes to connect the shore power and water connections before I took off in search of a hot shower.

The steaming hot water was incredibly refreshing. I washed the salt and sweat of the last few months off in the shower basin. Cruisers joke that "Hollywood" showers are heavenly. While they are one of the few things that I missed when cruising, the freedom of the lifestyle outweighed the lack of a daily hot shower.

After a crazy amount of time enjoying the shower, I dressed and closed up the boat. The coffee hadn't filled me, and my stomach was growling. I climbed the stairs from the marina toward the Tilly Inn. The inn was built in the mid-1930s. The facade had been recently refurbished, and the exterior Gothic aesthetics had been sandblasted. The double doors on the southeast corner lead into the Manta Club.

The windows of the bar were opened, allowing the Atlantic air to flow through the bar. The bar was designed to allow the natural light to enter the eastern and southern windows. At night, the dark wood paneling and mahogany bar created a near gloomy atmosphere. The television over the bar was showing SportsCenter.

"If it isn't the resident SEAL," a short, dark-haired man in a tailored suit said from the other side of the bar. "Must be back begging for his job."

"I wasn't a SEAL, Mike," I mumbled to him.

"It's Michael," he corrected.

I smiled at him. "It's Marine."

"Whatever, a buzz cut is a buzz cut," Michael Seine barked. "You would think that the military would have taught you respect for authority."

I slid onto a barstool. Hunter, the bartender, slid a cold Swamp Ape IPA in front of me.

"Kind of early for a beer," Michael snipped.

"Being married to the boss doesn't make you the boss," I retorted as I took a swallow from the bottle.

"You don't get to talk to me like that," Michael's voice harshened.

"Michael, don't speak that way to my staff," a blond woman said from the landing leading to the hotel's lobby.

Michael glared at the woman, grumbling under his breath.

"Don't you have a meeting?" she asked.

Michael glanced at his watch. He scrambled to gather the papers he had spread over the bar. He scurried past the woman. "Bye, Missy."

"Bye, Felicia," Hunter muttered behind the bar.

I chuckled to myself.

"Glad to see you made it back, Chase," Missy said as she walked towards the bar. "How was your trip?"

"Pretty relaxing."

"Where all did you go?" Hunter asked.

"Just down through the Abacos and Eleuthera and back up West Side. Stayed a month in West Side."

"Sounds lonely," Missy purred.

"Catch any fish?" Hunter asked.

"Picked up a bunch. Got one sixty-pound yellow fin between Sandy Point and Dunmore. Ate my weight in conch too."

"You coming back to work?" Hunter asked.

"He better be," Missy replied.

I smiled. "Yeah, if you got some shifts."

"You could take my shift tomorrow," Hunter said, "I've been working almost six days in a row."

Missy furrowed her brow.

"Don't get me wrong, Missy," he stammered, "I love the money. Just my feet are tired."

"You're twenty-four. Nothing on you should get tired," she remarked.

A sheepish grin spread over his face.

"I can work tomorrow," I said.

"Chase, I have a stack of messages for you."

"Dude, when are you gonna get a phone?" Hunter laughed.

"When I want people to call me," I remarked.

"I also have your last check," Missy said, "in my office."

I drained my beer. "I'll be back," I told Hunter sliding the bottle across to him. Then I followed Missy into the hotel lobby.

Her office is on the second floor, away from the other offices on the first floor. Her assistant only works part-time, and when we entered the outer office, it was apparent that this wasn't part of that time. Her door read, "Melissa Seine - Manager." An understatement since she owned one hundred percent of Teleti Hospitality, which is the parent company for The Tilly Inn. Missy was in her early twenties when her father died and left the company to her. However, she had been running it since she graduated from the University of Florida.

As her door shut behind me, she rasped, "Gah, I have missed you."

Her lips pressed against mine passionately. My hands moved to her hips immediately; I pushed her against the door and kissed her neck.

"Are you telling me you've been celibate for four months?" I breathed in her ear.

"Hell, no," she said, pushing me toward the couch against the wall, " but you are my favorite."

I sank into the cushions as she unbuttoned her blouse and straddled me. Her breasts were against my face, and I kissed them. She pulled my shirt off and dragged her finger-nails along my back. Within a minute, we were entwined on the couch.

When we finally collapsed, we were on the floor, the

couch cushions pushed away. Missy curled up in the crook of my arm, still running her fingers over my body.

"Damn, I missed you," she sighed and bit my ear.

I rolled her onto her back and kissed her lips and started working down her neck.

"Stop that," she moaned. "I have to get back to work."

"I don't, though." My mouth moved lower, and a guttural moan came out of her.

2

"Tell me something," I said as we lay on the floor panting after our second go-round.

"What?" Missy asked, her head resting on my chest.

"Why do you put up with that dick of a husband? I mean, you are pretty self-sufficient. You obviously don't love each other. What is it?"

"He's a decent father," she said.

"But a shitty husband?"

"I didn't say that. He's okay."

"'He's okay' is the most romantic thing."

"Chase, get your head out of your ass. We all can't spend our days acting like we are Jack Sparrow. Marriage isn't always about romance."

I laughed. "Jack Sparrow?"

"I don't know any other pirates."

"So, what's it about?"

"What?" she asked. "Marriage?"

I nodded.

"Status, I guess."

Shaking my head, I asked, "What do you mean?"

Missy pushed up off me and crossed her legs. "When my mother married my father, it was against her family's wishes. He was a dirty Italian, and the Drexlers were a good, Jewish family with clout in the community."

She stood up and reached for her bra. She continued, "Michael is a 'good, Jewish boy' who is even a successful lawyer. Thus, he gives me status in the Jewish community, something that you would be surprised helps every day in running this place."

I shrugged and began to dress. "Was there ever any love?"

"I don't know. Probably. I was certainly head over heels for Michael in college. He was doting and sweet. Probably an average lover, but then I'm sure in college I wasn't much more than a starfish."

"Then you have certainly improved," I joked.

Missy walked around her desk in just her bra and panties, a very sexy red matching set. She didn't look like a mother of two teenagers. Hell, she'd almost pass for a teenager herself.

"What are you grinning at?" she asked.

"I was just thinking that I bet your daughter's boyfriends must spend a lot of time at your house."

She smiled slyly.

"Here are some messages for you," she dropped a small stack of notes on the corner of her desk.

I pulled my shorts on and lifted them and started thumbing through them. Two were from my sister.

"Did you get situated at the marina?" Missy asked.

I glanced at her as she buttoned her blouse. "Yeah, right down on Dock C."

It was an unspoken invitation. She'd show up sometime

late when Michael was away. I guessed that she looked for the lights on *Carina* before she trudged down to the marina, but I didn't ask.

The truth was I didn't spend a lot of time dating. My last serious girlfriend was in the eleventh grade. I turned eighteen during the summer before my senior year, took the GED, and enlisted in the Marines. The last I heard from Lauren was that she was married with two boys. Marriage or even dating was so far off my radar. However, Missy was still more than a convenience.

Four messages were from Tristan Locke. Tristan Locke. I stared at the name on the yellow paper. I hadn't talked to Tristan in over two years, maybe three. He and I served in Afghanistan together. Tristan was the youngest in our unit, and he couldn't think past the end of his nose. He was always getting into some trouble or another. Tristan, myself, and Jay Delp, another guy from our unit, ended up in a bar brawl with seven members of the Afghan Army after Tristan sashayed up to one and asked him to dance. We three Marines prevailed, but our reward was being ninja punched for three days in our quarters.

Tristan had his faults, but I owed him my life. Our unit was tasked with an incursion into an enemy camp. Tristan saved me from a bullet in the back.

He got a dishonorable discharge after I got out. He claimed he was framed. He never got convicted, but during a raid on a camp, fifty kilos of heroin went missing. He said they never convicted because there was no evidence. I wasn't sure. I loved the kid, but as I said, he didn't think past his nose.

The next message was from my sister in Arkansas.

The last message was from Kayla Locke. Tristan's sister? I couldn't remember if he had a sister. Maybe a wife.

"I talked to her," Missy said. "She said it was important."

"Did she say what she wanted?"

Missy shrugged as she slipped her shoes back on her feet. "She didn't say. Just that she needed to talk to you."

"We better get back before Hunter starts to think something," I said.

Missy laughed and said, "I'm sure Hunter knows something is up."

"What if Michael finds out?"

"Whatever," she muttered as she kissed me, "he does his own thing. Come on, let's go."

I followed Missy out of the office.

"I need to head to the front desk," she said instead of saying goodbye.

Skipping steps two at a time, I jogged down the stairs to the Manta Club. Hunter was still behind the bar talking to a customer. I sat to Hunter's left. He glanced my way and reached into a cooler to grab another beer. He slid it in front of me.

"Can you hand me the phone?" I asked Hunter.

Grabbing the phone from under the bar, he set it in front of me. "Glad you're back," he said, "I've been working six days for a month."

"Take a few days off then," I said. "I can jump in tomorrow."

"That's great," Hunter said. His mind was already turning over how to spend a day off.

I dialed the number from Tristan's message. The phone went straight to voice mail. I left a message with my number, then I tried the number for Kayla. Three rings and the voice mail answered -another message.

Hanging up the phone, I decided to call my sister back later. It would be just another phone call berating my life choices. I could wait until I felt a need to self-flagellate. Some would say that she means well, but I don't think that's true. She's saddled with a husband, an ex-husband, and three kids. She resents me for leaving so early. She wants to be rescued from her crappy life; I dodged that bullet. If I had stayed, then I'd have ended up divorced and miserable. Probably working at the cotton gin or driving a John Deere in circles around a field. The thought made me cringe.

I drank the beer slowly, waiting on Hunter to make his way back toward my end of the bar.

"Hunter," I called as he got closer, "can I get a tuna sandwich?"

"Sure, how do you want it?"

"Seared, with fries."

Hunter keyed the order into the computer. A boisterous voice bellowed, "That sounds good! I'll have that!"

I looked up at the corner of the bar to see Wilson Peterson bobbling around the bar. Peterson, the mayor of West Palm Beach, is a jovial regular. He eats lunch and the occasional dinner, but he has made the Manta Club his Friday afternoon haunt for years. By four o'clock on any Friday, the bar starts to fill with lawyers, elected officials, appointed officials, and several of other people seeking to trade political clout. Today wasn't Friday, so this was just another lunch.

"Chase, you're back from your trip," he stated.

"Got in last night," I said.

"Can I join you?" Peterson asked.

"Sure," I said. "You aren't meeting anyone?"

"No, just hungry," he answered. He looked to Hunter and said, "I'll just get an iced tea. Sweet."

Hunter poured his tea before moving to the customers

on the other side. The television started blasting the music for the noon news.

"Breaking news. Another home invasion ends with the homeowner in critical condition," the female anchor said.

"Shit," Peterson mumbled. "More of this."

I reached over the bar to grab the remote that we kept on the shelf. Muting the volume, I asked, "What's been happening?"

"These home invasions. We've had five in the last two months. This time they only beat the owner into a coma. Last time they killed the owner."

"Cops have anything?" I asked.

He shrugged. "They only take high dollar jewelry and cash. The phone won't stop in my office. Damn political nightmare."

I shrugged back. What else could you do?

"How was your trip?" he asked, changing the subject.

"Great. I'm already beginning to hate civilization," I said, glancing at the television. "But, I have to do a little work before I can get back out there."

Peterson looked across the bar where Hunter was talking to a brunette in her thirties. "I may have a little opportunity for you to make some money," he remarked.

I cocked my head. "Doing what?"

Wilson Peterson narrowed his eyes and said, "This must be under the strictest confidence."

I nodded.

"This could ruin me, so I need your assurance that you will keep this close to the chest."

"I will," I promised.

Peterson swiveled his head around again to make sure no one was in earshot. "I'm being blackmailed."

I sat quietly, staring at him.

He continued, "Someone has a very compromising video of me. They want me to pay them fifty-thousand dollars, or they will release it on the internet."

"What do you want from me?" I asked.

"Chase, everyone talks about you. I know you don't advertise it, but I know you were Special Forces or something."

I shook my head. "Force Recon."

"Right," Peterson said as if that was exactly what he said. "I don't feel comfortable carrying that much cash. I was hoping you would deliver it for me."

"Wilson, why don't you call the police?"

"This can't get out."

I stared at him. His eyes were shifty, but he was a politician. I liked Wilson, but like any politician, I assumed he was lying.

"You want me to carry fifty-thousand dollars in cash and deliver it? Where?"

He shook his head. "I don't know yet."

"Do you want to find out who it is and stop them?" I asked. I was waiting for the next proposition to be for me to remove the threat. Not something I take lightly.

"Oh, no," he assured me. "I just want you to take the money. I'll pay you for the trouble. Five thousand dollars."

I scratched the back of my head. Hunter approached us again, and I ordered another beer. Peterson got a refill on his iced tea. Hunter beelined back to the attractive female customer.

"If you pay the money, nothing will stop them from wanting more later."

"I don't have a lot of choice," he stated. "This can't get out."

"I have to ask," I said, "what's on the video? I don't need details, just generally."

"It's a sex tape."

"You're single," I said, "What do you care?"

The look on his face answered that. I could take a couple of guesses. His partner might not be single. Or female. Or it was more than just your average Sunday afternoon sex. An image of the rotund mayor in a sex swing gave me a shiver.

"Fine," I replied, "I'll help you. Do you know when the drop-off will be?"

He shook his head. "Not yet. I was told to have the money ready, and they would message me."

"You just want me to go along with you?"

"No, I was hoping you would go for me. I don't want to be caught up with whoever is doing this."

"Wilson, you need to reconsider. Paying them won't ensure they will destroy the video. They may come back in a week, or a month, wanting more money."

"It's the only way," Peterson insisted. "I just need you to deliver the money. I'll pay you well for your time."

Shaking my head, I asked, "You trust me with fifty-thousand dollars?"

Peterson looked at me. "I think so. I've got a good read on people. You always shoot straight."

Hunter appeared with our sandwiches. The garlic aioli that the chef put on the sandwich mixed with the aroma of spices reminded me that I hadn't eaten yet today.

"Thanks," I said to Hunter, who dropped off our silverware and moved back to flirt with the girl.

"When they call, you can reach me here."

"I appreciate this, Chase."

"Understand something," I said. "I do shoot straight, so I'm warning you ahead of time. If something goes bad, or I get the hinkiest feeling that something is wrong, I'm calling it off."

Peterson nodded. "I understand. This should be straight forward."

"Where is the money coming from?" I asked.

"What do you mean?" Peterson asked.

"The fifty-thousand dollars? Where are you getting the cash?"

"The bank. It's my money if that's what you're asking."

I unwrapped the roll of silverware and put the napkin on my lap. "Sorry, Wilson, that's exactly what I'm asking."

"The cash is legitimate," he assured me.

I nodded as I picked up my sandwich.

When I bit into the sandwich, the juices from the tuna and aioli dripped onto the plate. My thoughts turned over how long I could disappear in the Exumas with a five-thousand-dollar head start. That would buy a few six-packs of Sands Beer.

3

The man in the salmon polo shirt waved me over. From Georgia, he told me. I guessed he was here on business. Nothing about him said he was a tourist. He had been nursing a bourbon and Coke while watching a replay of a Bears-Cowboy game from 1996. At one point, I heard him mumbling under his breath at the screen and wondered if he was aware the game was over twenty-four years ago.

"Can I see a menu?" he asked.

I pulled a menu from behind the register and slipped it onto the bar next to him. "Another bourbon?" I asked, looking at his almost empty tumbler.

He nodded.

Great night to start back to work. Wednesdays are often slow, but tonight was exceptionally so. That was the business, sporadic even in paradise.

I had Bourbon and Coke and two others at the bar, Stella Artois and Merlot. None of them were together, and all were male, which meant they didn't want to chat each other up. All of them were staying at the Tilly. Salesmen, most likely.

Nights like this, I was praying for a decent-looking business-woman to stroll in for dinner before heading to her room. Then the mixture at the bar gets interesting. Inevitably, one of the three men will start a conversation with her. Sometimes two, or even all three, will vie for her attention. That's when the show starts. Rarely does it get too exciting, but occasionally, sparks fly.

Not tonight. There are just never enough traveling businesswomen that hang out in bars.

I gave Bourbon and Coke his drink and took his order for a hamburger and fries. He was boring, staring at a twenty-four-year-old match that didn't matter then and barely sipping his drink. Here he is in South Florida, home to some of the best seafood on the planet, and the man orders a burger. Well-done. With American cheese.

Kristy stood by the serving station, scrolling through her phone, waiting on a guest to sit at a table.

"Bored?" I asked her.

She curled her lip at me as if I was getting on her case.

She was new. At least new to me. I don't know how long she had been working as a cocktail waitress, but she wasn't here when I left for my trip. Too young for me. She might have been nineteen.

"Just slow," she said.

"Yeah," I agreed. "So, you go to school or anything?"

"Yeah, I'm taking online classes." She returned to scrolling through her phone.

Apparently, we weren't going to be best of friends tonight.

I made my rounds around the bar. Stella Artois needed another beer and a Cuban sandwich. Merlot wanted another glass of red and to know if I knew a good place for dinner. I always loved that question, as if the food here wasn't good enough for dinner. It's always the guys that order the house wine that suddenly become gourmands.

"Bimini Twist is good." It was. Served the same seafood we do for about twice as much, but he would consider the higher prices a meter of quality.

"Where is it?" Merlot asked.

"Got a car?" I asked.

Merlot shook his head.

"The concierge can get you a cab. It's a bit too far to walk."

Merlot nodded, and I was willing to bet myself that he'd end up ordering here after all.

A woman walked in from the hotel with a toddler holding her hand. I glanced at Kristy. Her eyes rolled, which was the look I expected. Kids in a bar always elicit that reaction. She walked toward the woman to seat her.

Bourbon and Coke's hamburger arrived, and I delivered it to him with a roll of silverware and a bottle of ketchup. He seemed satisfied not to carry on a long conversation and disappeared into his sports of yore.

"Chase," I heard Kristy call me around the bar. When I looked her way, she said, "This lady would like to talk to you."

The woman and her daughter were moving to one of the tables near the window. She looked to be in her late twenties with blond hair and tan skin. She was pretty but didn't take care of herself. The yellowed hair had the stiff look that the combination of salt and sun creates. In contrast, her daughter was wearing a little sundress with pink bows in her hair.

"Can you watch my guys?" I asked Kristy.

She shrugged, and I took that as a 'yes.' I took the two steps toward the table in a quick stride.

"Hi, can I help you?" I asked, standing by her table.

"Are you Chase Gordon?" Her voice drawled in a soft tone.

"Yes," I answered.

"I'm Kayla Locke. This is Abbie. I'm Tristan's wife."

"Oh," was all I said. Her face was somber, and I felt a blow to my gut. Her message was still in the pocket of my shorts. I hadn't tried to call her again since yesterday.

I sat down at the table. "What's wrong?" I muttered.

"I don't know where he is," she said.

"Tristan?"

"Yes, he's been gone for over a month. I haven't heard from him in over two weeks." Her eyes widened and moistened.

"Kayla, I haven't talked to him in years," I said, leaving out the four messages I had from him.

"I know, I'm sorry. Tristan just always talked about you. 'Go to Chase,' he'd say if something were to happen to him."

"Why me?"

"He trusted you. He talked about you all the time."

I grabbed her hand. I wasn't sure what I was supposed to do in this situation. "Kayla, I don't know what you want me to do."

Shaking her head, she said, "I don't know. I don't know what to do."

Abbie started pulling at her mother until Kayla lifted her into her lap. The girl reached up and stroked her mother's hair while she sang softly.

"He's never been gone this long before."

"Where does he go?" I asked.

"He usually goes on 'fishing trips.' That's what he calls it. He's really smuggling drugs, but he wants to pretend that's not it. For us."

"Drugs?" I sighed. The kid hadn't changed. That kind of work never ended well.

"He tried getting work, but the dishonorable kept following him. This started as a last resort, but the money was real good."

"How long do these," I paused, looking at Abbie staring at me, and continued, "'fishing trips' usually take?"

"A few days. Maybe a week."

"Does he have a boat?"

"Yeah, but it's still in the slip."

"How does he get the," I glanced at the little girl, "...uh...fish?"

"In his boat," Kayla said.

"Did he say he was going on a 'fishing trip?'" I asked. The subterfuge seemed futile since Abbie seemed to be in her own world, playing with her mother's buttons on her blouse.

"I don't think so. Something happened last month, but he didn't talk about it. He was worried about getting more money."

"Chase," Kristy said from the bar.

"Excuse me, Kayla. Do you guys want something to eat?"

Abbie's head twisted toward me and nodded.

Kayla shook her head. "No, Abbie. Thank you, though."

"Give me a minute, okay?"

I ran behind the bar to close out Stella Artois. Merlot also wanted to order the filet and snapper combo. I knew I'd win that bet.

I ordered a plate of chicken tenders and a grilled chicken for Kayla and Abbie.

"Kristy," I asked, "would you grab a chocolate milk from the kitchen and a soda for me?"

Kristy rolled her eyes and traipsed toward the kitchen.

I sat back down at the table with Kayla. "Alright, what happened last month?"

Kayla shook her head. "I don't know," she answered. "Not exactly. He was bitching about the Coast Guard. He said all they could do was cruise around on their boats. They weren't real military."

"You said you talked to him a couple of weeks ago. What did he say?"

"He said he had a job that was going to keep him busy."

I sighed. "No idea what kind of job, I guess?"

"No."

I looked over towards the bar. Missy had entered and stood by the bar, looking in my direction. I nodded at her, and she turned and left the club. Kristy passed her carrying a glass of chocolate milk. She stopped at the bar and grabbed a glass of soda. She brought the drinks to the table.

"You didn't have to," Kayla said.

I smiled, "No, I did it mostly for Abbie." I pushed the chocolate milk to Abbie. "Do you like chocolate milk?"

Abbie grinned and bobbed her head. Kayla handed the glass to Abbie. "Be careful, Abs," she warned.

Abbie sipped the milk and smiled at me. Her lip was coated in brown milk.

"I ordered her some chicken tenders," I said. "I hope that's okay."

"Oh," Kayla said, "I can't afford that."

I cocked my head. "It's my treat. Are you strapped financially?"

"Yeah," she dropped her head, "usually Tristan would've brought some money by now."

I sighed. Tristan had stepped into it. I know he made some bad decisions, but Tristan was loyal. The Marine I knew wouldn't have abandoned his wife and daughter like this. The best guess I had was that the issue with the Coast Guard was likely a boarding. He probably dumped whatever contraband he was carrying on board. The owners of the drugs would be less than happy if he came back empty-handed. I hoped that he was hiding out while trying to find a way out of the situation and not dumped in the Glades somewhere.

"Hang on," I said, and I walked behind the bar. I swiped my card and opened the register. I counted out five-hundred dollars. That would be my weekend pay, but I could figure that out later.

I returned to the table as Kristy brought the girls' meals to them.

"Here," I said, handing the wad of twenties to Kayla. "Maybe this will help until we find him."

"I can't take that," she said, pushing the money back.

"Kayla," I looked into her eyes, "do you know why Tristan sent you to me?"

"You're his friend."

"No, we aren't friends. We're more than that," I explained. "He knew I would take care of you. We were brothers. I owe him my life. So, don't insult that by not taking this."

A smile crossed her lips as she nodded. She slipped the bills into her pocket. She lifted Abbie from her lap and put her in a chair. "Here, honey, Mr. Gordon bought you some chicken fingers. What do you tell him?"

Abbie beamed, "Tankoo, Mista Gordon."

Winking at her, I said, "How about you call me Chase. Even Uncle Chase is fine. I'm no 'mister'."

Abbie nodded. "Tankoo, Shase."

"How old are you, sweetie?"

The girl held up four fingers. She tried to lower her

pinky finger, but it kept straightening. Finally, she used her other hand to hold it down and display three fingers.

I added, "If it's alright with Mommy, we do have some ice cream."

"Oh, you don't have to," Kayla insisted.

"If you don't eat it with me, I have to eat it by myself."

Abbie looked to her mother, imploring with her eyes.

"Eat your chicken, and we'll see."

Abbie began dipping the chicken into the carafe of honey mustard. She growled like a lion before chomping her teeth into the chicken.

"Abbie, baby," Kayla said, "chew with your mouth closed."

The girl's head bobbed in time with the open mouth chewing.

"Do you know where Tristan usually went for these pickups?"

"I don't. He never told me anything. He wanted to pretend it was legit with me, I think."

"Where does he berth his boat?"

"It's down at Boynton Inlet. The marina there."

I sat back. "Do you mind if I go take a look at the boat?"

"Not at all. Do you think it will help?"

I shrugged. "Maybe. I doubt it, but maybe. What kind of boat is it?"

"It's a Bertram. Her name is *Kristol*."

4

My head was reclined against the cockpit cushion with my eyes closed. A King's X song was drifting from a boat three slips down. Two guys were moving about the deck of the Pearson earlier. They had arrived during the afternoon while I was still at the Manta Club. I didn't mind, so far. Both had been extremely congenial when I returned to the boat. The music was at least good and barely audible, and they seemed to be settling in the cockpit with their beer.

A glass of dark rum with a splash of pineapple juice, borrowed from the bar, rested on the gunwale. Well, mostly, there was just ice in the glass. The rum and juice had disappeared as I pondered what kind of trouble Tristan might have. The problem was going to require a bit more rum.

The wind carried laughter over the water from a small group on a houseboat across the marina. It was probably the *SeaHorse*. They were retired and loved their sundowners. They had an open invitation if they were on deck. Steve retired from real estate in Indianapolis, and Mariane was a former accountant. Both loved their beer and wine, respec-

tively. They were what I call twice-a-weekers at the Manta.
They popped in for one drink and dinner about twice a
week. They preferred to drink on the *SeaHorse* with friends.

A refill seemed in order. But the rum was sitting on the
counter in the galley, and I was quite comfortable where I
was. The stars were a great deal dimmer here than when I
was anchored in the Exumas, where each distant star could
be made out clearly as they trailed and traced along the
constellations. Even now, though, with the pollution of light
from the shore, the night sky was something to marvel. Or
maybe to just stare at while I mulled over the problem with
Tristan.

If I was right, Tristan might be up to his eyeballs with a
drug distributor. From what little Kayla told me, I guessed
that he might have been boarded, which his employer
would likely not like. While I don't have any first-hand
knowledge, I imagine that there isn't a lot of understanding
and compassion in that business. I suppose that point of
view could make sense. Anyone could claim to be forced to
dump their cargo before being boarded when, in fact, they
got a little too greedy. Drug dealers have an image to
uphold.

Trying to take advantage of that kind of situation
seemed stupid enough for Tristan to think he could pull off.
He would see a big payday, and Tristan thought he was
smarter than most people. He wasn't, as is often the case for
people like that.

My mind kept thinking about Kayla and Abbie. How
does someone leave his loved ones in this position?

Tristan's childhood resembled that, though. His father
walked out when Tristan was eight or nine. According to
Tristan, his father found a new family. I took that to mean
that he married a woman with children. He always thought

that his father just forgot about Tristan and his mom. When we served together, he had no qualms about showing his disdain for his father.

After that, Tristan began to get in trouble. He once told me about the first time he went to jail after being arrested for shoplifting a six-pack of Smirnoff Ice. Jail never taught him anything, and he ended up bouncing through the juvenile system in Birmingham, Alabama, until he was eighteen. His PO pushed him to join the Marines, hoping that he would turn around with a little discipline. While he served under me, he seemed to be fine. Not exactly level-headed, but at least not self-destructive. After our unit dissolved, he got back into trouble. When he was bounced out of the Corps, I guess he never landed on his feet. Didn't know how to, I surmised.

Not a skill one should be missing when there are a wife and baby at home.

"You look like you need another drink," Missy said from the dock. She smiled down at me. She had changed into a thin white sundress that fluttered around her knees. Her hair was pulled back, save two to three blond strands that danced in the Atlantic breeze.

Lifting my empty glass, I said, "I do, but the damned rum is all the way below."

"It seems active down here," she commented, looking toward the boat three slips over.

"They got in this afternoon. They are staying quiet."

"What are they listening to?" she asked.

"I don't know this one," I answered, listening to an electric guitar reverbing in the air. "It sounds like the eighties metal they were playing earlier, though."

"May I come aboard?" she asked demurely as if my answer mattered.

"Aye, lass. Step aboard." Standing, I extended my right hand to her and waved an invitation with my left.

She grasped my hand for support and stepped down. *Carina* shifted and rocked as Missy's foot pushed the side of the boat down. The gentle rocking subsided. Missy bent over me and kissed my lips before she took my glass from me and disappeared below deck.

"Where's Michael?" I asked with only a slightly judgmental tone. Missy's visits to *Carina* seemed to only happen when they coincided with one of Michael's trips, usually to visit wherever his current girlfriend lived. While I obviously didn't have a problem with the moral ambiguity about my relationship with Missy, I struggled to understand the one between her and Michael. The two were usually civil but never loving.

"He drove up to Orlando. Said he had a meeting, but I'm sure he's visiting that teeny bopper."

"The Disney princess?" I asked.

"She's not a princess anymore," Missy rebutted from below. "She's a concierge now."

"You stalking her on Facebook?" I asked.

Appearing at the companionway, Missy handed me a fresh drink. "Just enough to make sure he can't screw me ever. Better to know more than he does."

The cocktail was stronger than my first two. The woman was a heavy-handed pour or trying to get me drunk.

"Just wait," I said, "he'll be suggesting you need a new concierge for the Tilly."

"That'll be a cold day in hell," she snapped.

"You do sound jealous," I joked. "That might be a bit hypocritical."

"Not at all. Michael can stick it in whoever he wants. That's his business," she said. "But, the Tilly is mine."

"At least if she worked at the Tilly, you could keep an eye on her."

She rolled her eyes.

"Who knows, he may have the boat wired for video," I joked. "He might feel the same way."

"If he is watching us, then he needs to start taking the initiative to learn a thing or two from you." She slumped onto the other cockpit bench.

"Long day?"

She nodded. "Yeah, we have a group coming in tomorrow, and there's an audit by the bankers."

"See, you might need a new concierge."

She shot me a look that said, "Shut up." Maybe it was a little harsher than that.

"Who's home with Paige?" I asked.

"She's seventeen," Missy said. "She doesn't need a babysitter, although she'd probably love you to babysit her."

"That might be awkward." I drank the cocktail.

"She's got a huge crush on you," Missy teased. "Last time she saw you, she talked about you for an hour."

I laughed. "Who doesn't feel that way about me?"

"It is a little weird hearing my daughter go on about you," she commented.

I smiled, "I hope you know that I have no intentions with Paige."

"Too bad. She'd love to take you to prom," she joked before she added, "Looked like you have had your share of female admirers lately."

"What?" I asked.

"The girl today," she said. "The one with the baby."

"Oh, Kayla. I think that baby was like three or four."

"Yeah, still a little rugrat. Not yours, I hope," Missy commented.

I glanced at Missy. "No, that's not my style."

She shrugged. "You never know. You gave her a wad of cash."

Shaking my head, I said, "I didn't think you were the jealous type."

"I'm not. Just better to know more." She lifted her knee and let her skirt slide up her leg.

"It's not like you didn't have kids before we met."

"Kid. Just the one," she said. "That was the girl from the message, right?"

I answered, "Yeah. Kayla's the wife of an old Marine buddy."

The ice jingled in the glass as Missy took a drink. "Where was your buddy?" she asked. "He know you are having lunch with his family?"

"Missing. She hasn't seen him in a month."

Her face grew somber. "Oh, I see."

"She hoped I knew where he might be. Tristan told her to come see me if there was ever an emergency."

"Do you?" she asked. "Know where he is?"

I shook my head. "No, he's in trouble. He's always done stupid things. He is one of those people that leaps before he looks, but he has a heart of gold. I can't imagine he would leave his family without a good reason."

"Like what?"

"I'm scared to find out," I said as I drained the rest of my cocktail. "But I have an idea." The rum was working its way to my extremities, but it wasn't making me feel any better about Tristan. The question that continued to run through my head was what was the only thing that would keep him away.

"You're going to help her," she said. "You feel obligated because he said you would help? That doesn't make sense."

"When I was in Afghanistan," I began, "our unit was sent in to extract a target. A warlord in the Taliban, supposedly. Who knows? We infiltrated a building. I was on point, meaning I lead the men in."

"I know what 'point' means, asshole," she snapped.

"Sorry, I just over-explain, I guess."

"Whatever," she waved off my comment. "It's called 'mansplaining.' Go on."

"I thought the first floor was cleared. I was about to move upstairs. Tristan opened fire on a door behind me. A nine-year-old kid with a Kalashnikov assault rifle aimed at me. He killed the kid, and the group upstairs came down hot. We were lucky to get out of there."

"Damn," Missy whispered.

"Tristan took it hard, killing that kid. He saved my life, and I don't doubt he'd have done it again. But I know it messed him up."

"You think you owe him," she said matter-of-factly.

"Over there, you owe everyone in your unit."

"What are you going to do?" she asked.

I rested my glass on the cockpit table. "Not sure. According to Kayla, the kid was smuggling drugs on his boat. That seems like a good start."

"His boat," she asked, "or the drugs."

"I guess the boat. I have no idea who he was smuggling drugs for."

Missy set her glass down and moved across the cockpit to my lap. "I'm sure you'll find him, but how about we do something else tonight?"

Her lips touched mine, and I tasted the lime from her cocktail. Her hands stroked my cheeks as she kissed me; I wrapped my arms around her waist and pulled her firmly into my lap. She breathed heavily as I kissed her neck and moved my hands under her blouse. Her skin was soft and cool. My mouth moved down her neck to kiss the top of her breasts, peeking through the loosed button.

"Down below," I mumbled.

"What?" she breathed.

Pulling back and looking her in the eyes, I said, "I want you down below."

She shifted her weight to her feet and ran her hand over my shorts. "Oh, me first, this time," she said with a smile and slipped down the companionway.

I rolled to my feet and followed her, leaving the two empty glasses sitting in the starlight.

5

I don't own a car anymore, not since I bought *Carina*. When I decided to spend months cruising, a car seemed like a ridiculous expense. The marina has a complimentary car for transients to run to the store. I promised Randy that I'd get the oil changed today while I was out. I squeezed out of the Toyota Corolla. Living on a boat should make me used to cramped spaces. I think it does the opposite. I love my space, and most days I spend my time on deck, stretched out in some fashion.

The parking lot for the Boynton Marina was raised about twenty feet above the waterline. Boynton Inlet is a gap in the barrier island protecting most of the towns along east Florida that opens up to the Atlantic Ocean. The marina is situated on the west side of the barrier island. The slips were mostly filled. Not surprising for mid-morning on a Thursday. Tomorrow the boats would be heading out for the weekend. Today, the docks were quiet.

The walkway rocked as I walked across it. There was no breeze; the bluff stifled the Atlantic breeze. Florida heat can hide behind a coastal breeze, but when the air is shielded, the heat becomes oppressive fast. Ironically, that works for the mosquitoes too.

Beads of sweat formed on my forehead. I thought that four years in Afghanistan would have made me immune to the heat. That didn't seem to matter. I drip sweat all the time. I wiped my brow, the first of many times I was sure while I traipsed among the docked boats. Marinas are notoriously hot. They are usually protected from the wind and waves, a perfect storm for still, humid air. When I'm out cruising, I try to stay far away from them. Luckily, the Tilly's marina faced the bay inlet, and the breeze remained consistent.

A few retired liveaboards were moving about on deck. Flicking my wrist, I gave one man a one-finger wave of acknowledgment as he cleaned the deck of his Beneteau sailboat. The transom was embossed with the name *C'est Vie*. He responded with a smile and a nod.

"G' day," he said as he scrubbed the cockpit.

"Hi," I responded. "Can you give me some directions?"

"Sure thing," he said, straightening up.

"Looking for the dockmaster," I said.

"The office is over there," he said, pointing toward the west. "Store's open, but I don't think Nick is there."

"You know where a Bertram might be berthed?"

"I know of two here," the sailor said. "There's one over there." He pointed toward the south.

My eyes followed his fingers, but I didn't see the boat.

"The other is toward the other side of the marina, in one of the covered slips. You know her name?"

"*Kristol,* I think."

"Ah," he said knowingly. "That would be the one on the south dock."

"Thank you," I said.

"Is it for sale?" he asked warily.

I shook my head, "I don't think so."

"You with the bank?" he questioned.

Smiling congenially, I answered, "No, it belongs to my friend."

He lifted an eyebrow curiously. "It's in need of some TLC," he said sharply.

"Are you getting her ready to head out?" I asked, diverting the conversation.

The brown face cracked a smile, "Just got back from Cuba."

"Sweet," I whistled. "That's on my agenda soon. I rolled in from the Exumas a few days ago."

He perked up, "I'm going back across next month. What do you have?"

"Tartan 40."

He nodded with a smile.

The next few minutes were passed as we discussed our different vessels and places we had both been. He was a retired part-time cruiser like me, which meant we had a few things in common.

After a few more minutes and a divergence toward crab-bing techniques and great anchorages, I thanked him for his time and headed toward the second Bertram. Call it a hunch, but knowing Tristan, I guessed that he didn't main-tain the same maintenance protocols that kept *Carina* and *C'est Vie* shipshape.

The sailor was right; the Bertram required care. The ultraviolet rays had cracked and faded the gel coat, and the brightwork was gray and begging for some teak oil. The lettering on the stern read *Kristol.*

The green buildup that seemed inevitable on the water was covering the gunwales and cockpit. Nothing that several hours with a pressure washer and some elbow grease couldn't remove. My stomach turned at the thought of what the bottom might look like.

Even with Kayla's permission, I did a double-take over my shoulders to see if anyone was around before I stepped across the gunwale. The companionway was locked, and I didn't have a key. When Kayla didn't have the keys, I figured I'd get the opportunity to practice my lock tumbling skills. I was adequate at picking locks, something I picked up as a teenager. It was a summer job helping a local locksmith, not a misspent youth.

Eight minutes. That's how long it took me. Like I said, adequate.

A musty smell washed out when I opened the companionway as I stepped into the salon of the Bertram. The inside was a mess. Maybe a sort of statement on Tristan's life in general. However, the navigation table was open, and charts were scattered on the floor. It was the charts that were out that got my attention-one for the coastline around Panama City and one for the Texas coastline. No matter how messy he might be, those two charts were beyond useless here. Whether it was Tristan or someone else, the navigation table had been rifled through.

I picked up the loose charts, looking through them as I rolled them back up. On the corner of the Texas chart was a phone number scrawled on the corner. Ripping the corner, I tore the number off. Folding it up, I slipped it into my pocket.

The galley would have been nice, but it needed some updating. A microwave was installed in one of the cabinets. I opened it to find the inside looked like a crime scene.

"Cover a damn dish, kid," I whispered.

The small refrigerator had developed a mold collection.

The little food that was in there was mostly staples. Some butter, sliced American cheese, and a couple of cans of Busch beer. Inside the oven was a small toolbox.

Opening the little red toolbox, I found a handheld GPS chart reader along with a battery-operated VHF radio. It was a trick a lot of sailors used. Even I did it. It always seemed more important on a sailboat, but I suppose even power-boats could use it. The idea is that if lightning strikes the boat, or even near it, the electronics can often get fried, and using the toolbox inside the oven created a simple Faraday Cage. Ideally, the backup will be protected from an electrical overload.

I returned the electronics to the toolbox and the toolbox to the oven. Venturing into the front cabin, I found piles of clothes where Tristan had shed dirty clothes and forgotten to take them for laundry. My lip curled at the thought of having to live in this derelict.

The boat shifted as someone stepped on board. I turned aft to see two men stepping through the companionway. Both were Latino, but I couldn't guess their exact ancestry. The second thing I noticed was that each one had a nine millimeter Glock in their respective hands.

"Hello," I said with some trepidation. They were blocking the only way out of the Bertram.

"Who are you?"

"Dockmaster," I lied. "The owner asked me to pick up his laundry."

The one in front wore a black linen jacket and cocked his head. He had two thin lines of facial hair along his jawline. His hair was short and styled in little spikes with a significant amount of hair gel. The other was bigger. His face was rugged, and he spent more time working to build his biceps, triceps, and everything else than he ever spent on his hair.

"Try again," Spiky Hair said. "Where is Tristan Locke?"

I lifted my hands slowly. "I wish I knew."

"Where is Locke?" he repeated.

"I don't know," I said. "I'm looking for him."

"What are you looking for?"

"Certainly not clean underwear," I said.

"You think you are funny," Spiky snarled and stepped closer.

Too close. My hand flicked forward and snatched the barrel of the gun out of his hand. My other hand grabbed Spiky by the forearm and pulled him toward me.

Facing the real muscle, I had the 9 mm leveled at him with Spiky Hair's neck caught in my elbow.

"Let's be reasonable," I said calmly. "This is a marina, and every boater you passed watched the two of you."

Muscles stared at me. I pushed Spiky forward, using him as a shield.

"What do you guys want with Tristan?" I asked.

Muscles didn't answer.

"What about you?" I asked Spiky as I tightened my arm around his throat.

"You'll regret this," he choked out.

"I already do," I said. "You got hair gel all over my shirt."

For a split second, I saw the corner of Muscles' mouth twitch. I turned Spiky so that Muscles was now forward, and my back was to the companionway. Spiky started thrashing, and Muscles' pupils dilated. I pulled the trigger, grazing Muscles' shoulder enough that he jerked his arm down. My hand slapped against the side of Spikey's head, and I shoved him into Muscles.

Turning, I scrambled out of the companionway as two

gunshots rang out behind me. My foot hit the bench and launched me up and over the side of the Bertram's cockpit. I hit the water and kicked down. The water was murky and brown, but I swam away from the sunlight. The shadowy, dark shapes were, I hoped, created by the dock's walkways.

My arms made several butterfly strokes, and I came up under the dock walkway. Grabbing a support beam, I pulled my head up between two black flotation platforms. The slimy algae that coated the beam, as well as everything else under here, oozed between my fingers.

Muffled voices were above me. The splashing of the ocean and the creaking of the dock made deciphering anything they said impossible. The walkway rocked as they passed over my hiding spot. One of them was almost shouting as they walked past. I could make out those words; unfortunately, they seemed to imply my relationship with my mother was much closer than it should have been.

A small school of cichlids swarmed as I dislodged the algae growing about me. A few nipped at my legs, grabbing dead skin cells. I hung on the beam letting the fish school around me for another few minutes before I submerged again. My head popped back up a second later in the sunshine. I stroked over to aft of the *Kristol*.

The boarding ladder was still upright, and I pushed myself up out of the water until I could grasp one of the cleats on the side of the Bertram. I tried to grab the ladder, but it was tied off securely. I wasn't going to release it easily. Instead, my free hand grasped the dock line. I put my weight onto it, and the Bertram pulled toward the side of the slip. I threw my leg up against the dock and pushed my body up toward the Bertram's cockpit. Once I got my fingers around the stainless-steel railing, I was able to pull myself the rest of the way onto the boat.

"That seemed like a lot of work," a voice said.

I looked up to see an auburn-haired woman smiling at me from the dock.

"You know there is a ladder at the front of your boat," she said. She pointed toward a ladder on the other side of the Bertram's nose.

"No, I didn't," I confessed.

She laughed at me.

6

———

Gin and Tonic was ordering his third round. His girlfriend, Frozen Strawberry Margarita, was still working on the first one. Thankfully, I hate making frozen drinks. I think it's a rule among bartenders, but in South Florida, it's a necessary evil. The Manta Club isn't set up like so many of the tiki bars around the coastline. There isn't a big machine that churns out frozen *daiquiris*, *margaritas*, *piña coladas*, or whatever other frozen crap tourists like to drink. Instead, I worked out of a two-quart mixer, which means my icy cocktails are actually hand-crafted. We even carry fresh citrus and fruits instead of the frozen jugs of mixes that are half sugar.

I might hate making the damned things, but at least, I make good ones.

Kristy was talking to a table near the fireplace. She was taking their drink orders, and I watched, trying to guess what they were wanting. The man was a bottled beer kind of guy. Though, the woman struck me as "just a Diet Coke" type.

The dinner rush would be hitting soon. I had Bobby the barback stock the beer and load up the ice.

Hunter was ready to leave when I got here, but I couldn't fault him much. I was running late after having spent a half-hour trying to get the smell of algae and dead fish off me. My wet clothes were draped across the lifelines on *Carina*, waiting for me to do the laundry I was supposed to do two days ago. The last thing I wanted was to let the cabin start smelling like the bottom of a marina. I made a mental note to do my laundry when I got off tonight.

"I need a Malibu and Pineapple and Macallan neat," Kristy said from the service station.

I was wrong again. "Please tell me the Malibu is for her."

Kristy smiled at me and didn't answer. She might be warming up to me now.

"Did he specify which Macallan?"

She shook her head.

"Eighteen-year," I told her.

We had the eighteen-year and the twenty-five-year Macallan. Both are on the back shelf. Reaching over the three other rows of liquor, I grabbed the eighteen-year-old scotch and poured a couple of ounces into a short glass before returning it to its nesting place. Scooping some ice into a tall glass, I added an ounce of Malibu Rum and topped the rest of the glass with the pineapple juice that Bobby had juiced earlier. I dropped a cherry and a paper straw into the glass.

"Thank you," Kristy said as she trayed the drinks up and took them back to her table.

Leaning against the bar, I checked the wadded ball of paper that I left under one of the lights. The phone number that I had torn from Tristan's chart had not weathered the dip in the sea as well as I had. I had forgotten about it until I was in the shower. I pulled it out of my pocket to find the thin paper had meshed together in an asymmetrical ball. Several attempts to unwad the mess were unsuccessful. Short of an archaeological laboratory, I didn't see very good chances of salvaging it.

I consoled myself with the fact that it was probably a long shot. The charts could have been used, and that number was over twenty years old.

I would work the paper a little at a time. If I get something, then good. If not, I wasn't going to dwell on it too much.

Kristy was back at the computer plugging the couple's order into the system. Her eyes flicked up over the monitor at me before they went back to the screen.

I circled the bar to check on Gin and Tonic and Frozen Strawberry Margarita. She asked to see a menu, and I pulled one up from under the bar. She smiled at me.

Stephanie Akins, the anchor for Channel Six News, popped up on the television that Gin and Tonic was watching. "Another home invasion near Hillsboro Beach, tune in at 5:30."

Wilson Peterson walked through the door. He saw the screen and rolled his eyes. I acknowledged him with a nod as he moved around to sit at the other end of the bar.

"Can I get the crab cakes?" Frozen Strawberry Margarita asked cheerily.

"Absolutely," I answered. I asked Gin and Tonic, "Anything for you, sir?"

"Those firecracker shrimp look good. Are they?"

"Very," I said, "but they are hot."

"Sounds good."

I passed Peterson and asked, "Want a martini?"

The mayor was always a dirty martini drinker. He probably thought it made him seem worldly when he first started drinking them.

"Yeah, Chase," he answered. "Thanks."

I keyed the couple's appetizers into the computer. Then I grabbed the Ketel One Vodka from the shelf to start Peterson's martini.

"You still like it really dirty?" I asked him.

"Pornographic, as you say."

I added a heavy dose of olive juice from the condiment tray into the cocktail shaker. After a vigorous shaking, the metal shaker began to frost on the outside. I strained the salty, olive-colored vodka into a frozen martini glass. Ice crystals floated on the surface, and I dropped a frozen olive into the glass.

"Thank you," Peterson said as he took the first sip. "No one does it quite as good as you do, Chase."

I shrugged. The process wasn't exactly rocket science. Maybe thermodynamics, but I'm not even sure what that is. Who knows?

"I got a call today," Peterson said in a hushed tone. "I am supposed to make the drop tomorrow."

I nodded. "A call?" I asked. "Do you have the number it came from?"

Peterson nodded. "I had it checked. It's a prepaid phone that was bought in Fort Lauderdale. No way to find out who bought it."

"How did you check it?" I asked curiously.

"I am the mayor. I have plenty of officers looking to curry favor," he responded with a smug look.

"When will the drop happen?"

"I'll be told tomorrow. I'm supposed to be ready at any time."

Wiping the bar in front of him for the second time, I said, "I'm off tomorrow. I can go anytime."

"Thanks, Chase."

"Wilson," I said, "you need to reconsider calling the cops. There is no guarantee that they will do what they say."

The mayor pursed his lips and said, "I know, but it's complicated."

"I understand complicated," I assured him.

"This means a lot to me, Chase," he said.

"You want some food?" I asked.

"Olives are food," he said.

"Then, enjoy your dinner," I quipped.

Bobby opened the beer cooler and looked at the fully stocked fridge.

"I got a firecracker and crab cakes in the kitchen," I told him.

"Got it," he said, grateful for something to do.

A man stepped through the door and strode to the bar. He was wearing a cheap suit that hadn't been pressed in a couple of wearings. He was graying on both his head and in the five o'clock shadow that was coming in patches. A pair of wire-framed bifocals were pressed against the bridge of his nose.

`"How's it going?" I asked as I approached him. "What can I get you?"

"Are you Chase Gordon?" he asked.

The hairs on my neck stiffened. Another quick examination of him screamed bureaucrat. I couldn't decide what breed he might be.

"I am," I said slowly.

He pulled his wallet out and flashed an identification. "Van Kohl. DEA." He was pocketing his wallet before the last syllable left his lip.

"You mind if I take a closer look at that ID?" I asked.

He peered over the top of his glasses. His left middle finger pushed the glasses back on his nose. He was wearing a shiny gold wedding ring on his ring finger. He removed his wallet again and reopened it.

"Mind taking it out for me?" I asked. It's a question I get to ask a lot as a bartender. Always easier to spot the fakes when they are in my hand. I didn't doubt that he was DEA, but at this moment, he was in my bar. That made me in charge. We both needed to know that right now.

His face twisted a bit. It wasn't a question he got much, I guessed. He pulled the card free and let me read it.

I know what all the state cards look like, but a card for one of the alphabet agencies was not something I saw much. It certainly looked real-no novelty stamp or cheesy fake name that floated around the internet.

I handed it back to him. "What can I do for the DEA?" I asked.

"Mr. Gordon, were you at the Boynton Marina earlier today?" he asked as he slid his Drug Enforcement Agency card back into his wallet.

"Why do you ask?"

"Are you going to make things difficult?" he narrowed his eyes as he asked.

"Just want to know what is going on."

"I could make this official. Walk you out of here in cuffs, and we can go somewhere and have this conversation there."

"We could," I said, nodding. "That conversation would consist of me asking for my lawyer and waiting for you to file some charges. Since you would have to take me out of here, it would be a little public. The whole thing would be very counter-productive on your part. On my part, I would lose a day or two in your holding facility. When I get out, then I would talk to my friend, Stephanie Akins. Do you know her? She's the anchor on Channel Six."

I don't actually know her, but since her name was fresh in my mind, it seemed like a good one to drop.

"On the other hand," I said, "you could be a little more forthright and tell me what is going on. Then I can decide if I want to talk to you."

"You were identified in an incident at Boynton Marina. Two witnesses have picked you out as having been there."

I smiled. "Was one that cute brunette?"

"Were you there?" he asked.

"I was."

"What were you doing there?"

"I was checking on a friend's boat."

"Tristan Locke?"

I stared at him for a full second before I nodded.

"Where is Mr. Locke?" Agent Kohl asked.

"I don't know. I was there at the behest of his wife."

Kohl looked at me.

"How are you involved with Mr. Locke?" he asked.

"Since you were able to identify me before you arrived, you already pulled my service record. That means you already know the answer to that."

Kohl glared at me. "When did you last talk to Locke?"

"I don't know. Few years ago."

Bobby walked into the bar carrying a tray with my firecracker shrimp and crab cakes. He set the tray on the bar for me.

"Agent Kohl, I don't know where he is. If you don't mind, I'm working. If you aren't ordering, then I think you should move along."

He laid a card on the bar. "I'm looking for Locke. He needs to talk to me. It's in his best interest."

I picked up the card and read it.

"What is he into?" I asked.

"Maybe read the card," Kohl snapped as he stood and walked out of the bar.

I tossed his card onto the cash register next to my wadded ball with the phone number I found on Tristan's boat. Grabbing the two appetizers, I took them to Gin and Tonic and Frozen Strawberry Margarita.

Placing two sets of silverware rolls next to them, I asked, "Do you need anything else?"

"Another round," Gin and Tonic said.

"Can I get a water too?" Frozen Strawberry Margarita asked.

When I mixed their drinks and dropped them off, I stopped in front of Peterson.

"I have a question," I said.

"The answer is 'yes, I need another martini.'"

Smiling, I said, "Okay, but my question is different. You have officers looking to curry favor. Do you know anyone that deals with the drug trade around here?"

Peterson cocked an eyebrow. "Yeah, Tom Schilling is the detective that leads that up."

"Does he work with the DEA much?" I asked.

"All the time. Probably much to his own chagrin."

"Think you could ask him to talk to me?"

"Sure, can I ask what's going on?" the mayor queried.

"That depends," I said, "can I ask what's on the tape?"

Peterson nodded. "Fair point. I'll give him a call."

7

The settee in my salon was piled with clean clothes. After closing the Manta down, I spent a couple of hours hanging out in the marina's laundromat with a stiff drink and the latest David Berens novel. At half-past two, I dumped the load onto the cushions and collapsed into my berth. As the water for my coffee heated, I stared at the pile. I'd separate later, but for now, I could pick through and find something for today.

Peterson expected another call today with instructions, but I was hoping it wouldn't be first thing. He made a call for me last night to Tom Schilling's office and told him to expect me this morning. He knew where I would be if the call came through while I was at the police department.

Kohl's visit to me last night gave me pause. I was already more than a little intrigued by Spikey's and Muscles' appearance on Tristan's boat. They were hired guns. The pieces of Tristan's puzzle were starting to come together. Kohl had managed to put several into the right place for me last night.

He or at least someone at the DEA was watching either

Tristan's boat or Spikey and Muscles. Maybe both. Somehow, I doubted that Tristan, Spikey, or Muscles was the DEA's primary focus. I was a little curious who that might be. Hopefully, the detective that Peterson mentioned could offer a clue to the man behind the curtain.

The kettle whistled as the water boiled. I poured the steaming water into my French press and let science turn the coffee grounds and water into a magical elixir. I realize that calling coffee a mixture of science and magic is somewhat contradictory, but I like to think of it in both terms.

Dropping on the settee next to my fresh laundry, I took the initiative to pair socks and fold underwear while I waited. The mundane task let me move around in my head a little. Besides some confirmation that Tristan was into some shady activities, I realized that his employer was looking for him as well. That meant that he hadn't been permanently retired by whoever was funding his drug-running enterprise.

After five minutes, I had several neat stacks of clothes, ready to be stowed away. I poured my coffee in a large stainless-steel insulated cup. The first sip hit my throat before I climbed out of the companionway.

West Palm Beach and all of South Florida had the same weather every day. Hot with a chance of showers. I loved it. Having grown up in northern Arkansas, I was used to hot summers, but every winter, I found myself cursing the cold. As a kid, I spent my summers on the lake and rivers. Swimming, water-skiing, and lots of canoeing. I tried football in my sophomore year of high school. It's not that I minded the game, I enjoyed it. The issue I had was sacrificing my summers for training. That one July and August, I spent practicing with the team every day netted a losing season and two lost months of water-skiing. I didn't sign up the next year, much to the disappointment of both of my parents. That wasn't the first or the last time that they were convinced I failed them.

Randy was adjusting the dock lines on one of the marina's rental pontoon boats as I walked toward him. He glanced up from his knees.

"Morning, Chase," he waved.

"Hey, Randy, how's it going?"

The dockmaster contorted his face. "These kids don't know how to tie up a boat to save their lives."

I wasn't sure what kids he meant. Maybe some of the high school students he hires as dockhands.

"I'm going to borrow the car. Anyone using it today?

He shook his head. "Guess it's you now," he laughed.

"I'll be back in a couple of hours," I told him.

He waved me away with a "see ya later" and went to retie the stern lines on the pontoon.

The West Palm Beach Police Department is about ten minutes from the marina, and I stopped a block away at The Pink Flamingo for a couple of their waffle sandwiches. By the time I got to the diner, I had finished all thirty-two ounces of my coffee. I got a small coffee, opting to let them keep a paper cup and just fill my big coffee cup.

I devoured one of the waffle sandwiches on my walk to the police department. Tom Schilling's desk was in the middle of a bullpen of about eight other desks.

"Detective Schilling?" I asked as I approached.

The balding, overweight detective looked up from his computer monitor.

I extended a hand. "My name is Chase Gordon. I think Mayor Peterson may have called ahead."

The detective rolled his eyes as subtly as he probably could. "Yeah, I think he called the chief."

He hadn't offered me a seat yet, and I tried to smile patiently. "I appreciate your time. I brought you a bacon, egg, and cheese waffle sandwich from the Flamingo."

He nodded slightly, but his eyes widened. "Thank you," he said, taking the bag. "Why don't you sit down? I don't usually get that many VIPs around here."

Ignoring the jab, I sat down opposite him.

He unwrapped the sandwich and took a big bite. "What can I do for you?" he mumbled through waffle, egg, and bacon.

"I'm interested in the drug trade in South Florida."

"You writing a book or something?"

"Something," I answered.

"'Kay," he swallowed. "That's a broad subject."

"How about let's narrow it to drug smuggling?"

"Still pretty broad," the detective stated.

"Let's say I have a boat-something with a nice range. I wanted to pick up extra money. How does that work?"

Schilling put the uneaten half of his sandwich down on the desk. He leaned back in his chair and peered at me over the desk. "It varies. Generally, a courier will drop a load, could be a package, a bale, something. It's usually going to be some set coordinates offshore. You could take your boat and pick up the load. You bring it ashore and pray that you don't get boarded."

"How often do these smugglers get boarded?" I asked.

"Honestly, not enough to stop the traffic. In the last ten years, the amount of cocaine that has been smuggled through South Florida has increased by five-hundred percent. Every year tourists find hundreds of pounds of cocaine washed onshore. The traffic just keeps growing, and there's no way to really slow it down.

"The boats that do get boarded are usually the ones

making dumb mistakes. They look like they are up to no good. Best way to avoid detection would be to have a multi-million-dollar yacht. The Coasties might board, but they won't look too hard. No one wants to upset rich constituents."

I nodded along.

"When I get back to shore with the drugs?" I asked.

"If you aren't freelancing, then you meet whoever paid you to do the pickup and hand it all over to them."

"If I was a freelancer?"

"You'd sell it yourself," Schilling answered. "But you better stay under the radar, because at that point, the law is the least of your concerns."

I cocked an eyebrow.

He continued, "The big boys in the drug trade are big because they don't like competition. If a guy is horning in on their business, then it's not like the corporate world. He isn't bought out by the big guy. He's dragged out into the swamp and shot."

"Nasty business," I said.

"Indeed," he commented as he took another bite of sandwich.

"Who around here is the big boy then?" I asked.

Detective Schilling swallowed. "Exactly what are you interested in this for?"

"I have a friend. An old Marine buddy that may have gotten in over his head with some of these folks. He's just trying to keep his family fed, and he may have made some bad decisions."

"You think you can help him out of those decisions, somehow?"

I shrugged. "I doubt it. Those kinds of consequences are

hard to avoid. The man saved my life, though, so if I don't at least try..."

Schilling nodded knowingly. "The big dog around here is going to be Julio Moreno. He controls most of the drug trade between Cuba and Tallahassee, maybe even farther north than that. He's dangerous, and if your friend is working for him, he is in for a world of hurt. His best bet is to bail out. Maybe negotiate a state deal. I know the DEA is all over Moreno right now. If they could make a case stick, he'd end up in jail for the rest of our lives."

"That's a big 'if'," I said. "I am willing to bet he doesn't have enough of the goods to negotiate a decent deal. Then his family is in danger, and he'll end up knifed in the back in some prison shower."

The detective's face offered a conceding look. "This might be one of those cases where the answers aren't any better than the questions."

"How big is Moreno's operation?"

Schilling shrugged.

"What happens if you guys," I paused, "the DEA and state can make a case against him?"

"He'll go to jail, and someone in his organization will step into his place. Or another organization will fill his shoes. Although, right now, he has such a grip, I imagine that he'd run the operation from his prison cell."

"What can you get him on?" I asked.

"Ideally, murder, racketeering, and a long list of charges we'd like to slap him with. Realistically, it will be whatever we can actually tie directly to him."

I sat back in my chair and thought for a second. Schilling finished his sandwich off and wadded the wrapper into a ball. He tossed the ball of greasy paper into the trash can.

"Your wheels seem to be turning," he noted.

"Sounds like my friend's best bet is to get away cleanly and stay as far away as he can."

"Truthfully," Schilling said, "yes. I think Moreno's wake has destroyed countless lives, and it's not hard to get sucked into that. Desperate men and all."

"Thank you for your candor," I said.

Schilling nodded. "I appreciate the sandwich. I understand the drive you have to help your buddy. I had one just like that. We were in the Army over in Desert Storm. He could never adjust to real life, though. Drowned himself in alcohol, and when that wasn't enough, it was heroin. He'd show up at the door of one of us from the unit at least once a year. Every one of us tried to help him. Get him a job, get him into rehab, whatever we could. He would repay us by stealing from us and lying to us. It didn't matter though; he was still a brother. Until he shot a couple of cops in Georgia. He was holed up in a motel outside Macon, Georgia."

Schilling's eyes drifted toward the ceiling. "I guess he didn't want to be taken alive. He charged out shooting. The bastard was a crack shot, too. He took out two Georgia staties before they unloaded into him. Turns out, he had killed another guy when he tried to rob his house. That's why he was on the run."

I knew what he was saying. Some people can't be helped.

"Did this guy have a family?" I asked.

Schilling shook his head. "No, a mom and a sister, but no wife and kids."

"I have to at least help his wife and kid," I said.

Schilling's head bobbed up and down in understanding.

"Just be prepared for the worst," he said. "I've seen it as a cop too much. No one prepares for the worst, and when it happens, it crushes them."

8

The rest of the day was spent on boat chores. I didn't want to be too far from the marina or the Tilly when Peterson called. Missy scolded me again as I came through the Tilly about getting a cell phone.

"Not gonna happen," I told her.

She shook her head as I passed through the Manta Club. "We aren't your personal answering service," she called after me.

I waved back at her over my shoulder.

Randy was behind the counter at the marina store. I grabbed a Dr. Pepper and told him I was expecting a call.

"No problem," he said as he pushed my change back to me.

"You still got that little pressure washer?" I asked.

"Yeah, you want to borrow it?"

"If you don't mind. I need to scrub *Carina's* topside."

"It's over in the storage room," he said, pointing behind the store where all the tools and extra lines were kept.

"Thanks, Randy."

The power washer was one of the small electric ones, but it would do to wash some of the salt and grime from the deck. Rolling the washer to my slip, I watched the activity around the marina. Two guys in a flatboat were fishing in the middle of the marina. A common but annoying occurrence. It never really bothers me until I try to get my forty-foot behemoth out of the dock with some dumbass refusing to reel in his line and make way for me.

The rest of the afternoon involved me in my swimsuit, spraying the salt residue off the hull. Sweat was drenching my shirt by the time I finally came out of it.

"What time does the show end?" Missy asked from the dock.

Surprised, I shut off the sprayer and turned.

"You just came to catch a glimpse," I joked.

"You have a message," she responded. "That's all."

"You could have called on the radio," I pointed out.

She grinned slyly. "I never said I didn't want a look," she said. "Here."

She handed a slip of paper to me. No name, just a number.

"He didn't say who it was," she said. "Is this about your friend?"

"No," I said, unplugging the power washer. "A favor for someone else."

"You going to be around tonight?"

"At some point," I said. I didn't know how long Peterson's drop was going to take me. "I hope to be in bed tonight. What time is it?"

"Good," she said. "4:36." She turned and walked back up the walkway to the Tilly's entrance.

My eyes followed her as she walked away, something I'm sure she was expecting to happen. When she vanished into the inn, I jumped onto the dock and cut the water faucet off. I disconnected everything and carried the washer back to the tool room.

"Can I use the phone?" I asked Randy when I came into the store.

"Sure, use my office," he said.

Randy's office was more of a closet. The smell of beef jerky and menthol cigarettes hung in the air. The desk was covered with invoices and notes. A poster on the wall mapped out the marina with slip numbers and docks.

The receiver on the phone was gritty from grease-covered hands handling it for years. I dialed the number.

"Hello," Peterson said after the first ring.

"Wilson, it's Chase."

"Thank goodness. Can you meet me at the Manta in fifteen minutes?"

"Yeah, Wilson. See you then."

He hung up, and I considered that if I rushed, I could squeeze in a quick shower before meeting him.

Wilson Peterson was already at the bar when I walked through the door. He was seated at the far end of the bar. The dinner crowd was beginning to filter in with the Tilly's guests. Locals were usually fifteen to twenty minutes behind the guests.

Peterson had a Corona Light in front of him. I slipped onto the stool next to him. Hunter appeared in front of me.

"Whatcha need, Chase?"

"Give me a Tecate," I said.

Hunter vanished to grab my beer.

"The drop is supposed to be forty-five minutes after sunset at Dehrer Park." Peterson pointed at a package on the floor next to his stool. His foot was resting on it.

"Okay," I said as Hunter set a cold bottle of beer in front

of me. When he went back to his other guests, I asked, "Wilson, have you thought about letting me at least try to figure out who is doing this?"

The mayor shook his head. "No, let's just get this taken care of. There is an extra five grand in an envelope for you."

I nodded my appreciation curtly. "Do you plan on staying here?" I asked him. "Or do you want to go along?"

"I'll wait here."

"Wilson, this is a lot of money. I wouldn't fault you for having any doubts or worries about it."

"Chase," Peterson said calmly. "I have faith in you. Otherwise, I wouldn't have come to you."

"I appreciate that," I told him. The truth was I was a little worried myself. The mayor wasn't being upfront about everything, and while I liked the guy, I didn't trust him much. He was a politician, after all. Despite that, I didn't get the feeling that the man was trying to swindle me. He was genuinely concerned about something. It wasn't a sex tape unless the sex was less than vanilla.

I drank half of my beer. "Where in the park am I supposed to go?"

"There's a palm tree behind the pavilion. About a hundred feet, they said. Leave the package there and walk back out."

Turning the bottle up, I finished the rest of my beer. I dropped six dollars on the bar and grabbed the package.

"I'll be back then," I said.

"Thank you, Chase," the mayor said.

Throwing a two-finger salute to Hunter, I walked out the entrance toward the marina. Randy was leaving as I headed toward the parking lot.

"You taking the car?" he asked.

"If you don't mind. I'll fill it up."

"Great, see you tomorrow, man." He climbed up into his 2006 Trailblazer to head home.

Dehrer Park is, like everything else around here, only a ten-minute drive. It's right off I-95, and across the street from the zoo. The park was beginning to empty as dusk approached. I drove the little Corolla through the parking lot, examining the cars. Dehrer Park is designed for walking and running, and most of the people heading out were wearing jogging attire for their after-work runs.

Not wanting to scare the blackmailer off, I left the park. The southern entrance was near a neighborhood, and I parked on one of the side streets that was opposite the small pond. I watched as the sun sank below the horizon. A few stragglers trickled out of the park, only a few people were left.

The sign at both entrances stated that the park closed at dark-a smart play on the blackmailer's part. I could make the drop without drawing a lot of attention, as long as I didn't stay around too long. I had to be quick. The odds of a cop showing up increased with every second I was there.

It also meant that the blackmailer couldn't stick around. Complicated, to say the least.

Peterson had used an old Amazon box. He taped it up and put it and my envelope in a large plastic shopping bag. With no knowledge of how much fifty-thousand dollars weighs, it felt heavy enough. I counted the hundred-dollar bills in my envelope. It's hard not to smile when I make five grand that easily.

The sun had been down for ten minutes. I needed to wait another half hour before I drove in there. But if I walked, I thought, I could make it in well under thirty minutes, and there would be less chance of being noticed by the police.

With the Amazon box under my arm, I locked the Corolla and walked toward the park. The circular path that rounded the pond was the quickest route, but it was the most visible. In order to maintain a covert approach, I cut across the field along the tree line.

Within twenty minutes of leaving the car, I was staring across the parking lot at the empty pavilion. Crouching behind a row of trees, I waited. My eyes had long ago adjusted to the dark. A crescent moon hung halfway in the sky to the southeast. The stars were mostly drowned out by the lights of the city, which were sufficient enough to let me make out features in the dark.

Unfortunately, there was no one to see. The park was empty. I checked my watch; sunset was exactly forty-one minutes ago-time for me to move.

I crossed the parking lot. Behind the pavilion was a walking path that arched toward the northwest. Intersecting it was a narrow, dirt path made unofficially by those radical walkers that just can't stay on the concrete sidewalk. The angle of the track made it directly behind the pavilion. My foot stepped gingerly onto the dirt. The area was wooded, and the last thing I wanted was to step on was some cold-blooded creature. South Florida was loaded with those types of critters. All you need to get an alligator is have a body of water. The damned things would flock to a puddle if it was deep enough.

Pacing off the distance, I stopped after what I estimated to be about a hundred feet. In front of me, two palm trees towered in the night. I glanced around for any movement. My breath held momentarily in my chest as I listened for someone in the woods with me. There was no one. I was positive I was alone.

The Amazon package rested against one of the palms. I

stepped back and looked around again. I couldn't see anything moving in the park.

My time was up. No one was going to come while I was still here. Retreating, I tried to keep an eye over my shoulder for any movement. Still, I was alone. I double-timed it back to the car, and I waited.

And I waited. No vehicles entered the park.

Half an hour passed, and still nothing. I waited a bit longer. Peterson said he didn't want me to try and find out who was blackmailing him, but he was also lying to me about something. My curiosity was intense. Besides, I recall what Missy said about it being better to know about Michael than be surprised. The same thing applies here. I would prefer to know if I am going to be railroaded by Peterson or his blackmailer before it happened.

After an hour, I considered going back to see if the package was still there. That seemed unwise. If I was watching, so could the blackmailer.

Who would leave that much cash in a park? The answer was simple. No one would. They did the same thing I did. They came in on foot. Through the woods that backed up to the interstate. Easy-peasy. Just park in the breakdown lane on I-95 and traipse through the woods. The entire venture would take ten minutes. The parking lot was visible from the highway, and they could just wait until they saw me walk across it. They could have been in the park and back before I made it to my car.

Wish I had thought of that earlier, I scolded myself.

I started the car and drove back to the Tilly. Before I went north on I-95, I took a peek from the interstate. My suspicions were correct. The breakdown lane heading north provided the perfect place to watch my approach and departure.

The Manta was busy when I came through. Peterson was still sitting at the bar. A few of his cronies had stopped in and were crowded around him. He looked up at me as I entered. I gave him a nod before I passed through the bar to the marina exit.

9

My body was dragging when I finally made it up to the Manta Club to open the bar. Missy showed up around half past midnight. I was already asleep in the v-berth when she woke me, climbing into the bed. She kept me up until close to four before she kissed me goodnight and slipped off the boat.

The opening shift was never fun. Hunter was pretty good about leaving the bar in good shape, so it's just a matter of cutting fruit and adding ice to the bins. The bar opened at ten, but only a handful of people ever showed up before 11:30. This might be South Florida, but only the hard-core start drinking that early. Even on vacation.

Taylor, our other barback, wasn't scheduled until noon. No point, we didn't get busy until the lunch rush. Until then. I leaned against the keg cooler and watched The Price is Right. I didn't mind Drew Carey, but I felt like his talent was wasted here. Plus, he was no Bob Barker.

"Chase." I heard a voice from the door. Looking around the center of the bar, I saw Kayla standing at the door.

"Kayla," I asked surprised. "What's up?"

Abbie wasn't with her, and Kayla looked a little disheveled. Her hair was pulled back but not really brushed. The cotton dress she was wearing was wrinkled. She walked over to the bar.

"You don't look okay," I commented.

"Two men came to the house yesterday, looking for Tristan."

She started tearing up. The girl had been holding it in, and the dam was about to break.

"Sit down, Kayla," I told her. "Let me get you something to drink."

She nodded fiercely.

"You want coffee, or, maybe, a Coke?"

"Can I get a Sprite?" she asked, as a single tear escaped and ran down her cheek.

Filling a glass with Sprite from the soda gun hanging over the ice bin, I added a couple of maraschino cherries to the glass. She smiled slightly when she saw the cherries.

"When did these men come by?"

She took a sip of the Sprite. "Last night, about nine. Abbie was already asleep."

"Where is Abbie?" I asked.

"She's staying with a friend," she explained.

"Were these two men Latino?"

She nodded.

"One was small with nicely styled hair, the other a big guy?"

She nodded again. "How did you know?"

"I met them on the *Kristol* the other day."

Her eyes flashed with fear. "You didn't tell me."

"No, I didn't. I wasn't sure what to tell you yet," I stated. "What did they want?"

"They said Tristan owed them money. They think I know where he is."

I listened.

"They came to my house." Her voice started getting agitated. "My little girl was there."

"I know," I empathized.

"What the hell was Tristan thinking?" she snapped. "Where is he?"

"Do you have any family here?"

She shook her head. "My mom lives in Sanford."

"Near Orlando?" I asked.

She nodded.

"Listen, can you take Abbie and stay with her? At least for a few days."

"Do you think that they will be back?"

"I'm afraid so. They said Tristan owed twenty-five grand. That's not something they are going to just let slide."

The dam broke, and she started crying. I handed her a beverage napkin. Not exactly a tissue, but the best I could do at a bar.

"We don't have that kind of money," she blubbered.

"Can you go to your mom's for a bit?" I repeated.

She nodded. "I'll call her today."

A man in his seventies walked in. He craned his head as he checked out the pretty girl crying at the bar. I ignored him as he walked around to the other side of my bar.

"Don't go anywhere," I told Kayla.

The old man wanted a rum and Coke, but he wanted to be cool, so he asked for a *Cuba Libre*. The only difference is the lime, which I add anyway to a rum and Coke. I'm lazy. I don't want to have to get it later when the customer realizes they ordered it wrong.

"Want some food?" I asked the man.

"No, I'm just waiting on my wife," he said.

"Where are you from?"

"Philly."

"Great sandwiches," I said. Sometimes finding common ground is tough. Who wants to talk about a big broken bell? But steak sandwiches covered in cheese. That's a bigger demographic.

"Is that girl alright?" he prodded.

"She's fine," I said. "She was just emotionally moved by the cherries in her drink."

He rolled his eyes at me. He was going to leave the same tip no matter what. Even if he doesn't, being snarky is the bartender's inalienable right.

Kayla was staring at the half-empty glass of Sprite. I topped the glass off with more Sprite.

"There is some good news, though," I pointed out.

"What's that?" she asked.

"If these guys work for the guy that Tristan was running drugs for, then we know they are looking for him. That means that they didn't do anything to him yet."

She looked up from her glass. "Yet."

"Well, it's only a little good news. We have to deal with the situation as it unfolds."

She nodded.

I didn't want to keep anything from her, and the involvement of the DEA and Agent Kohl was something she needed to be aware of.

"Have you had any visits from an agent in the DEA?"

Her face was shocked. Then worried.

"No, is the DEA looking for Tristan?"

I nodded slowly. "I think they might be watching his boat. Probably you too."

"What do I do?"

"Nothing," I said. "Be careful what you say on any phone. Just in case."

"Are they going to arrest Tristan?"

Shaking my head, I answered, "I don't know. They might only suspect him. That might be why the Coast Guard boarded him. Tristan is small potatoes. They want the big boss, but they will use Tristan up and toss him out if it benefits them. He will need to be very careful."

Kayla started crying again. "I don't understand him."

I tried to soothe her. "Knowing Tristan, he thinks he is doing what is best for you and Abbie."

"Having him here is what's best," she said.

"I know," I responded.

"Listen, Kayla," I said, "I'm working a double today, but let me give you the number here."

I scrawled the Manta Club's direct line on a bev nap.

"Here," I handed her the napkin. "I want you to get home. Pack a bag for you and Abbie. Then drive to your mom's place. You have enough money to get there?"

She nodded slowly.

"Call me before you leave. Make sure you call me when you get to your mom's."

"Do you think they'll be waiting on me?"

I shook my head. "No, that was just to scare you and hopefully Tristan. They'll give you a day before they escalate. By then, you should be gone from here."

"Thank you so much," she muttered.

"Why don't you leave me a key to your place?" I suggested. "I want to look for anything that might tell me where Tristan went."

"I've already looked, though," she said.

"I know, but just in case." I added, "I promise not to throw any parties."

She smiled under the blond strands of hair hanging in her face.

"I'll leave you the extra key," she said.

"Do you have a mailbox on the street or on the house?"

"Street," she answered.

"Tape it to the bottom of the mailbox. Right under the front. No one will look there."

She nodded.

My peripheral vision caught a figure enter the bar, and I looked up to see Michael Seine stop inside the door, survey the bar, and smirk. He walked toward the bar with a smug look.

Ignoring him, I asked Kayla, "Do you need anything to eat before you go?"

"No, thank you. I better go."

I gave her an affirming nod. "Call me," I reiterated.

She stood with a demure smile and left the bar. I watched her leave.

"Can't blame you for staring," Michael sneered. "She's a little hottie."

Cutting my eyes to him, I snarled as politely as I could, "What do you need, Mike?"

"It's Michael," he huffed.

"I know," I responded.

"Give me a Weller and water," he ordered. "I'm having lunch with Missy."

Pulling the bourbon from the shelf, I mixed his drink. I'll admit I was a little light-handed in my pour.

"I thought you were out of town," I commented as I set the cocktail in front of him.

"I bet you did," he remarked. "I just got back."

"Get enough of the mouse?"

He just glared at me. I left him and circled the bar to

check on Rum and Coke. He ordered another and asked for a menu. His wife was still shopping, he informed me.

Missy came through the door as I was typing in Rum and Coke's Shrimp Po-boy order. A quick smile flashed at me before Michael turned to look at her. I poured her an iced tea and set it on the bar in front of her.

"You should have asked her what she wanted," Michael snapped. "Maybe she wanted a real drink with lunch."

"My bad," I said. Looking at Missy, I asked, "What can I get you, ma'am?"

"An iced tea is fine," she said. She looked at Michael and said, "I don't drink while I'm at work. I always have iced tea."

He let out a "harrumph."

"What can I get you?" I asked.

Missy answered, "Put me in a club sandwich."

"No tomatoes?" I asked.

She nodded, and I looked at Michael, who stared at me glumly. "Give me a Cuban."

Taylor walked in as I finished ordering their food.

"Hey, Chase," the nineteen-year-old kid said. He was taking a sabbatical from school-his words, not mine. Right now, his dream was to become a bartender and get a job at one of the nightclubs in Miami. I can't fault the kid, there is a lot of money to be made down there.

"Sup, Taylor. I got a few orders in now," I told him. He nodded as he did his regular walk-through and verified that I had stocked all the beer and filled all the ice trays. His work ethic was admirable, and he wanted to learn all the tricks to bartending.

"Make it pink," I told him when he asked me what the main thing he needed to know.

"What do you mean?" he asked.

"If you don't know how to make a drink, and it's not an

obvious color, like a Blue Hawaiian, then make it pink. Most people don't know the difference between a Bay Breeze and a Sea Breeze."

That's always my go-to advice for learning to bartend.

Whenever Missy has lunch with Michael, I do my best to be as attentive as possible as far from them as possible. I'm sure it gives him a lot to overthink, but the fact is I don't like him, even if I wasn't sleeping with his wife.

Today was no different, and luckily the next hour proved busy as the lunch crowd started filling in the tables. There was no server on the schedule until this evening, but I was fine with that. I could manage the entire restaurant, and I liked the extra money.

By one-thirty, Taylor and I had hustled our asses off. When we were down to two tables, he asked me if he could grab a cigarette. I waved him off, and I started cleaning up from the rush. The last two tables paid their tabs, and I was ready to rest a bit. I spent the next ten minutes closing all the checks and cleaning the bar. Taylor would clean the tables when he got back.

When he returned from polluting his lungs, I took a quick break. I picked up the phone and called a number from memory.

"Delp," the voice on the other end answered.

Jay Delp served with me and Tristan in Afghanistan. He got out about the same time that I did. Now Jay is working up in Pensacola in the police department. He just made sergeant before I left for the Bahamas.

"Jay, it's Chase," I said.

"Chase, what's going on? You back from your trip?" He sounded excited to hear from me. He was always a bit energetic, but he is one of the very few guys I would want to watch my back.

"It's Tristan," I said. "Have you talked to him lately?"

"No, I haven't. It's been at least a year," Jay said. "What kind of trouble is he in?"

"Bad, I think. His wife came to see me. He's disappeared. Been gone a month, but she hasn't heard from him in weeks."

"Shit," Jay's Mississippi accent dragged the word out for several syllables.

"Couple of thugs are looking for him too. He's been running drugs, I think. Might have dumped a load before the Coasties boarded him."

"That damned kid," Jay said into the phone.

"My sentiments too." I added, "It gets better. The DEA is sniffing around for him too. An agent Van Kohl has already come to visit me."

"Way to dive into the deep end, Chase. What can I do?"

"I'm thinking that the main drug line through here is run by a Julio Moreno. Can you see what is officially out there? Don't overstep any bounds, though."

"Let me poke a little. See what I can find out."

"Thanks, Jay."

"No need, Chase. You know if it gets hairy, I can be down there in a flash."

"I know," I responded.

"You find that kid, you beat the ever-loving shit outta him. You got me?"

"Got it."

10

My feet were sore. Not that I can complain. There were points at Parris Island when my feet were bleeding at the end of the day. Now, I'd just classify it as sore.

Kristy was doing her side work as Bobby carried the last of the dirty dishes to the kitchen to be washed.

"I need this drink taken off so I can close the ticket," she bitched at me.

Since I operate as the supervisor when I'm behind the bar, I have the authority to adjust or change the tickets. I have to type in my PIN and swipe the "manager" card. One of Kristy's customers didn't like that there was grapefruit juice in their Greyhound. The mind is left to ponder some folks. I removed the Greyhound so that she could close the check to exact change.

"You need me to do anything else?" she asked.

"Everything stocked?"

"Yeah."

"Then go on."

She spread two twenty-dollar bills on the bar for me. "Thanks, Chase," she said as she skipped toward the door.

She stopped Bobby as he came through the door and handed him a folded wad of bills.

"Anyone going for a drink?" she asked both of us.

I shook my head. "No, I've been on my feet since open."

"I'll go." Bobby jumped at the chance to have a drink with the girl. "You need anything else, Chase?"

Looking over the bar, everything looked stocked. "I'm good. See ya'll later."

His face lit up, and the two left together. They'd probably hit Marty's down the street. The little pub stayed open till three, and the kitchen was cooking until two.

I started turning off the lights when the phone rang. Surprised, I thought it might be Kayla calling again. She had phoned around six when she made it to Orlando. It could easily be someone checking to see if we were still open.

"Manta," I said into the receiver.

"Hey," Missy said over the phone.

"Hey, back."

"You done up there?" she asked.

"Yeah," I said. "Are you still here?"

"In my office," she said.

"You alright?" I asked.

"Yeah, just a long day. Why don't you bring a bottle of wine down? I need a drink."

Missy preferred Pinot Noir, and I grabbed an Erath Pinot Noir, two glasses, and a wine tool. The hotel was quiet now. A couple of guests passed through the lobby. I saw Natalie, the overnight clerk behind the counter. She appeared to be intensely working on her computer. Plugging in the day's numbers, I guessed.

The hallway leading to Missy's office was a dead zone.

The only other office personnel she had on staff were nine-to-fivers. I opened her door to see her seated behind her desk. She was wearing the same black suit with a white button-down blouse that I saw her in at lunch. She'd removed the jacket, and the top button of her blouse was loose. She was staring at her computer, and her mouth widened into a grin when I came through the door.

"Working late," I commented.

"Eh" was all she said.

Twisting the corkscrew, I pulled the cork free with an almost silent pop.

"What's wrong?" I asked when I handed her a glass. I sank into the couch on her back wall with my drink.

"I'm married to an ass, that's all."

"No argument from me," I added. "You don't want to go home, huh?"

"Paige is at a friend's, so it would be just the two of us at the house. That might be unbearable."

I drank the wine and held my tongue. She stood up and walked around the desk. Her skirt slid up her thigh as she sat beside me.

"Do you want to talk about it?" I asked.

"No," she said.

I leaned in to kiss her. Her hand pressed against my shirt, and for a split second, it occurred to me that I was coming off a fourteen-hour shift and might not smell as fresh as I could. When her lips moved to my neck, I forgot about that.

My fingers unbuttoned her blouse, and my hand slipped into her shirt and caressed her skin. In seconds, we were both mostly naked, and the wine completely ignored.

When we finally collapsed, she was draped across me on the floor, both of us catching our breath. Her face nestled against my chest, and her fingers traced patterns down my body.

"I want another," she whispered.

"I need at least ten minutes," I told her.

She pulled her leg over me, staring down at me. Her hips started moving rhythmically until a smile appeared on her face.

"There it is!" she exclaimed excitedly.

When she finished, she rolled off me onto the floor, panting. I turned my head to look at her. "Want to talk about it now?" I asked.

She smacked me playfully. "I do not," she stated, and she climbed to her feet. I watched her every move, studying the lithe form and toned muscles developed from two hours in the hotel's fitness center every day.

"You know," I suggested, "you could hire someone to run the Tilly, and we could sail off to the islands together."

"There's Paige."

"I have an extra cabin."

She laughed. "Yes, that's what I need. My seventeen-year-old daughter vying for the attention of my boyfriend twenty-four hours a day."

"She'd never get it," I told her.

"Doesn't matter," she said as she slid the straps of her bra onto her shoulder. "We'd never work out."

I shrugged. "It would be fun, though."

She gave me a wry grin. "It's fun now," she said. "You know I don't need saving, don't you?"

I lifted my hands. "I know that for sure."

"Good, where did that come from then?"

"Maybe I just like your companionship," I offered.

"Bullshit," she said. Her eyes moved to the security monitor on her desk.

"What is it?" I asked.

"This man's been sitting in the east portico for hours. I saw him before you came down here."

Pushing up to my feet, I moved around her desk to look at the screen.

"I thought he was just grabbing a cigarette earlier," she said.

I groaned. "That's the bodybuilder from Tristan's boat."

Missy twisted her head to stare at me. "The one that tried to kill you?"

"He didn't try hard," I said. "They paid a visit to Kayla last night. I sent her to stay with her mother; I guess they might know she is gone."

"There were two of them, right?" Missy asked as she buttoned her blouse.

I grabbed my pants and started dressing. "Yeah."

"Maybe the other one is still following her."

"Damn," I muttered. The time on Missy's computer read 1:30 a.m. I didn't want to call Kayla and scare her if it was nothing.

I made a quick decision. "I'm going to take him away from the inn."

"Chase, that's dangerous."

"The last thing either of us wants is a scene to happen here. You don't want the publicity, and I'd just as soon not lead them to *Carina*. I can handle him."

"What if the other guy is out there too?"

"This time, I won't be boxed into the cabin of a boat," I assured her. "I'll be a little more ready for them."

She stared at me glumly.

"I don't plan to start a fight. I just want to redirect him elsewhere."

I leaned down and kissed her. "You know, you are going to regret not running off to the islands with me."

She put the palm of her hand on my cheek. "I don't have the luxury of regret."

Slipping out of her office, I tried to be discreet and avoid any of the inn's staff. There were already plenty of rumors, and while I don't care, it matters to Missy. The thought of the two of us running off together was pleasant, but I knew she was right. We were never a forever-together type of people. Marriage and love were not part of her plan, and I knew that. Understand it, no. But I knew it was what she thought. Somehow her success with the Tilly was marginalized in her head if she didn't have a successful family.

On the other hand, I wasn't ready to be tied down. Not to a person or a place. It's not like I play the field with women everywhere. Missy has been my only relationship over the last couple of years. I just had plenty of years where I was told where to go and when to go. Now, I like to go when I damned well pleased.

Back in the Manta, I could see Muscles sitting on the portico overlooking the marina and the Manta Club's marina exit. When I left, he'd take an extra minute to get there from the upper level.

Walking away from the window, I went behind the bar. I picked up the bar knife that we use to cut up fruit. It was a five-inch-long butcher knife. In a cocktail glass next to the register was a small collection of rubber bands. I found three of the wider ones. Rolling my sleeves up, I bound the knife to my forearm with the rubber bands. The handle rested just below the palm of my left hand so that I could pull it easily. My sleeves covered the blade, and I left the left cuff unbuttoned.

Venturing into the night, I felt the breeze coming over

the marina. There is a sidewalk path that leads north parallel to the marina. I started down the footpath slow enough that Muscles had time to catch up, but not so slow that he suspected anything.

North of the marina was a private dock that was part of the condominiums. The walkway leads down to the condominiums, an idea that Missy promoted to drive business from the condos to the Manta Club. The complex added a stretch of concrete that forked off toward the dock. That path went along the parking garage and the bluff overlooking the bay.

My tail was behind me when I went toward the docks. Squeezing into an alcove, I waited in the dark. Somewhere around ninety seconds later, eighty-seven to be exact, Muscles passed my hiding space. He was oblivious to my presence. When he had passed, I took a second to check that Spikey Hair was not around.

I thought about stepping out behind him and saying something glib like, "Are you looking for me?" But I was reminded of a commander I once had that drove home the idea that if someone might want to kill you, then don't give them a chance. Instead of being snarky, I whipped the knife free of my arm and hit him from behind. The man was all muscle, and it felt a little like hitting a wall. Unfortunately, years of weight training and bodybuilding don't make up for combat training. Muscles was off-balance, and my tackle buckled his knees, sending him face-first into the concrete. I was back on my feet, holding the knife ready to strike.

Muscles was still fast for his size. He was rebounding to his feet. The silhouette of a gun came up, and I slashed down on his forearm. The goon let out a quick grunt, and his gun clattered across the sidewalk.

He was more of a fighter than I gave him credit for. He lunged at me, letting me drive the knife into his bicep before he knocked me to the ground. Rolling to my feet, I watched as the man ran back toward the street.

I picked up the nine-millimeter Glock that he dropped. Considering the number of kids that traipse along these paths, I didn't want to leave it. I slipped it into my belt above my butt. Muscles was gone now. I started back along the path. Just because I never saw Spikey around didn't mean that he or someone else wasn't waiting on me. My guess was that he was alone, or someone would have popped up during the scuffle.

Quiet was all around. I walked along the dark path keeping my ears and eyes tuned for any movement. On the walkway to the marina, I froze. Light poured out of the porthole in my boat. My pace slowed as I peeked into the window.

I sighed with relief when I saw Missy moving around the galley. The boat rocked as I stepped aboard.

"You're here," I said as I stepped through the companionway.

She smiled. "Hope that's okay," she said. "What happened?"

"I lost the bar knife, but otherwise, I'm fine."

She handed me a slip of paper.

"What's this?"

"I searched the surveillance video after you left. Your man arrived in an old Honda Del Sol. Tricked out. This is his license plate."

My eyes lit up, and I leaned in and kissed her. "That's perfect," I told her.

"You mind if I stay the night?" she asked.

"Are you reconsidering running off with me?"

"Not tonight," she said as she crawled up into the v-berth. "I just want to fall asleep with you."

11

The inside of *Carina* stays dark with the blinds over the portholes closed. The effect left me confused as to how long I had been asleep. Years of sleeping in many uncomfortable positions gave me the ability to "sleep fast" as a sergeant once ordered me. Even now, I sometimes had to train myself to sleep more than two or three hours. Some days I'd force myself back to sleep just to make sure I was actually rested and not just fooled by the Marine endurance.

Today was a little different. Even in the darkened cabin, I was alert. I didn't care about going back to sleep. Missy's naked body was pressed against me, and I didn't want to move just yet. The v-berth was filled with a floral aroma that came off her. Her silky skin was cool against my chest, and I let my eyes close as I enjoyed the peace.

By the time I dealt with Muscles last night and made it back to the boat, it was well after three in the morning. Now, the interior was only illuminated enough to indicate it was morning, and my internal clock said it was well past mid-morning.

Missy stirred in her sleep and rolled over. It was evident that she wasn't used to the cramped quarters in the v-berth. While it is roughly a queen-sized bed, the walls on the side can create a claustrophobic feeling if one isn't used to it. Personally, I love my bed, and the gentle swaying of the waves helps me sleep all the better.

She rarely stayed the night with me. Even on nights when Michael was traveling, she would go back to her home. I didn't mind. Something was freeing about a relationship with very few expectations. On the other hand, mornings like this were very nice. I enjoyed having someone to fall asleep with on occasion.

Eventually, my bladder got the best of me. Without stirring Missy, I shimmied out from under her and pulled myself out of the berth. My bare feet touched the sole of the cabin, and *Carina* shifted gently in the slip. The head was in the aft of the boat, which was nice since I slept in the forward berth. I shuffled to relieve myself before I started looking for coffee.

Priorities are important.

Missy was still curled up in the sheets. A soft heaving of breath came from the front. Her bare leg protruded from under the covers displaying the taut muscles in her calf and thigh. I admired the curve from her ankle to her knee as I stood over the stove in my boxers, waiting on the water to boil for the coffee.

She was a beautiful woman with a complicated soul. I wish I understood the attraction I felt for her. There was more to her than simply her looks. We differed in so many areas that I knew we would never last a month in a committed relationship. It was the subject of many conversations. She liked certain amenities, like room service and high-end clothes. She abhorred sweating for any reason that wasn't gym related. I could live off-grid forever if I had the chance.

Still, there was this undeniable connection. I might classify my feelings for Missy in the love category, but I certainly did not put them in the "in love" category. But I remembered the day I met her clearly. There was a crazy spark of attraction. She was interviewing me for the bartender position about three years ago. As soon as I knew that she was married, I decided to steer away from her. But I couldn't shake the magnetism I felt toward her. We laughed together at work, and soon I was anticipating her coming by the bar to check on things. In fact, I started to think that she was coming by the Manta Club more often when I was there.

She finally made the first move. One night after the club had closed, she waited until the rest of the staff left for the night. She orchestrated a reason for talking to me. Something mundane about adding new keg taps. Missy was behind the bar, bending over and looking at the lines running from the kegs to the tap. The next thing I remember was her leaning in and hitting me with a swift playful kiss that devolved into a passionate few minutes on the top of the kegerator. Any resolve I had to keep our relationship platonic buckled.

That kiss was one of the few in my life I remember wanting as badly as I did.

The longest conversation we ever had about our relationship was the one last night about sailing to the islands together. It wasn't some dream I had. I never expected or wanted much more than the relationship we currently had. She was right last night. We wouldn't work together in the long term. She needed status, and I could never offer her that. Instead, I was little more than a guilty respite from the drudgery of her life.

"Missy!" a voice shouted from the dock. "Missy, do you hear me? I know you're there!"

I opened the companionway and popped my head up. A red-faced Michael stood at the bow of *Carina*. He looked out of place in his Italian suit. His forehead peppered with beads of sweat.

"What the hell?" I asked.

"Where is she?" Michael demanded.

"Who?" I feigned ignorance.

"You damned well know who."

Rising out of the companionway, I stood up in the cockpit. "Missy? She's not here. Why don't you get out of here before you cause a scene?"

He charged down the dock toward me. "I want to see her right now."

His foot touched the side of the cockpit as he attempted to board my boat. My right hand caught his arm and shoved him back onto the dock.

"Do not set foot on my boat," I told him sternly.

He straightened up. "Or what?" he asked. "What do you think you are going to do?"

He made a move as if he was going to try again. I came out of the cockpit and stood in front of him. "I will knock you on your ass."

"Where is that whore?" he shouted.

I hit him in the nose. I felt the crunch, and Michael fell down. He almost rolled into the water, except I caught his arm and pulled him back firmly on the dock.

"How dare you?" he muttered. "I'm going to make you pay for that."

My hand wrapped around his upper arm, and I lifted him up. Blood trickled from his misshapen nose.

"No, you won't," I said firmly. "You are going to go

home now and clean up. You will adjust your attitude and never come back down here again. Do you understand me?"

He glared at me. "You don't get to talk to me like that!" he howled.

"My suggestion is that you get something on that nose before you bleed all over that five-hundred-dollar shirt."

He looked down suddenly, sending droplets of blood onto his shirt and tie. Biting my lip, I resisted the smile trying to force its way onto my face.

I stared at him, letting my body remain tense. "Now get the hell out of here."

"I own this marina; I'll have you thrown out."

My grip on his arm tightened. "No, your wife owns this marina. Why don't you tell her that I broke your nose when you called her a 'whore?' She can decide if I need to be kicked out. You leave now, or I will make sure you can't use this arm for another six weeks."

His eyes widened. He stepped back slowly. His narrowed eyes maintained a lock on mine as he attempted to keep some sense of self-assurance.

"You had better apologize to your wife when you see her. You never talk about any woman like that in front of me again. Do you understand?"

He pulled against my grip. I released his arm and motioned for him to leave. His hand wiped the blood from his nose, leaving a trail across his cheek. He stumbled away from me. I watched as he walked away.

One of the guys from the boat two slips over walked past. He gave me a look, probably because I was standing on the dock in my underwear.

"Hope that didn't disturb you," I said, pointing at the retreating Michael.

"No, but I thought you handled the whole thing gracefully, considering."

I shrugged as the man continued past. A figure was ambling toward me. Wilson Peterson passed the other sailor and stared at me.

"Chase?"

"Wilson," I said. "It's a long story. Is everything alright?"

"You were right," he said, "they want another twenty-thousand."

I sighed. "Wilson, can we go to the police now?"

He shook his head. "I told them this was the last I was willing to pay."

"They won't believe you," I remarked.

"I'll give you another two grand to make the delivery."

Breathing out with some exasperation, I said, "Wilson, I will, but you have to think about putting a stop to this."

He shook his head. "Just this last time, Chase."

I watched the man's face, and even though I was the one standing in public in my underwear, I felt that he was the one with shame covering him.

"I'll do it," I stated. "At this rate, you might be funding a good year in the islands."

"Thank you, Chase," he said. "I'll call when they set up a time."

"Today?"

"Maybe," he answered. He extended a hand and retracted it awkwardly as he took another look at me in just boxers.

"Call me, Wilson. Either at the Manta or at the store."

He nodded and walked off.

I looked around to see very few people taking much notice of me. Turning back, I boarded *Carina* and stepped down below.

"I'm so sorry," Missy stuttered. "I didn't think he'd come here."

She was standing in the cabin, and I guessed that she had watched everything from the portholes.

"What's going on, Missy?"

"He's mad. The Disney princess broke it off, I think. He came back from Orlando in a mood. He says that he wants to work on our marriage. He demanded that we start acting like a married couple."

Settling on the settee, I asked, "What does that mean?"

"He means that if he can't get any from his girl, then it has to come from me."

I cocked an eyebrow.

She continued, "I took a little offense at that. How dare he think he can come and go from this marriage anytime he wants?"

"That's why you didn't want to go home last night?"

"Paige wasn't home. Normally we don't air the laundry while she's there."

I nodded along.

"This hasn't been a marriage in years, and I'll be damned if he thinks he can demand anything from me."

"He's going to be back," I said. "Not here, but at the Tilly."

She sank onto the settee next to me. "Can I just stay here?"

"As long as you want," I said. "Course, I have to go open the Manta in a bit."

"Your boss said you can take the day off," she had a demure smile cross her lips.

"My boss still needs someone there," I pointed out. "But Hunter will be there by four, and I'll bring you some dinner."

She pulled me closer and pressed her lips against mine. I pulled her over into my lap and continued to kiss her.

"What time do you have to be there?" she whispered in my ear.

"I think my schedule says ten."

She slid off my lap and onto the floor. Her fingers tugged on the elastic band on my boxer shorts.

"I think you can at least be a few minutes late," she said lasciviously.

12

Bobby carried a club sandwich and a fried grouper from the kitchen. He set the two plates on the bar.

"Want me to drop these?" he asked eagerly.

We only had one table for lunch. I was fine with that. After the long day yesterday and the late night, I was happy to have a slow day. I nodded that it was fine for him to deliver the food. He wanted to make the jump to bartender, or even server, and he was happy to fill in whenever the opportunity presented itself.

A day like today was a good one for letting him have that opportunity. There weren't enough tips to go around.

I leaned against the beer cooler and watched the twelve o'clock news as it started. The weather was going to be typical. There was only a thirty percent chance of rain this afternoon, but there was an easterly wind. I was already thinking about heading back across the stream. I could at least make it to Bimini for the weekend. Easily squeeze in some snorkeling.

Fiddling with the paper that Missy gave me last night, I

thought again about Tristan. I picked up the phone and dialed Jay's number.

"Delp," he answered.

"Hey, it's Chase."

"Any word from Tristan?" he asked.

"No, I'm hoping you have something for me," I said.

"On Moreno? A little." I heard him take a drink of something. "He's definitely the subject of someone's investigation, but the details are sketchy."

"What does that mean?" I asked.

"It usually means, the department investigating doesn't want whatever evidence they do find being fed to the subject from some cop on his payroll. Better to keep one hand from knowing what the other is doing."

"What do you know?"

"Julio Moreno was born in Miami, but probably raised in Havana. Maybe back and forth from Cuba to the States. Again, the info is incomplete. He has a couple of arrests in Miami. One is a juvenile arrest when he was fourteen, and the other was assault when he was nineteen. The assault charge was beaten. He had witnesses that stated the victim struck first. Mind you, the victim ended up in a wheelchair for the rest of his life."

"Sounds like he had a good start."

"When I reached out to some of our contacts with the DEA, the response I got was to send any pertinent evidence to them. They would loop me in later."

"Guessing that's not the most productive route," I remarked.

"Like dealing with the State Department if you know what I mean. They assume their turds are smarter than I am, so no need to share their shit with me."

"Thanks. Maybe we can go a different way. I have something," I said into the phone. "Can you run a plate number for me?"

"Yeah," he answered.

I rattled off the numbers. "One of the guys that I met on Tristan's boat came to visit me yesterday. This tag was on the car he ran off in."

Jay chuckled, "I'm guessing you gave him something to think about if he fled."

"Well..."

I heard him do something on the other end. Then he said, "Easy. Here it is. The car is registered to Ponce Alvarez. His address is in Miami. 3462 Flowering Trail."

"Thank you, Jay."

"What's your plan, then?"

"I'm pretty sure that this guy, whoever he is, is working for Julio Moreno. Those same guys visited Tristan's wife, so I need to make sure that Moreno doesn't think that's acceptable."

"Sounds like they are looking for him too," Delp replied. "That means they didn't kill him, yet."

"I know. Any good news is nice, but I want to know where that little son of a bitch is. I want to confirm my suspicion that Tristan's boat was searched too."

"I might be able to help you with that. I know a guy in the Coasties down there," Delp said "I'll give him a call. What's the name of his boat?"

"The *Kristol*. Give him my number here if you want."

"You sure I can't come down with you? Maybe a badge would help smooth the way with the locals."

"No," I said into the receiver. "It's not the locals that are the problem right now. These goons haven't tossed anything at me that I can't handle."

"Chase, you know they might be figuring that out."

"Good," I stated.

"Not necessarily," he pointed out. "They might try to find something to toss at you that you can't handle."

"I guess I'll burn that bridge when I get there," I said.

"Keep me apprised," he stated.

"You got it." I added, "Thanks."

Hanging up the phone, I leaned against the bar and stared absent-mindedly at the wall. Tristan had me focusing on two fronts. Ponce Alvarez and his friend with the spiked hair were looking hard for Tristan. That means they wouldn't lead me to him, so there wasn't a lot of point in focusing on them. Except they now involved Tristan's family. Right now, it seems Tristan had left no clues to his whereabouts. That was equally disturbing. For all his faults, Tristan didn't seem the type to not at least check in with Kayla.

All those thoughts raced through my head at one time. He might be dead, but at least Alvarez and his friends didn't kill him. Or he might just be hiding, and Alvarez and friends had every intention of killing him if he didn't have their money. Maybe even if he did have their money, just to prove a point to others.

The sound of a stool scooting echoed around the bar. I walked around to see Agent Kohl sitting at the bar.

"Damn," I said.

"That's some terrible customer service," Kohl replied. "I'd complain to the management, but since you spent the night with her last night, I don't think there would be a lot of consequences."

"Oh no," I feigned disbelief, "the mighty federal agent has been keeping tabs on me. What a shock? I can't believe it."

Kohl stared at me with an annoyed look.

"Agent Kohl," I said, "I've spent several years dealing with people like you in the service. Some guy whose head is so far up his ass he has no way to see what was actually happening."

"Gordon," he hissed, "you have no idea what I know."

I leaned over the bar and drew closer to his face. "I know that if you bring Missy up again in any type of threatening manner, you will be eating everything through a straw. I don't care how much time I might get for that."

He blinked at me. He understood me, but he wasn't about to give in.

"Want to tell me where you were two nights ago?" he asked.

"Not really," I said. "Besides, I figure you are about to tell me anyway."

"You aren't making this easy on yourself, Gordon."

I leaned against the bar, still holding eye contact with the agent. He wanted to fluster me. Very few people could do that; Marines don't get flustered.

"I don't need to make it easy."

Kohl adjusted his ass on the stool. "What were you doing at Dehrer Park?"

I cocked an eyebrow. "I was enjoying an evening stroll."

"When the park was closed?"

"I don't like crowds."

"That's illegal," he said.

"Then issue me a citation."

His eyes narrowed. "I'm going to tell you what I think."

I waved my hand toward him as if to tell him to go on.

"I think you were carrying a package of drugs and dropping them off with someone."

I nodded along with him. "I don't suppose you saw the person I was delivering these alleged drugs to."

He didn't answer. Which was an answer itself.

"I have no affiliation with Julio Moreno."

"Other than the knife fight you had with one of his guys last night?"

"We didn't exchange names."

Kohl folded his hands. "Let me lay my cards on the table."

"Good," I stated, "because your bluffing game is shit."

He rolled his eyes. "How about we cut out the tough guy crap. I get it. You aren't intimidated. That probably makes you stupid or something."

"I've been called worse."

"I don't know how you are involved. Are you looking for Locke? Maybe his wife asked you to."

"I was just checking the man's boat for her."

He nodded. "Right," he said sarcastically. "Just in the wrong place at the wrong time."

"Story of my life."

"Look, Locke is in some deep shit. That is if Moreno hasn't already killed him."

"Listen, Kohl, I haven't any idea if Julio Moreno is involved with Tristan. If he is, I would want to work to get him away from that life. That's my only concern in this whole thing. I want Tristan and his family to be safe."

"He needs to come to me," Kohl said. "I can get him a deal. Put his family someplace safe."

"If he even knows anything about Moreno," I said.

"No, if he's in the organization, we can use whatever information he has."

I nodded as if I believed everything Kohl said. The truth was more likely to be far from that. If Tristan had any actionable information about Moreno, then he could write whatever deal he wanted. What was more likely was that all he ever did was deal with a middleman, and Moreno never entered the scene. In that case, Tristan might end up with a lighter sentence in a prison where someone working for Moreno could put a knife in him. Or worse, the feds would convince him to stay in the organization and try to work his way closer to Moreno. That was a death sentence for Tristan and maybe his family.

No, the only way to save Tristan, if he was even still alive, was to help him extricate himself and his family without the federal government's assistance. There were a lot of "buts" floating around that idea. But I had to find him first. But I had to get him away from Moreno. But I had to keep the DEA away from Tristan.

"I don't know where he is," I explained.

"But you're looking for him?"

"I don't have any idea where to look for him." That wasn't a lie.

Kohl unfolded his hands. "Who were you meeting at Dehrer Park then?"

I laughed. "I'm an idiot. You thought I was meeting Tristan, didn't you?"

Kohl didn't share in my amusement.

"That was another matter completely," I assured him.

His face indicated that he didn't find me truthful.

"Before you ask, that's a private matter altogether."

Kohl said, "We need to work together on this."

I smiled. "If you will forgive my skepticism, I don't trust you to have my best interest in mind, much less Tristan's or his family's. Moreno is a big fish. I bet if you lead the takedown of him, you get to write your ticket anywhere in the DEA. Maybe even bigger than that. Am I right?"

"Moreno is a killer. He's responsible for the murder of hundreds of people. I want to stop him."

"I am sure," I conceded. "But the boon to your career wouldn't be bad either."

He lifted his hands with some exasperation. "Fine, we won't work together. That means if you get in my way, then I'll be arresting you for obstruction of justice."

"That must mean you have some concrete evidence against Tristan," I said. "Otherwise, it's just speculation. Maybe circumstantial. In which case, I'm not really obstructing justice.

"Unless you have some evidence you want to show me," I added.

He pushed away from the bar, scraping the stool's legs across the hardwood floor. "Gordon, you are stepping in shit that you can't get off your boot."

"My boots. My problem. Perhaps at this point, you should realize these little conversations aren't fruitful. If you want to arrest me, lay a charge on me. If you don't have anything, get the hell out. You are taking up space at my bar."

The DEA agent attempted to stare me down. He snarled at me when I didn't blink, and he turned around and stormed out of the Manta Club.

13

Flowering Trail Road wasn't as alluring as its name might make it seem. Instead of trails of flowers, the sidewalks were lined with four-foot chain-link fences surrounding typical lower-middle-class single-family homes. I say typical, but I mean for Florida. Houses, where I'm from in rural Arkansas, didn't look like these cinder block structures with flat roofs.

I can't say I care one way or the other. From the moment I turned eighteen, I hadn't lived in a house. For years it was barracks, and when I was finally discharged, I bought *Carina* and moved onboard her while I cleaned her up.

Ponce Alvarez's home was nearly identical to every other house. The wood trim on his house was rotted while most of the other homes had some fresher paint and some evidence of recent maintenance. The yard was void of toys, while the rest showed some signs of children in the homes.

An audacious blue Honda Del Sol with yellow stripes swooping up the doors and an aftermarket spoiler that rose at least eight inches off the trunk sat in the driveway. It was the only car there.

The tree in the front yard was laden with Spanish moss that hung almost to the grassless, dirt yard.

I sat in Missy's BMW. She was still hanging low on *Carina*, and I didn't want to monopolize the marina's Toyota. Plus, if the DEA was following me, then they would have a hard time in a new car. I hadn't been looking for anyone following me before my interaction with Kohl, but now I was double-checking my mirror and doing some extra evasive maneuvers. I was reasonably confident that no one had tailed me.

The window was down, but the sun was already turning the car into a little oven. There was no breeze to offer any relief. However, I didn't know how long I would be sitting, and running the air seemed like a waste of gas. My body doesn't mind the heat, and when I get back to the marina, I could shower before heading to bed. If Missy was going to be staying another night, then she might appreciate me washing the sticky Florida sweat and grime off me.

Following Alvarez wasn't going to produce a lot of results. At least as far as helping me find Tristan. Unless Moreno's guys found him first. Those chances seemed thin if they hadn't turned anything up yet. I was more interested in how the operation worked and who was involved. Alvarez and his friend had turned to threatening Kayla and Abbie in order to find Tristan. That needed to be stopped now. Protecting the girls in Tristan's life was a slightly higher priority. I knew that he'd expect me to protect them before finding him. At least, I hoped the kid I served with still thought that way, despite whatever mistakes he had made lately.

Two toddlers, wearing only diapers, were jumping through a sprinkler while their mother hung laundry on a makeshift clothesline. Their giggles were audible across the street. My eyes caught the young mother who had a half-smile on her face as she listened to her kids playing gleefully.

A few doors down, another woman shouted something to the young mother. They spoke in Spanish across the yards. The second woman said something, and both looked in my direction. I offered a small wave. A gesture meant to convey that I was harmless. The women appeared to think otherwise. The young mother hurriedly hung the last of her laundry before ushering the wet tots into the house.

The sprinkler slowed to a smaller and smaller arc of water. Until the metal contraption seemed to only spit a tiny spurt every second or so. Then the water was gone.

Way to go, Chase, I told myself. You ruined those kids' afternoon.

The smell of asphalt baking in the sun floated up from the street. It reminded me of the aroma that hit me every time I stepped off a plane in the desert. The sun seemed to warm the tar mixture until it released that smell. I was strangely comforted by the memory it triggered.

Missy had a few CDs in the car, but her taste in music tended toward the shitty. In fact, on a scale of crap to pure utter shite, her music collection was, in my opinion, on the far end. I groaned as I flipped through Bruno Mars, Justin Bieber, and Destiny's Child. Giving up on the CDs, I started tuning the radio instead until I found a classic rock station that was playing Van Morrison's "Into the Mystic." With a half-grin, I leaned back as I watched Alvarez's house.

The music didn't help to make anything happen. The afternoon was waning. A couple of hours passed while I sat on Flowering Trail.

Finally, when I was near the point of giving up, Ponce Alvarez came out of his house. By now, my forehead was

bubbled with sweat. My shirt was sticking to my back, and I
hastened to imagine how I was starting to smell.

He was talking on the phone. He stood under the
Spanish moss talking. He pulled on a piece of moss until it
came free. He idly dropped it on the ground. When he
seemed to be through with his conversation, he stuck the
phone in his pocket and climbed into his Del Sol and
backed out of the drive. I waited as he reversed into the
street and started in the other direction. When the little
blue and yellow Honda had driven down the road a block, I
began to follow him, staying a decent distance back and
hoping that he didn't notice the silver BMW in his rearview
mirror.

We drove through several neighborhoods and along
some side streets. I spend very little time in Miami. If I go
much farther than the Costco in West Palm Beach, it's an
extraordinary occasion. Urban sprawl tends to turn my
stomach. My childhood was spent in a community of fewer
than fifty people, my elementary, junior, and high school
were all housed in the same building. The same nine kids
followed me from kindergarten through graduation. Well,
my high school graduation occurred on my second night on
Parris Island. I would like my neighbors several miles away
if I had my wish.

As I said, I don't come to Miami much, and I couldn't tell
you where we were going. The neighborhoods we were
entering were growing visibly more rundown. The businesses that had signs had them in Spanish. Many buildings
were just boarded up, the owners or tenants surrendering to
the decay.

When Alvarez stopped, we were on a populated thor-
oughfare through the western side of Miami. He parked on
the street. I found a spot half a block away, trying to remain

inconspicuous. The block we were on was a little less dilapidated than some we had driven past.

Alvarez crossed the street and entered a small diner. The elaborately hand-painted sign hanging over the double window facing the street showed a great deal more pride in the restaurant than some of the other businesses on the street displayed. Small print under the name stated, "Cuban Restaurant" and "*Comida de Cuba.*"

Sitting in the BMW, I sank down in the driver's seat and watched the front of the diner. The street was lined with cars, most older but well-maintained. A few spots held newer, sportier models. Chuckling to myself, I noted that there wasn't a single minivan in sight.

This time, the engine stayed on. The air was cooling the interior and keeping the sweat at bay. As I said, I didn't mind the heat, but the sweat might be offensive to anyone with olfactory glands.

While I stared at the door of Padrino's, I fiddled with the radio until I found another station playing some Sting. That seemed as good as anything else.

Thirty minutes passed. Or at least close to that. The door to the diner opened, and Alvarez came out with his buddy, the spiky-haired smart-ass. The two got into the Del Sol and pulled away from the curb. I took a moment and considered whether to follow the two of them or check out Padrino's. The latter seemed like a better idea. Something about the restaurant didn't fit in the neighborhood. Someone was keeping a nice joint open in a wasteland. There has to be a good reason for that.

Besides, I was a little hungry.

Unless the two goons were on their way to find Tristan, letting them go wasn't a big deal.

Locking up the car, I started toward the little cafe. The

alarm beeped as I set it. The last thing I wanted to do was explain to Missy how something happened to her BMW. Truthfully, I doubted she would care-especially given her current state of mind.

Inside Padrino's, there were seven tables. Most were empty, but two in the back corner were occupied. The center of that group was a tall, thin man, probably of Cuban descent. His hair was flecked with gray, and he was the one in charge. Two men sat at the table with him, and a third man sat at the next table alone. The scar across the face of the one sitting alone reminded me of a man from the church where my parents dragged me as a kid. The story was that the man's wife unloaded two rounds of birdshot in his face when she caught him with one of the Sunday school teachers. I don't remember what happened to that teacher.

A neon sign scrolled over the table, reading "Cristal." Two cans of beer sporting the same name were sitting on the table.

A small counter stood close to the door. A beautiful young girl was behind the counter; she looked at me curiously.

"*¿Necesitas una mesa?*"

"*No habla español,*" I explained.

"Do you need a table?" she asked gracefully.

"Can I order it to-go?"

She nodded and passed me a menu. I scanned the listed items in Spanish. While I don't speak Spanish, I can manage reading it.

"Can I get a *Media Noche*?" I asked.

She wrote my order on a pad and smiled at me before she walked into the back.

"Good choice," an accented voice came from the table in the corner.

I turned and saw that the man in the center was speaking. "Thanks," I said.

"You should come back for the *boliche* sometime," he commented.

My face must have displayed my confusion. He added, "It's *carne*...beef. Stuffed beef. Very good. Tender and delicious."

"That sounds good," I said. "I'll come back."

"How did you find Padrino's?" he asked. His tone and demeanor were docile, but his eyes reminded me of something sinister I had seen in the eyes of a Taliban warlord before he detonated a bomb, killing several innocent Afghans in a square.

"It was recommended," I said. "I thought it would be good to try it."

The smile he had sent shivers up my spine. "Where are you from?" he asked.

I returned his smile with one that was filled with Arkansas charm. "Originally, a cow farm in Arkansas."

"Originally?"

"I move around a lot now. In fact, I am planning to visit Cuba soon. I wanted to sample some food before I go."

"I am sorry," he said with a humble tone. "I don't remember your name."

"We didn't exchange names, so you can't be faulted for that."

He smiled again. His teeth were impressively white. Eerily white.

"*Señor*," the girl said from behind the counter. She held a white paper bag.

I bowed my head to the man. "It's been a pleasure," I said before turning to pay the young girl.

"Be sure to come back for the *boliche*," he said to my back.

"Certainly," I said as I left the cafeteria. I had a suspicion that the man I met was Alvarez and Spike's boss, and possibly Julio Moreno himself.

Whoever he was, he was dangerous. I wondered if he knew who I was, or if he just suspected me of being a federal agent.

Glancing over my shoulder, I saw the scarred man that had been sitting alone coming out of Padrino's. He turned down the sidewalk behind me.

14

This time I didn't have a butcher knife strapped to my arm. I made a couple of quick assumptions. The first was that Scar was very likely carrying a firearm, and if I wasn't careful, it might make my day turn for the worst. That meant that whatever I did next needed to provide me with the upper hand, or at the very least even the playing field.

The second was that I needed to lose Scar before I got to Missy's car. Trying to get into and start the car would put me in a vulnerable spot. Not to mention getting it out of the parking spot I maneuvered into earlier. He'd have plenty of opportunities to put a bullet or two into me, or worse—into the BMW.

No, I was going to have to take a walk and lose him.

The third thing I assumed was a little more heartbreaking. I was never going to get a chance to try the sandwich in my bag.

Increasing my pace fractionally, I tried to increase the distance between us without going into a full sprint. I could outrun Scar easily. He was big and strong, that was evident from looking at him. He was used to winning fights. Not against someone who knew how to fight, though. He thought he was scary. I could see that in his eyes in Padrino's. Intimidation isn't strength.

I was now a little farther ahead of Scar. Ticking the seconds off in my head, I counted a ten-second lead on him at our current speed. As soon as I reached the end of the block, I took a left. The instant that I was out of his line of vision, I sprinted down the street. I counted off seven seconds. Then I slowed to my original pace.

He made the turn behind me. Now I had a significant lead on him. Unless he decided to charge me or shoot me, I gave myself a little room to work. I decided to force his hand. When a small break in traffic appeared, I jogged across the street in the middle of the block.

When I stepped off the street onto the other sidewalk, I took a quick right down an alley. A quick glance confirmed my tail was trying to time the traffic so he could cross. I broke into another run. The alley was short enough that I was able to race through it before Scar even made it to this side of the street.

I could lose him now, or I could wait and confront him. Confronting him was more visceral. There was nothing to gain from it. Losing him was the smarter option.

Besides, I might still be able to enjoy the *Media Noche* in my bag.

The alley hit the next street, and I went right. I could make the block and get back to the BMW while he tried to figure out which way I went. My feet pounded against the sidewalk as I jogged up the block.

When I reached the corner, a delivery van pulled up in front of me. The side door slid open, and Agent Kohl stared at me.

"Get in," he ordered.

"Am I under arrest?"

He rolled his eyes. "Get in the damn van, or you will be."

I took a quick survey in my head. Kohl wasn't going to try and kill me. At least, I didn't think he would. Scar, on the other hand, could very well try just that. The decision was easy. I obeyed Kohl and climbed into the back. "I hope this doesn't end up with me in a black site somewhere."

"Drive, Ken," Kohl ordered the driver.

The van pulled off the curb, and I glanced out the side window to see Scar come out of the alley.

"The man following you is Esteban Velázquez. He's an enforcer for Moreno. He is a person of interest in numerous murders, including three drug enforcement agents about ten years ago."

The van bounced and jarred as it drove over the roads of this unmaintained neighborhood. Road work didn't seem a priority around here, and judging from the facades of many of the buildings, neither did regular upkeep. This was a forgotten section of Miami that most of the denizens of West Palm Beach would never see. The neighborhood was as war-torn as many places I saw in Afghanistan and Iraq. This didn't feel like America.

"You think he wanted to take my sandwich?"

"He doesn't get involved unless someone else ends up dead," Kohl stated.

I bit my tongue, mainly because I had nothing to add. My sixth sense was telling me when Moreno's goon started following me that he had that exact plan.

"Care to tell me why you were having lunch with Julio Moreno?" Kohl asked.

"You weren't following me today," I stated firmly.

"We were," Kohl responded, "until you decided to give my agents the slip."

I shrugged. "I like my privacy."

Kohl narrowed his eyes, a trait I wondered if he did with everyone, or if I was just special.

"That means that you are watching Padrino's because it is Moreno's little hangout. Am I right?"

"You seem to have been following Ponce Alvarez. How did you pick up on him?"

We stared at each other for a few seconds.

Kohl broke the silence, "Gordon, you keep stepping on my toes here. It seems you won't go away."

"I'm just trying to find a good sandwich."

Kohl smirked, maybe at my wit. Probably not, though. "Why don't I tell you what I know about you?" he suggested.

I shrugged. "If you've been following me, then you know enough, I'm sure."

"Not everything," he stated. "I know that Alvarez and Cabrera visited Locke's home the other night. Now, his wife and daughter are nowhere to be found. Then, you and Alvarez have a little altercation at the Tilly Inn. Next thing I know, you are showing up at Moreno's restaurant. Do tell me again how you aren't involved. Are you protecting the wife or Locke?"

"Which one is Cabrera?" I asked.

"Short guy. Greasy hair."

"Spiked?"

He nodded.

"Let me ask you something, Kohl," I started. "If your wife and daughter got a visit from the two of them, what would you want Ken up there to do about it?"

Kohl glanced at the driver whose eyes looked back in the

rearview mirror. "Are you saying that Tristan Locke asked you to protect his wife?"

I shook my head. "No, he didn't."

"Have you talked to him?"

I shook my head again. "I have a feeling that he's dead."

That was the first time I mentioned my thoughts. They had been milling around my head for the last day.

"You think Moreno had him killed?"

"No," I answered. "Alvarez and Carbera..."

"Cabrera," he corrected me.

"Right," I continued, "Alvarez and Cabrera were looking for him. I don't think they would be doing that if they killed him."

"Then what makes you think he is dead?" Kohl asked.

My eyes cut to Ken driving through a nicer stretch of neighborhood. Maybe the delivery van circling Moreno's block was a little too obvious. While I worried that Tristan was dead, I wasn't sure. The last thing I wanted was to find out that I had given the evidence to have him convicted or worse. My steps needed to be taken gingerly.

"Let me state unequivocally that everything I know is pure supposition."

Kohl nodded. "In other words, off the record and inadmissible."

"Exactly," I said, "and getting me to testify is not going to be in your case's best interest."

Reluctantly, Kohl seemed to agree.

"Tristan may or may not have been involved in something with Moreno. Enough so that now Moreno thinks he owes him a lot of money. However, he, or at least his goons, are still looking for him, so they haven't done anything to him yet. Moreno thinks that he is still out there in hiding. Alvarez and..."

"Cabrera," Kohl supplied.

"Right," I said. "I can't seem to get that. Cabrera. The two of them now go to his wife and try to strong-arm her, hoping that he is talking to her. Thinking maybe threatening his family would bring him out."

Kohl listened. Even Ken seemed to be intent on my theory.

I continued, "This is the part that makes me think he is already dead. He hasn't talked to his wife in a long time. That seems unusual for someone like Tristan. I know that I haven't really talked to him in years, but he was loyal and devoted. He needs to get that kind of affection. He might go off on his own, but he'd still need to talk to his wife and daughter."

"And he hasn't?" Ken asked from the driver's seat.

"Right."

Kohl asked, "Do you think someone killed him?"

"Seems likely. You might want to check any John Does. Kayla hasn't involved the police, so there isn't a missing person case open."

"Who would kill him?"

"Consider this," I suggested. "If you were in debt to someone like Moreno, what are your options?"

Ken spouted, "Find the money to pay him back."

"Otherwise, he is going to kill you, right?" I asked.

Ken nodded. Kohl said, "You think he got involved with someone else?"

I shrugged. "I don't actually know shit. That's the problem. As far as I am concerned, though, whether Tristan was involved with Moreno or not—his family stays protected."

"From Moreno?" Kohl asked.

"He seems to be the most viable threat."

"And you are doing this out of the kindness of your heart?"

I glared at Kohl. "I'm doing this because it's what a brother does."

"You're willing to go up against the biggest drug cartel in Florida for her?"

"Kohl, if you don't get it, then I guess, I can never explain it to you," I stated. "Suffice it to say, yes, I am willing to go up against Moreno to help this woman and her child."

My peripheral vision caught Ken gesturing in agreement.

"Fine, Gordon," Kohl agreed. "We are going to check any John Does against Locke, but if we can't get his cooperation, then we can't help his family."

"No offense, Agent Kohl," I said, "I don't think you could help him even with his cooperation. Whatever involvement he had with Moreno was marginal, and I assure you, Moreno was well-shielded from Tristan's involvement."

"Doesn't mean he can't help our case," Kohl said defiantly.

"Not enough to justify the sacrifice he might make. It's not that I don't trust you, Kohl, but I know how the government cogs rotate. They don't tend to work in favor of the little mouse caught in between the gears. He might make it messy for the powers that be, but he ends up squished every time."

Kohl's face twisted. "I protect my CIs," he announced firmly.

"I don't doubt you intend to," I told him. "Just you don't call all the shots, do you? American bureaucracy beats the little guy almost always."

"Cynical, aren't you?"

I shrugged. "I watched brothers and sisters fight and die

in battles that should have never been engaged. Because somebody higher up wanted to attempt a strategic move. Some worked, but most were abject failures. Let's say that I trust you. I do not trust your superiors or their superiors. Not to protect a guy who might have been doing shady things just to feed his family."

Kohl remained silent. Ken took another glimpse at me in the mirror, his eyes were empathetic. He served somewhere. He held himself like a soldier, not that Kohl was unprofessional. There is just something that is trained into your core during training that never goes away. Not if you were a good soldier.

"Hey, Ken," I said, "if you guys aren't arresting me, can you drop me close to my car?"

He glanced at Kohl, who gave a curt nod of his head.

I added, "I assume you know where I parked."

15

The Manta Club was busy. The late afternoon crowd was filling in. Local bankers, lawyers, and other white-collared folks were coming in for an hour or two of socializing and networking. I wasn't working behind the bar. Really, I wasn't working at all.

Hunter was slinging drinks for the crowd, and I was enjoying a rum and orange juice. Most drinkers fall into a routine. Beer drinkers rarely range far from beer. Hardcore drinkers will swallow anything with alcohol, and price versus punch is usually the deciding factor. Social drinkers stick to the cocktail *du jour*. Once it was the Cosmo, now it seems the Moscow Mule is the rage. My drink of choice varies, I can appreciate a good whiskey or a nice local beer. Today I felt like something fruity. I do live in South Florida, and fruity drinks are always acceptable.

"You need anything to eat?" Hunter asked as he passed by me.

"I'll wait till the rush is gone," I assured him.

He gave me an appreciative gesture. I took a sip of my drink. Over the rim of the glass, I caught Michael walking into the bar. I hadn't seen Missy since this morning. She wasn't on board *Carina* when I returned from Miami. She might have gone to her office or even home for a bit. In truth, I didn't give it much thought until just now.

Michael walked over and sat next to me at the bar.

"Chase." His greeting was solemn and sharp.

"Michael." He hadn't started snidely, and I didn't see any reason to fire the first shot.

"About this morning," he started.

Hunter appeared in front of him. "Get you a drink, Michael?" he asked.

"Maker's and Coke," the lawyer said.

Hunter tapped the bar in front of Michael before turning to grab the wax-necked bottle of bourbon.

"Anyway," he continued. "About this morning. I'm sorry for causing a scene."

I acknowledged his apology with a nod. He had more burdens on his shoulders, and he was about to unburden them. I wanted to see what was coming next before I considered giving him the satisfaction of a verbal acceptance.

"I was out of line," he said under his breath as Hunter placed a napkin on the bar in front of Michael, followed by a tall thin glass filled with bourbon and cola.

"Yeah, you were," I reaffirmed to him.

He dropped his head, and I waited. He was about to tell me about his problems. I've been around long enough to recognize the signs.

"You probably know as much about our relationship as I do," he said.

Resisting all urges, I refrained from giving any sign of agreement.

"I guess it's a sham," he muttered. "Our marriage, that is."

He took a drink from the paper straw in his glass. He made a face, pulled it out of the drink, and dropped it on the bar.

"I suppose it always was," he continued.

Listening, I took another drink and thought that I was going to need a double next time. The next time would be very soon. I chugged the rest of my glass.

"We are just roommates," he sighed.

Hunter locked eyes with me for a second, and I gave him the subtle signal that I needed another. My hand flashed two fingers, indicating I wanted a double. Without breaking his stride, Hunter nodded and continued to make a gin and tonic.

"What do you want exactly?" I asked Michael.

"I know that you and Missy are," he paused, "close."

Raising my hand, I stopped him. Hunter replaced my glass with another full one that was a much paler orange. I took a gulp before continuing. Hunter had more than doubled the rum. I needed it to get through a conversation with Michael.

"Michael," I started, "let's not get into shit that you don't want to dig up. As I understand it, you aren't exactly the faithful, devoted type. I don't understand the dynamics of your marriage. And honestly, I don't want to. I don't actually like you. You are a smug, entitled asshat. But at some point, Missy didn't think that, so there must be something worthwhile inside you.

"If you want my opinion, Michael, and I doubt you do, this isn't about me and Missy. You feel deflated because whatever girl you were banging up north dumped you or something. I wouldn't suggest you try to wrest control of your relationship from Missy. She doesn't need you, and you should realize that. She isn't going to complete you. Neither is the next young girl you decide to sleep with."

He stared at me. His eyes began to burn. "You think you know everything," he snapped.

"Look," I snarled at him, "you brought this over here. Don't get pissy with me because you suddenly found out what I think about you. If you didn't already know that, then you are an effing moron."

"I know how you feel about me. You are sleeping with my wife!" His voice escalated, and Hunter's head turned toward us.

"Michael, you hold your voice down, or you and I are going outside, even if I have to drag you by the hair." My eyes narrowed, and I added, "I think you know that I'll do it, too."

The rage that flared in his eyes changed to shock, maybe fear.

"Now, I don't care what you think is going on. You have a problem with anything to do with your wife, you go to her. Don't drag me into it."

"You're already in it," he hissed.

My head cocked sideways as I looked at this pathetic man. "Grow a pair," I told him. "I don't answer to you; I don't think Missy answers to you. You want to change something, work on your own damned self. Stop wallowing, and certainly, don't try to muddy the rest of us because you think it will make you feel better."

He downed the Maker's and Coke quickly and pushed the glass away from him. He grunted something at me that I couldn't understand before he walked away from the bar.

When he disappeared through the doors, Hunter walked over and picked up his glass. "Didn't wait for the check again," he said.

"Charge it to his house account. Be sure to throw twenty percent on there."

"Sounded like he bought your drinks too," he quipped.

Smiling, I said, "I doubt he likes me enough."

"Yeah," Hunter said, "he was getting pretty loud for a second there."

We shared a look. His face assured his discretion.

"He's a jackass," Hunter added as he took Michael's glass.

"That's being awfully nice of you."

He laughed as he walked across the bar to another guest.

"Chase," I heard someone say.

My head turned to see Peterson straddle the stool next to me.

"I got a call," he said. "They want it dropped in twenty minutes."

"That's quick."

"Yeah, I had to haul ass over here to see you."

"Where?"

"The bridge over Lake Clarke on I-95. You have to drop it off the bridge on the southbound side."

"Twenty minutes?" I asked again. Luckily, I still had the keys to Missy's BMW. Even with that, the time frame was a tight squeeze. Just getting onto I-95 would take ten minutes.

He nodded. A small package was in his hand. He pushed it toward me. "Can you make it?"

Two grand was a good two-months' expenses in the Bahamas. My fingers wrapped around the package. "Yeah, I can do it," I promised him.

I dropped a twenty-dollar bill on the bar. Hunter charged my drinks to Michael. "I'll be back, Hunter," I told him as I hurried out of the Manta Club.

The traffic was past the heaviest point, but even at a

quarter after six, the movement was slow going. Once I got on the interstate, it was stop-and-go for the next mile, and that took me nearly ten minutes. The drop was supposed to happen in six minutes. I assumed that no one synchronized watches or anything, but I wasn't sure what the average time was a blackmailer waits for his drop.

The tight timeline would ensure that little could be done to surveil the drop point. Perhaps I was spotted at Dehrer Park. Or maybe, my drug enforcement tail was spotted. My eyes were scanning for anyone following me, but with the number of headlights coming on as the sun faded, it was impossible to determine. The rush to reach the bridge didn't leave me any time to lose a tail, either.

Five minutes.

The lake was off to the west. I wasn't familiar with it except to drive past it. There was a channel that connected it to the Atlantic, but I didn't think I could squeeze *Carina* under the concrete bridges. Besides, I never felt an inclination to try. These types of lakes covered the area fed by the glades and dumped into the ocean somewhere down the trail.

The next exit was past the bridge and the off-ramp was clogged. The taillights in front of me crept forward.

Four minutes.

My fingers tapped on the steering wheel as if they could will the drivers in front of me to move faster. They failed miserably.

The orange sky stretched eastward. From the raised interstate, I could look out toward the black night crawling across the ocean toward land.

The lights ahead started moving a little faster. I pulled over into the break-down lane and raced forward.

Three minutes.

The traffic was moving, and as I crested the bridge, I could see a tow truck moving a car off the interstate, allowing the cars to flow more freely.

Opening the package, I found the envelope for me. I glimpsed inside to count twenty bills. Stuffing that envelope in my shorts, I turned my hazard flashers on and got out of the car. Peering over the bridge, I didn't see anything except water below.

Was I just supposed to drop the package? Twenty grand sinking to the bottom of the canal seemed like a scary endeavor.

It was time. Peterson said to drop it over the side. I looked again. Extending my hand out, I let the package fall from my grip. A second and a half passed before the cardboard box splashed into the water. I could see it floating, bobbing up and down with the waves.

Was I willing to jump in after it?

It's twenty-thousand dollars.

The answer was yes, I would.

My eyes stayed locked on the white box drifting in the water. The nose of a boat came from under the bridge. A white center console fishing boat edged into view. The hardtop bimini blocked my vision. I didn't know the make of the vessel, but it was sporting a 225-horsepower Yamaha motor on the back. The driver reached out from under the awning and scooped the box up with a fishing net. When the net and package were on board, he vanished again under the cover. I could make out that it was a thin white male. Even his height was hard to discern when looking from above. A ball cap with a marlin on it shielded his face from me too.

The motor screamed as he pressed the throttle down. The boat raced away, leaving a trail of waves rolling out of its wake. The boat had a name on the transom, though-*King of Hookers*. Classy, I thought.

The fishing boat sped down the channel into Lake Clarke. The fading sunlight only reflected in glints off the waves it left behind. In less than a minute, the vessel curved along the bend of the shoreline and disappeared onto the lake.

I stared off after it for a minute or two after it was gone from sight. The drop was smart, and I wondered why he would prominently display the name of his boat. Those center consoles are a dime a dozen around here.

The answer was that the boat wasn't his. He picked a great spot, limited the time to prepare for anything shady, and left himself multiple avenues to get away. Stealing a boat was the smart thing too. Even if I traced the vessel, I would get nothing from it.

For a second, I considered that he was smart enough to deserve the seventy thousand he made this week. Still, I knew that if he wasn't found, Peterson would always look over his shoulder. Whatever the man had on him, it was enough to keep the mayor scared and enough for him to shell out a fee to me that would keep me on the boat for the next five years.

I got back into the car and pulled back onto the interstate.

16

Peterson was still at the bar when I returned. The crowd had diminished some, but he had a couple of guys trying to vie for his attention like he had double D's and a sign that said "Available."

He peeked up from his conversation to see me take a seat up at a stool across from him. With no indication that he had any interest in my return, he continued talking to a balding man wearing a two-thousand-dollar suit that looked like he had just put it on.

Hunter walked by and asked, "You back? Want another drink?"

"Yeah, and can you order me a burger? Medium rare with that smoked *brie* they have back there."

Hunter moved around the bar. In less than a minute, he dropped a drink off.

"Hey there," Missy sidled up next to me. "I heard Michael was in earlier."

The blood rushed to my cheeks, and I felt the flush of heat in my face.

"I'm so sorry about that," she offered.

"It's fine. He seemed wound up pretty tight."

She shook her head slowly. "That's no excuse. I have to talk to him. I just don't want to."

"Then don't do it yet," I suggested. "Let the bastard stew a bit. Michael needs to find his peace. Maybe you do, too."

She looked at me. "I have an idea of what needs to happen."

"But..."

She shrugged. "I have to work on payroll and approve Chef's new menu."

"Sounds like fun."

"You hear anything from your Marine buddy?"

"No," I answered. "He has gotten in with some bad guys."

Missy cringed. "Think he's okay?"

"I really don't," I said. "Maybe I'm wrong, but my gut tells me he's gone."

Her hand covered mine gingerly. "Oh, Chase, I'm sorry."

My hand turned and squeezed hers. "The kid made his bed, I suppose."

Hunter came around the center of the bar carrying my cheeseburger. Missy released my hand and retracted her arm like a whip. Hunter didn't appear fazed by the intimacy we were sharing.

"You know, you can never fire Hunter," I pointed out as I lifted the bun on my burger to check the accuracy of my order.

"Hell," she joked, "I was just going to sleep with him."

I laughed. "I figured you already had."

"Keep it up," she snapped, "and I just might."

She stood up. "I have work to do. Can I crash with you tonight?"

"Want I should invite Hunter too?"

She grinned. "You think it requires both of you?"

When she walked away, I picked up the burger and took a bite. As I chewed, I noticed Peterson's group had dwindled. He excused himself from the two guys still talking. He moved around to me.

"Everything good, Chase?"

"Yeah," I said when I swallowed. "I saw the guy. He was in a fishing boat. Picked it up and jetted off toward the lake."

"You saw him?" Peterson asked excitedly.

"Not enough to identify him," I explained. "The boat, though, was named *King of Hookers* in case you want to pursue it."

"*King of Hookers*?"

"Classy, right?"

Peterson said, "Thank you for this, Chase."

I lifted my hands. "Don't thank me. I didn't do anything. I haven't helped you at all."

He gave me a curt nod, and another constituent of his grabbed his arm. With that, the mayor moved back into political mode. I finished my burger and flagged Hunter down for my check.

The night was clear, save a few cumulus clouds churning past the moon. My skin tingled as the breeze from the ocean rushed in. Strands of hair caught the wind and danced around my head. I walked along the sidewalk, where Alvarez had followed me.

My thoughts about Tristan were jumbled. At what point should I tell my concerns to Kayla? Was I jumping the gun here? There was no proof that he was dead. If we were still in the desert, would I be so quick to decide he could be left behind without really knowing?

Laughter rode on the wind from somewhere. I glanced back to see two couples on the Tilly's patio. They were in their forties. Not locals either, this was a getaway for them.

I turned back to continue my walk. A man stepped in front of me. The SIG Sauer that he was pointing at me was the first thing I noticed. He was Latino. Not Scar or Alvarez and whatever his name was. He wasn't as big as Scar or Alvarez, and if he wasn't holding a gun on me, I felt that I could take him in a fight. However, at this point, there was no opening for me.

I lifted my hands to about my mid-torso. There's the semblance of surrender while freeing my hands up to react if the opportunity presented itself. I was willing to lift them all the way if he insisted, but I had a feeling that he would accept it as surrender. Most people's egos make them think they are far more superior than they are. Add in a weapon, and they become cocky.

"*Vamos*," he ordered.

My high school Spanish still needed brushing up, but I was pretty sure it meant "Go." Plus, he waved his gun toward the road.

He stayed about six feet behind me, just far enough that I couldn't disarm him before he shot me-smart of him.

A black Hummer was parked on the street.

"*Entra*."

I turned and looked at him questioningly.

"*Entra*," he repeated.

"*No habla*," I explained.

The rear door opened. Light spilled out onto the asphalt from inside.

"Why don't you join me, Mister Gordon?" The voice was heavily accented, and the word "Mister" was enunciated with care and precision.

With a gun in my back, I accepted the invitation. Julio Moreno was seated in the back seat with Scar. I climbed in and sat on the seat, facing Moreno. The interior of the

Hummer was not stock. Two leather benches faced each other. LED strips along the ceiling cast a pale, bright light. The new guy sat next to me, facing forward.

"Mister Gordon," Moreno started, "how was your sandwich?"

"Very good. I don't suppose you brought me any of that... whatever it was?"

"*Boliche*," he said. "No, I thought we could have a talk."

"Well, talk," I replied.

Moreno's eyes narrowed. He studied me carefully. "I assume that since you are on good terms with the Drug Enforcement Agency, you know who I am."

"Good terms might be an exaggeration," I said. "But, yes, I know who you are."

Moreno looked at Scar and said, "*Buscalo*."

Scar ripped my shirt open and began to pat me down.

"*Nada*," he said to Moreno.

"That was great," I quipped. "Next time, why don't you buy me dinner before feeling me up?"

"Where is Tristan Locke?" Moreno demanded.

"Ah," I said, dragging the one syllable out. "I do not know that."

"You know something," he stated flatly.

"Lots," I confirmed. "Nothing about where Tristan is."

"He owes me a great deal of money." Moreno glared at me.

"Something like twenty-five grand, I hear. Am I right?"

A curt nod came from the man.

"What happened?" I asked, "Did Tristan say that the Coasties boarded him? He had to dump the drugs?"

"So he says," Moreno answered. "Though, that is not my concern."

"In your business, that's pocket change," I pointed out.

Moreno growled, "If you let the dog steal your scraps, before long, he will be taking the food from your mouth."

"I see. Good old gangster logic. I bet your employees go all out for Boss's Week, don't they."

"Is Locke working with Agent Kohl?" he asked.

"That I can answer," I said excitedly. "He is not. That's not Tristan's style."

"But you work with Kohl?" he asked.

"Again," I said, "I do not. Kohl is looking for any traction to get you with. He seems a bit desperate."

"Where is Locke?"

"I said, 'I don't know'." I added, "I know you didn't kill him, so there's that."

"Maybe he took my drugs and sold them. That kind of money can hide a man for a while."

"Maybe," I responded. "I don't think so."

Moreno stared at me. He seemed to be thinking. Then he asked, "Do you think he is still alive?"

My expression must have given away my thoughts. I was taken back by the question.

Moreno smiled, "But you don't know for sure, am I correct?"

I shook my head, "I don't know. I really don't."

"May I make a..." he paused as he looked for a word, "guess? Locke may have stolen my package and attempted to sell it to someone else. That person might have been greedy and decided that killing Locke meant he could have the money and the product."

That scenario hadn't occurred to me. If Tristan was dumb enough to get involved with Moreno, he might be dumb enough to think he could out-think him. Kayla mentioned him complaining about the Coast Guard, though.

"I'm afraid you have little to offer me," Moreno stated.

"But wait, there's more," I said. "If you act now, I'll throw in one of those towel things that never get wet."

"You make jokes," Moreno said. "Are you not afraid of me?"

"No, I'm not," I told him. "Wait, is that what you are going for?"

"What about your friend, Locke?" Moreno asked.

Smiling, I shook my head. "Nope, not afraid of him either, but between the two of you, he'd take the lead. Besides, you think he's dead now."

"I'm only making a guess," he said.

I remained still. Measuring in my head the distance from my arm to the SIG Sauer still pointed at my gut.

Moreno scowled. "Are you not afraid I'll find and hurt him or his family?"

"Mr. Moreno," I began. "May I call you Julio?"

Scar squinted at me. I wasn't sure if he spoke English or not. Judging from his reaction, I think he did.

"You may not," Moreno said.

Defiantly, I said, "Julio, I can only tell you this. If something were to happen to Tristan's family, then the number of days you get to spend above ground is going to be single digits."

"*Eres tonto*," he muttered. Then he translated, "You are a fool."

"*No, señor*," I corrected. "You are. What did you know about Tristan before you let him run drugs up and down the coast for you? What did you know about me before you dragged me into your car?"

His face twisted. "You were in the Army with Locke," he said confidently.

"Wrong," I said. My elbow popped up and caught the

gunman in the jaw as my right hand crossed my body and picked the SIG from his grip. The barrel of the SIG cracked Scar on the nose before he could draw his own gun. In the half a second that Scar was stunned, I elbowed the first guy again in his nose. This time an audible crack resounded through the Hummer.

The SIG was leveled at Moreno. I locked eyes with him. "Tell him to very slowly remove whatever weapon he has. I feel the least bit uncomfortable, and I will blow the back of your head off a second before I put one in his eye."

Moreno looked at Scar and nodded. Scar pulled a Colt .45 from his side, he held the gun by its barrel. I guess he did speak English.

I grabbed the grip and hit the guy next to me one more time, this time in the throat. He gasped for air. He was the closest to me, and that made him the most dangerous. Rules of engagement are that the most dangerous threat be eliminated first.

"Marine," I said bluntly. "We were both Marines."

"You are making a mistake," Moreno hissed through his teeth.

Holding both guns at Moreno and Scar, respectively, I asked, "You think I made a mistake? There are three of you inside a closed space and only one of me."

"You had surprise," Scar growled.

"Yes, and I won't get you that way again, will I?"

Scar bared his teeth slightly.

"Here's the thing," I explained. "What I said about going near Locke's family. I mean that. I can pick you with a rifle from seven hundred yards. I can wait days for you to stick your head out of the ground. Walk out of Padrino's with your belly full of borsch or whatever that shit is, and bam, you will be dead on the street."

"Not if I kill you first," Scar threatened.

I looked at Moreno. "Tristan and I were in a unit with four other Marines just like me. We are all alike, and if something happens to me, then Julio, my friend, you are going to be the number one target."

Scar bristled, and Moreno put a hand out to calm him.

"I seem to have underestimated you, Mister Gordon," he said calmly. "It is a mistake I don't tend to make."

"No," I responded, "I expect it isn't. Let's call a truce of sorts. I think perhaps this small change you have missing should just be written off. I'll stay clear of you, and you stay clear of me, Tristan, and his family. We can all live a much longer life that way."

Moreno said, "If Locke shows up, then we will decide the status of his debt at that time. However, I'll assure you that the decision will be civil. Will that be fair?"

"I'm a little sad I don't get to try the roast beef thing," I said.

"Hector," Moreno said to the man next to me, "please let Mister Gordon out."

Holding his bleeding nose and still trying to gasp for air, Hector struggled to get out of the car.

"Thank you, Señor Moreno," I offered. "I hope you don't mind if I keep the guns a bit longer. While you seem to be reasonable, wild hairs have caused all sorts of trouble in the past."

Moreno nodded as I stepped out. I retrained the SIG on Hector. While he was somewhat subdued, he was still the closest threat. He got back in the Hummer and shut the door. I backed away from the SUV as they pulled off the curb.

When the taillights were gone, I exhaled slowly.

17

My eyes opened, and I blinked a few times. I wasn't used to having the sun beam through the window to wake me up. Rolling my face away from the sun, I stared at Missy's naked form lying next to me.

After my encounter with Moreno, the best course of action, I thought, was to find a different place to spend the night. Moreno might decide that my insolence should be punished. Men like him don't always think of themselves as vulnerable. There was no point in letting him send Scar to kill me while I was sleeping in my berth.

Missy booked a room in the Tilly, and we decided to hide out here with a bottle of champagne.

But the flaw in this hotel was the east-facing windows. Everyone wants a view of the sea, but at six in the morning, the sun was a jarring wake-up call-my own fault for not closing the curtains before falling asleep.

Missy didn't seem fazed by the light. She breathed short, shallow breaths that huffed through her lips every second.

My watch said it was 6:20, and I contemplated taking a

shower. Instead, I let my head sink back into the pillow and thought about Tristan.

Moreno had all but confirmed that he hadn't found Tristan. My gut was still telling me that my friend had succumbed to a terrible fate. Maybe I was completely wrong about that. Perhaps, I was completely wrong about Tristan too. I assumed that the Tristan I had served with would never leave his wife and child. But the fact was that I didn't know the Tristan that got married and had a little girl.

Throw out all your assumptions, I told myself.

What if Tristan did steal Moreno's drugs? What if running drugs wasn't just a way to feed his family? I thought about what Detective Schilling said about the guy from his unit. Nothing could save him, no matter what Schilling and the other guys from his unit tried. Perhaps Tristan was just a low-rate criminal. Considering the circumstances that got him dishonorably discharged, the shoe might fit.

I felt confident that Moreno wasn't going to make a move against Kayla and Abbie right now. I needed to rethink Tristan's life. Where had he been hiding? Who was he associated with?

I sat up and stared out the open window.

"Where are you going?" Missy asked.

"Sorry, I woke you," I said.

"That's okay, but it's still early. What are you doing?"

"This Tristan thing is bothering me," I told her. "I'm going to do a little digging around."

"What about this drug dealer? Moran?"

"Moreno," I corrected. "I think I'm going to be wary, but I don't think he had anything to do with Tristan. Yet."

"You could just stay here for a bit," she suggested.

Twisting around, I lowered myself down and kissed her

lips. Her fingers coursed up through my hair, and she grabbed a handful.

I pulled away. "Why don't we put that on hold?"

She bit her lip. "I'll remember that later."

"Damn, woman," I growled, "you are insatiable."

"You can't go one more round?"

I laughed. "No, I'm gonna be walking funny all day as it is."

She threw a pillow at me as I went to the shower.

"Do you mind if I borrow your car again?" I asked over the sound of the running water.

"Can't today," she said, climbing into the shower with me. "I have to go to a Chamber of Commerce thing."

She started kissing my neck. My arms pulled her closer.

"I thought I said, 'later'."

"I know what you said." She kissed my chest.

My hands braced myself against the side of the shower as I lost all blood flow from my brain.

When she raised back up and kissed me, she said, "You owe me one."

"I thought I was already ahead by two."

She kissed me again. "You were, but you still owe me one."

I smiled. "Now," she said, "get out of the shower. I have to go to work."

Dripping on the floor, I toweled off. Missy was still in the shower when I finished dressing.

It was too early to call Kayla, but I wanted to talk to her in an hour or so. Tristan had to have a couple of friends around that he might have gone to if he needed a place to crash. If Kayla left me the key to her house, then maybe I could find something there that she missed.

I didn't want to monopolize the marina's car. Most

people would use an Uber or Lyft, but then most people have smartphones. I stopped by the concierge desk. The concierge on duty was William. Maybe Will. I didn't know. We were only on the nod across the way level of acquaintanceship.

"Hey," I said when I got to him.

"Hello, Chase," he said after what looked like a short struggle to place my name with my face. "What can I do for you?"

"Do you mind calling a cab for me?"

"Absolutely. Are you not working today?"

"Later, but I have to run some errands."

He nodded as he lifted the receiver on his desk. "I'll have them pick you up out front."

"Thanks."

On my way toward the front door, I stopped at the complimentary coffee station and grabbed a cup. When I plopped down on the bench outside the entrance of the Tilly Inn, I just soaked in the morning. The bartending life leaves me missing early mornings more often than not, but when I'm on the hook somewhere among some isolated islands, I enjoy the early mornings. I'll usually dive into the sea first thing for a snorkel and maybe a bit of spearfishing.

After only a couple of weeks back ashore, I was already thinking about heading back out. With Peterson's addition to my kitty, I didn't need to work as long as I thought I would need to. My brain was making little plans already. The Keys were a smooth sail south, and I could jump down to Cuba or over to the Caymans.

Eventually, I wanted to go through the Panama Canal and around the world. But I could spend a lifetime exploring the Caribbean, so I haven't got any set time for that destination.

The yellow taxi pulled up to the curb. I crumpled my empty coffee cup and deposited it in the trash bin.

A little incense holder on his dash filled the car with an aroma of spices. He was rail-thin, not like someone who was malnourished, but more like he hadn't succumbed to the American lifestyle of supersizing everything.

"Where to?" the cabbie asked me.

"3976 Long Shore. It should be out in Loxahatchee."

The driver typed the address into the GPS app on his phone. He clipped the phone into a holder clinging to the air vent over his radio.

The driver didn't seem interested in making small talk. It was a crapshoot. Sometimes cabbies will talk incessantly, and others are afraid to say a word. I didn't mind the quiet. The ride would give me time to catch some of the scenery. Like Miami, my travels don't venture too far inland.

He stuck to the main roads, and I wasn't sure exactly which ones we were traveling down. The businesses and commercial buildings began to taper off as we passed the Florida Turnpike. Golf courses and neighborhoods constructed atop what once was swampland passed us by. When he turned north, the scenery changed as we drove along the western side of a natural preserve.

My mind switched off after a while. Trees and Spanish moss racing past my view hypnotized me. When he came to a stop, I was jolted back.

I paid the driver and asked, "Can you wait a few minutes?" I held up a twenty-dollar bill.

The cabbie nodded without saying a word, and I held the bill forward for him to grab.

Tristan and Kayla lived in a small house, maybe eight hundred square feet. It was a small cube of cinder block painted and covered with chipped and broken stucco. The microscopic front yard was layered in rock and sand. A doll and a small toy Jeep were baking in the Florida sun, left no doubt by little Abbie. Modest attempts to make the house look like home were planted along the walkway. A hibiscus and a mango tree were on either side of the yard. It looked like they could only afford a plant or two at a time, and the gaps between anything planted seemed sad and large.

The front door was ajar, and I froze on the step. The wooden frame was splintered, where a foot had shoved the bolt through the wood. Glancing over my shoulder, I noticed the driver playing with his phone.

My toe pushed the door open. The inside looked like a tornado had ripped through it, a couch was sliced up and overturned. Things were scattered everywhere. I stepped in slowly, attempting to find an empty floor space to put my foot.

Don't touch anything, I reminded myself.

The search seemed both intense and thorough. The sheetrock walls were busted open, and gaping holes covered every wall. Even the ceiling had been ripped down.

This didn't feel like Moreno's work; he was more interested in sending a message. This devastation was visceral. Framed pictures of the Locke family were crushed underfoot. The frames were mostly intact, only the glass was broken.

The freezer door was open in the kitchen. Any food that had been in there was scattered on the floor in puddles. Some were beginning to smell as it rotted in the hotbox of a house. Drawers were flung around, and their contents scattered everywhere.

Even poor Abbie's room wasn't immune. Toys and stuffed animals were ripped and broken open. Her mattress was cut open and tossed aside.

The tank on the toilet was uncovered. The toilet itself was spared from the trashing that the rest of the house had endured. All of the air registers had been ripped from the wall. That made sense. They come in looking for something, and they started with the most logical and easiest-to-access hiding spots. The vents and toilet were early searches. As they didn't find what they were looking for, they got more frustrated.

Walking around to the back of the house, I found a tool shed. It hadn't escaped the search either. The door had been ripped open and hung loosely from one hinge. A hammer had been thrown through the window in the shed. Once I found a small handful of nails, I pulled the door the rest of the way off the hinge and carried it around to the front. Covering the busted door, I nailed the shed door over the opening. It was far from Fort Knox, but it might keep someone out of the house.

The awning over the front door had a small piece of wood where I hooked the hammer by its claw. I couldn't do much else here.

The ride back to the inn felt twice as long. Things were twisting in the wind.

When I was back, I found Joseph behind the bar. He works just a couple of days a week as a relief bartender. He's semi-retired in his sixties. He worked in Vegas back in the eighties, and he has some great stories about the orgy of excesses that coursed through Sin City back then.

"Mornin', Chase," he said as I came into the Manta. "Haven't seen you since you got back. How was your trip?"

"Great. I'm ready to head back out already."

He nodded. "Yeah, Janet doesn't want to have to use the head all the time. She'll let me go out for a few overnight fishing trips, but not longer than that."

"Sacrifices," I commented.

"Nah, I enjoy boating. I don't want it to become too much work."

"Can I borrow the phone?" I asked.

He tossed the cordless phone to me and returned to set up the bar. "You coming in later, right?" he asked.

"Yeah, I'm in at four," I answered as I dialed Kayla's number.

"Hello," she said.

"Kayla, it's Chase. Have you heard anything from Tristan?"

"Nothing. I keep thinking that he might just call or something. I'm so worried."

"I am still looking. I want you to stay up there with your mom. I don't know what Tristan has gotten involved in, but it's too dangerous for you and Abbie. At least until I figure a few things out."

Her deep breath was audible through the phone. "Is this because of those two men that came to the house?"

"No," I explained, "This seems to be something else. Those two men shouldn't cause any more trouble right now."

"What is it?" she asked, tears were in her voice. "What happened to Tristan?"

Right now didn't seem like the time to tell her about her house. That would only scare her more.

"At this point, I need to find anybody that Tristan knew. Do you know anyone that he might have gone to? Has he ever mentioned anyone by name?"

"Chase, I think you are the only person that he would go to around here. He doesn't have any family."

"Was he working anywhere in the last couple of years? Someone has to have had contact with him."

"He used to work at the Hometown Hardware over in Lake Park. That was last year. He started doing some construction work after that. I don't know with who. He was being paid in cash."

"Okay," I said, "like I said, I want you to stay up there. Don't come back without talking to me. Do you understand?"

"Yes."

"If you hear from Tristan, I need to know. He should know this, but tell him I want to help him."

"I will."

Her voice was demure and sad. I wondered if she was coming to the same thought I had. That Tristan was never coming home.

18

The phone rang, and my left hand reached for it as my right continued mixing a Grey Goose martini for the prim and proper woman seated at the back of the bar. Pinching the receiver between my cheek and shoulder, I answered, "Manta Club."

The voice on the other end said, "I need to speak with Chase Gordon."

"This is him. Can you hold one second?"

I dropped the phone from my chin to my hand as I carried the martini around to the woman on the backside of the bar. Giving me a nod without the slightest hint of a smile, she pressed her thin, red-stained lips to the glass. When she seemed satisfied, I lifted the phone back to my ear.

"Sorry about that. This is Chase."

"Chase, this is Rob Isip. Jay Delp called me about a boat named the *Kristol*."

I perked up. "Right. The Coastie...I mean, you're with the Coast Guard."

"Jay said you were a Jarhead," he commented. "Coastie. Only in this part of my life. I did twenty in the Navy first."

"Double dipping, huh?"

"The wife likes Fort Lauderdale, and it ain't cheap."

I laughed. "I hear that all wives aren't cheap."

Rob chuckled back. "I can't say. I'm only experienced in the one."

"I'll assume they all are, and I just try to avoid them at all costs."

"Might be wise," he laughed.

"Thanks for calling me back."

"Anytime. Jay said that you two have a friend from his Corps days that might be in over his head."

"Seems like it. What do you know about the *Kristol*?"

Rob answered, "I pulled reports. It looks like she was boarded about six weeks ago and searched. Nothing was found, and the vessel was permitted to continue on its way."

I shook my head. "Was there a reason that she was searched?"

"I can't say," he answered. He added, "I mean, I don't know from the report."

"Thanks, that helps a lot. Does it say if the owner was alone on the boat?"

"Yeah, just one person aboard. Name was Tristan Locke. Is that your buddy?"

"Yeah. I appreciate it. You get up here to West Palm much? Maybe we can grab a drink."

"Absolutely," he said. "You need anything, just let me know."

A thought popped in my head. "Yeah, I have another question you might help me with. Do you have any reports on stolen boats? I'm looking for one called *King of Hookers*."

"Classy name," he said. "Hang on."

He put me on hold, and I took a minute to do a pass by each of the customers at the bar. I was making a Dewar's on the rocks when Rob came back.

"Chase, I do have something."

"Great," I said as I slid the bottle of Dewars back into the bar well.

"The *King of Hookers* was stolen from a private dock in Jupiter. Sheriff's department got a call last night about it on Lake Clarke. Looks like it was close to the north side somewhere."

"Did the sheriff impound the boat?" I asked.

"Looks like the owner was called, and he retrieved it."

"Any chance that you have the owner's name?"

Rob paused. "I'm not sure I should share that. No offense."

"I understand."

"Is this still about your and Jay's friend?"

"No," I responded. "This was something else."

"You seem to have your hands in everything," he said.

"Normally, I do not. I like the quiet, easy life."

"Jay said you just got back from the Bahamas on your boat."

"After this week, I'm already tiring of people."

Rob laughed. "Sorry, I can't help you more."

"Thanks, Rob. I owe you one."

"Jay said you would take me and the wife out for a sunset sail sometime."

"Anytime," I promised him. "I only need a small excuse to head out."

"Great," he said gleefully. "I'll bring some beer."

I hung up and moved back to working the bar. Grey Goose Martini Lady was already almost finished with her drink. She motioned that she would like another. It's hard not to be impressed with a woman that drinks vodka like it was ice water.

The bar got busy with tourists and hotel guests. Nights like that are nice. Busy enough that the night doesn't drag by like a dead turtle and enough business that my tip jar fills. These tend to be quality gratuities over quantity.

By midnight, I was ready for a drink myself. Jerry, the kitchen supervisor, came through the doors carrying a plate.

"Yo', Chase!" he hollered. "Wanna trade a burger for a beer?"

Kristy and Bobby had just left. I try not to defy too many rules in front of them. I never drink when I'm on shift, but once the night is over, I have no problem with an after-shift round or two. I'm just careful about who I share them with. I've worked with barbacks and servers who couldn't understand that work and play shouldn't coincide. It probably stems from my years in the Corps. When on a mission, I was always focused and clear-headed. Not that bartending even remotely compares to the Marines.

"Yeah," I answered Jerry, "I'm starving."

He sat at the bar, and I poured two Coastline Lagers from the tap. I moved around and sat next to Jerry.

"How was your night?" I asked him.

"Had to fire Jeremy tonight."

I didn't know Jeremy very well. In fact, I just met him this week. The chef hired him while I was cruising, but my initial impression of him was that the kid has some serious issues. He disappeared for long periods of time mid-shift, and I'd noticed him near the sea wall smoking on more than one occasion. He had all the tell-tale signs of trouble.

"What did he do?" I asked.

"Damned kid is entitled. Spent an hour on a smoke

break. I found him out back with a joint and one of the housekeepers."

"Ah," I commented. Pretty much what I expected.

"Sent him home," Jerry said. "Let Chef deal with him tomorrow."

Jerry was an old Navy guy. I don't know much about his service. He was out before I was in high school, but he still carried that aura that real soldiers have instilled in them. I knew for a fact that Jerry enjoyed some recreational marijuana, but at work, he was a no-nonsense type.

"How was your night?" he asked.

"Pretty good," I assured him. "Steady."

"Am I interrupting?" Missy asked as she came through the door.

"No," Jerry answered. "We were just commiserating about the evening."

"I heard about your cook," she said to Jerry.

"Yeah," he replied as if there was no more explanation needed.

"Think he needs to go?" she asked him.

"Yeah," he said. "Kid's got no common sense or work ethic."

"I'll talk to Chef in the morning," she said.

Jerry nodded with little concern.

"How'd your Tristan thing go?" she asked me.

"It's getting complicated."

Jerry glanced at me.

"I have a friend from the Corps who has gone missing. He was into some bad stuff with some bad people."

Jerry listened and gave an understanding gesture. "They do something to him?" he asked.

"You know," I said, "I don't think so. Or at least the bad

people I know of haven't yet. I found his house broken into today."

Missy looked shocked. "The wife is still gone, right?"

I nodded. "They were looking for something."

Jerry shook his head. "I'm guessing this is drug-related."

"Seems to be. He was running drugs for the biggest dealer in the state."

"Think he stole from them?" Jerry asked.

"I don't know," I answered. "I am pretty sure that they haven't found him yet."

"Is he a Jeremy?" Jerry asked knowingly.

"Yeah. As long as I've known him."

"You won't be able to save him, you know?"

"I'm afraid that it's too late already."

"These kids," Jerry muttered before he drank the rest of his beer. "Sorry about that, Chase."

"It is what it is," I stated.

"Well, I gotta go finish up the order for Chef tomorrow," Jerry pushed his empty pint glass away. "Thanks, Chase. See ya, Missy."

When he was gone, Missy asked, "How did the wife take it?"

"The break-in?"

"Yeah," Missy responded.

"I haven't told her yet," I explained. "I didn't want to freak her out."

Missy shook her head. "You are an idiot."

I furrowed my brow at her.

"Look, I don't think that often. In this case, though, you are being one. I don't know this girl, but I think you should give her enough credit to handle this. Besides, her husband is missing, and she's already been approached by drug dealers looking for him. The poor thing is already freaked out. It's not fair of you to decide what she can handle or not."

"I am just trying to keep her safe," I replied.

"How is not telling her the truth going to keep her safe?" she asked. "If anything, knowing the danger is there is going to keep her alert and wary. Probably exactly the thing she needs to be right now."

I sighed.

Missy smiled, "You know I'm right. You just don't have enough relationship experience."

"Fine," I agreed, "I'll call her in the morning."

Missy grabbed one of the fries off my plate. She made a face. "It's cold."

Ignoring her complaint, I asked, "What are you doing about Michael?"

She peered at me through slits in her eyelids. "Paige is home, so I guess I need to be there when she gets up."

"That's not answering my question."

She looked at me with soft eyes. "Do you have any thoughts on what I can do?"

"I already said that we could just sail away."

She leaned over and kissed me.

"What was that for?" I asked.

"Because you offered to take me away," she said. "Even if you don't mean it, I like that you asked."

"How often have I had trouble saying what I think?" I questioned her. "If I ask, then I mean it."

Diverting the subject, she asked, "What about your friend? What are you going to do?"

"I've been thinking about him all day. If Moreno didn't kill him, he is either hiding out, or someone else did him in."

"Couldn't he have been in an accident?" she asked. "Maybe he fell overboard."

"It's unlikely," I said. "Not impossible, but there is no way to guess that. His boat is in dock, and he doesn't have another car. Anywhere he went would have to be with someone."

She nodded in understanding. "In which case, someone would know what happened to him."

"Exactly."

"Seems you need to find the 'someone'."

"The question is where to start."

She touched my hand. "The inn is sold out," she said, "I had to give away the room."

"Seems like you have to be getting home anyway."

"What about you?" she asked. "Don't you have a drug dealer after you?"

"I haven't seen hide nor hair of his guys," I commented. "But I'll be okay. I just don't want to worry about you in the mix."

I bent my head down and kissed her. "Why don't you go home?" I suggested.

Her hand drifted to my lap. "We could spend a few minutes in my office."

"I have to finish cleaning up. Plus, you are wearing me out."

Her eyes rolled. "I thought the Marines taught you stamina."

"Yeah, against enemy combatants, not voracious vixens."

Her eyes glittered. "You think I'm voracious."

"I'll still owe you one," I assured her, ignoring her snark.

"Fine," she stated as she stood up. Her fingers traced up my chest from my lap. "Don't think I'll let you forget it."

My hand slipped under her blouse and pulled her close

to me. My lips caressed hers, and I pulled back. She leaned in toward me closer. Her breath was heavy against my mouth.

"I promise I won't forget," I whispered as my mouth moved to kiss her neck.

"Damn you, Chase," she exhaled as she pushed away from me.

I watched her straighten her blouse and walk out of the bar. Her head turned back to me as she went through the door.

19

I drove past the bridge where the night before last, I had tossed a bag of money into the brackish waters. The next exit took me toward Forest Hill Boulevard. Rob didn't have a lot of information, but he said the boat was banging against another boat on the northern shore of Lake Clarke. Unfortunately, I'm not that familiar with the area around here. Or, as I've said before, I'm not familiar with anything south, north, or east of the Tilly Inn. Maybe that's a bit of an exaggeration.

There was a little park on the north shore. An American flag fluttered in the wind over a sign reading, "Town of Lake Clarke Shores." I can never tell when I cross a city limit. Individual municipalities cropped up here closer than neighbors in a duplex. Each one trying to find a way to tax and regulate its citizens, living in cookie-cutter homes with minimum square footage in the two to three thousand range.

The park must have been built for residents of the area. There was no parking, probably an attempt by the powers-that-be to prevent outsiders from enjoying the tranquil shoreline.

Across from the park was a dentist's office. I parked the marina's Corolla in a spot facing the lake. Forest Hill Boulevard separated me from the lake. Not that six lanes of traffic were a big hindrance.

The paths of the park were busy. Young mothers pushing strollers, single folks walking dogs of assorted sizes, and a couple of kids zipping along on skateboards.

If the *King of Hookers* was found around here, it might be difficult to establish where. Both the east and west shores of Lake Clarke were residential. Almost every house had a small dock with a boat of some type.

Staring across the water, I watched as a few boats zipped across the water. Two paddleboarders were working their way toward the park's shoreline. My feet shuffled through the grass toward the water.

The girls on the paddleboards were young. Maybe late teens or twenties. Both wearing bikinis showing off their bronzed skin. The girl in the front was peering at the surface of the water as she stroked along. The second one looked up at me. My hand came up in a wave, and I smiled at her.

"Hi there," she said as she glided near the shoreline.

"Hi," I responded. "Are you from around here?"

The first girl looked up. She turned her paddleboard toward shore.

The second girl answered me. "Yeah, we live over there." She pointed toward the western shore.

"What about you?" the first girl asked coyly.

"Closer to the ocean," I commented.

"That'd be nice," the second girl said. "I'm Kaitlin. This is Kari."

"Can I ask you guys a question?"

"Depends," Kari said. "What are you doing around here?"

"I'm looking for a boat that was stolen," I explained.

"That happens a lot," Kaitlin said. "Did someone steal your boat?"

I smiled. "No, my boat is safe."

"What is that tattoo you have?" Kaitlin asked, pointing at my arm.

My eyes glanced at the ink on my bicep. "It's a Marine tattoo."

"Does it mean anything?" she asked.

Grinning, I said, "It means I am a badass."

The girls both giggled.

"I heard that the sheriff found a boat yesterday around here."

The two girls looked at each other.

"I don't know about a boat," Kari commented, "but yesterday, when I was on my way to work, there was a sheriff boat over there."

She pointed to the opposite side of the lake.

"Do you know which house?"

"I'm not sure. Maybe the third one down."

"Thank you, ladies," I said.

"Wait, Mr. Marine," Kaitlin said. "You never told us your name."

"Or what kind of a boat you have," Kari added.

"I'm Chase."

"Hi Chase," they said in unison.

"Do you have a boat, for real?" Kari asked.

"I do. It's a forty-foot sailboat."

"That's so awesome," she cooed.

Kaitlin said, "Ignore her. She has a thing for boats."

I smiled. "Who doesn't?"

"Can we come for a sail sometime?" Kari asked.

"I'm not sure I can handle you both."

The girls giggled again.

"Maybe I'll see you around," I said. "I need to find out about this boat."

"You a cop or something?" Kaitlin asked.

"Not really," I said as I walked away from the two.

The sidewalk followed the shoreline towards the homes on the eastern shore. The path veered away from the lake toward the street. I walked past the first two houses. A woman was on her knees in the yard of the third house. She was bent over a flower bed with her head under a hibiscus in full bloom.

"Excuse me," I announced myself from the sidewalk.

The woman straightened up. Her head was covered by a wide-brimmed straw hat, she turned toward me. Her gloved hand, covered in dirt, pushed the rim of her hat back. Wide-eyed sunglasses shielded her eyes. Between the hat and the glasses, I couldn't make out her age.

"Yes," she responded as she rose to her feet.

"Hi," I started, "I was wondering if you had a second to answer a question."

"Are you selling something?" she asked as she pulled off the soil-covered gardening gloves.

"No, ma'am," I assured her. "I'm wondering about a boat that was recovered yesterday."

"Oh," she remarked.

"I was told that it might have been found on your dock," I explained.

"What exactly is your question?" she asked. "You seem to be hem-hawing around the subject."

"Hem-hawing," I repeated with a chuckle. "I'm sorry. I

guess I am. I'm curious if it was your dock, and if you happened to see the man that was in it."

"Good. Or at least better. You should be more direct," she told me. "The answer is yes. My husband found the boat early yesterday, banging against our runabout. We never saw anyone in it. He just tied it off and called the sheriff."

"He didn't see any sign of the thief around the shore?"

She pulled her glasses down to look at me. Emerald eyes stared at me with questions.

"Was it your boat?" she asked.

I smiled. She seemed astute, and no story I told would be accepted by those intuitive, green eyes.

"No," I told her. "However, I saw the man on the boat take something that wasn't his. I'm trying to find him so I can get it back."

"Very obtuse," she pointed out.

"True, and if I were able to tell you more, I would."

Her arms folded, and she stared at me across her yard. "I'm not sure that I'm going to be much help. The deputies hauled the boat away, but nothing was taken or disturbed on our property. My husband thought it broke loose from another dock at first. It wasn't until the deputies ran the registration that we found out it was stolen."

"Thank you for your time."

She gave me a little nod, and I turned and walked back toward the park. Stopping on the bank, I studied the shoreline. Anyone ditching a boat would need another form of transportation. I walked slowly along the grassy edge of the water. When I made it about a quarter of the way along the park's shore, I noticed a cut in the bank where someone drove a boat up onto the first foot or so of the shore. The rut was reasonably deep, and it was made with considerable force. Most people don't run the bow of their boat on shore since they don't want to damage the hull. If it were stolen though, then the driver wouldn't be as concerned about tearing up the boat.

From where I stood, I imagined myself jumping out of the boat and then pushing it back out onto the water. Maybe even leave the vessel in low gear so that it moved away from where I jumped out. By the time it was discovered, banging against someone's dock, I could be long gone.

Turning, I looked toward the street. If I was leaving here, the direct route would be the best. It was dark by the time the boat was ditched, and the less time milling around was the safest. I beelined toward the street. Across from me was the dental office where I parked the marina's Toyota.

A smile formed on my face. On the corner of the building was a camera aiming at the parking lot and the street.

I crossed the street and entered the office. The receptionist was a graying woman with short hair and thin-framed spectacles.

"Do you have an appointment?" she asked.

"No, ma'am. I do have a question, though."

She perked up in her chair. "What can I help you with?"

"I am trying to track a boat thief. He abandoned the boat the night before last in the park across the street. It's possible your cameras might have caught something."

"Oh," she remarked with raised eyebrows.

"I wonder if I could take a look at your security camera footage."

"Are you with the police?" she asked.

"No ma'am," I explained. I needed to keep Peterson out of the mix, and honesty was going to be a lot more complicated. So I lied. "The kid that stole the boat is a runaway. I'm trying to help the owner of the boat, and the parents keep the kid out of jail and get him back home."

She nodded. "I don't think I can just let you see our camera footage."

"I understand," I said, "but do you mind talking to your boss? I just want to find this kid before something bad happens to him."

"If you'll take a seat, I'll talk to Dr. Koenig."

I smiled at her. "Thank you so much."

Sitting in the stiff but padded wooden chair, I leafed through a saltwater fishing catalog. Those catalogs inevitably have ten things that ignite my desire to provision up and head out to sea. I was reading the description of the fishing rod and considering that my own was wearing. That mahi I snagged a few months ago put some strain on the rod. A stronger one might prove beneficial.

The door opened, and an attractive brunette in her forties appeared. She was wearing a white coat, and the name "Dr. Eliza Koenig" was emblazoned on the right side.

"I'm Dr. Koenig," she said. "Are you the one interested in our security cameras?"

Rising to my feet, I said, "Yes, doctor."

"You're looking for a runaway?" she asked skeptically.

"Yes," I extended a hand to the doctor. "I'm trying to get a bead on what car he got into. Unfortunately, there's been a stolen boat and some other possible issues that his family would like to head off before he gets too far in over his head."

"Are you a policeman?" she asked.

"No, ma'am. I'm a private investigator."

She nodded. "I can't let you take the footage, but I can allow you to look at it."

"That would be more than helpful."

She motioned for me to follow her. "The footage is accessible on any of our computers. I'm going to put Calvin with you," she explained. "I hope you understand."

An African American man, who was well over six feet and looked like a linebacker, appeared around the corner.

"I'm sorry," she said, "I didn't get your name."

"I'm Chase Gordon."

"Mr. Gordon, this is Calvin."

A sizable muscular hand gripped mine when I extended it. The vice-like grip was a rite of passage that dated back to the cavemen. Two brutes squaring off in the most amiable of contests. When the two cavemen have shown their strength, an unspoken decision is made, and the hands are released. The two may part as comrades or adversaries based solely on the perceived outcome. In this case, I felt an immediate kinship with Calvin.

"Calvin, can you take Mr. Gordon to Jeanette's office? You can use her computer."

"Yes, Dr. Koenig," the man answered. He looked at me before turning and walking down the hallway.

"Thank you, doctor," I said to her before following him.

Calvin ushered me into an office. "You can sit there," he said, pointing at a chair opposite the desk.

He typed rapidly on the keyboard. "When exactly am I looking?" he asked.

"It should be the night before last," I said. "From about 6:30." My guess was based on the time I saw the *King of Hookers* speed away from the drop. At best, the blackmailer could have made it to the northern shore of Lake Clarke in fifteen minutes, although that was being generous on my part.

"Okay," Calvin said, "I'm going to run it at four times, so we don't sit here all day."

"Of course," I agreed.

He turned the monitor so that I could see it as well. The camera was aimed perfectly at the driveway to the dental office's parking lot. The video was good quality, and even after the sun had set, the image was well-lit. The park was barely visible across Forest Hill Boulevard. Two cars were in the lot: a small Nissan and a Jeep Renegade. It took a second for my brain to decipher the image enough to recognize the top of the Jeep had kayak racks. It was a standard feature on vehicles belonging to the weekend warriors.

We watched cars whip past. The timestamp was flicking past the seconds.

"Who is this kid?" Calvin asked, breaking the silence.

I glanced up at the man. "His parents live over in WPB. He's an entitled shit, but they want to try and rein him in."

He nodded at the "WPB" reference to West Palm. The town was known for its affluent citizenry. Most of the working-class folks viewed the people from there with a certain cynicism and disdain. Calvin's expression assured me that he thought the same thing.

"How did you get to be a private detective?" he asked.

"I got out of the Marines with very few marketable skills," I replied. It wasn't a lie. There's not a lot of places looking to hire a guy whose primary training was the various methods he could kill a man.

"I get that," Calvin said. "I had a similar problem. Spent four years of high school and two years of college learning how to tackle a guy with a football. I was lucky enough to have three years playing for the Falcons before my knee bent the wrong way."

"Now you're learning the dental trade?" I asked.

He shrugged. "Being a never-was doesn't pay much, so I

took a course from one of those schools that advertise during Judge Judy."

"You like it?"

"Eh, it's okay. You like doing what you do?"

"Eh," I repeated him. "It beats getting a real job."

He leaned forward. "Hey, is that your kid?" He pointed at the screen.

"Can you rewind it?"

Calvin fiddled with the mouse, and the images started reversing.

"Hold it there," I said.

The screen showed a figure jogging across the parking lot. He climbed into the passenger seat of the Jeep, which backed out of the parking spot and took a right onto Forest Hill Boulevard.

"I think that might have been him," I said. "Could you make out the license plate?"

Calvin tried to get a clear freeze-frame of the Jeep's plate. "The angle isn't right," he finally remarked. "Let me try something else."

The monitor changed and showed the sidewalk leading up to the dentist's office. It also offered a view of the outside lane of Forest Hill Boulevard. Calvin advanced the frames slowly until the Jeep appeared in the corner. The second half of the plate was visible and read, "593."

I stared at the green Jeep with a couple of kayak holders and smiled.

20

Leaving Dr. Koenig's office, I realized that I still had a few hours before my shift at the Manta. I wasn't sure how the information I had gotten from the cameras would help me, or even if I should do anything with it. Peterson had been pretty clear that he didn't want to find his blackmailer. My curiosity got the better of me, though. Someone had something more than just a sex tape on the mayor.

I learned long ago that everyone has secrets. There are things that we each think would be the end of our world. Some folks cheat, some steal, some just think about it. No matter how much one thinks they want to know a person's secrets, they are usually wrong. It changes your perspective.

From my perspective, I liked Peterson, and I didn't care about his secret. Mainly because I didn't know it. If it was some horrid, despicable act, my actions might be different. Right now, I could argue plausible deniability. In my experience, the secrets people are desperate to hide usually end up being benign. At least as far as I'm concerned. I don't care if Peterson turns out to be gay, a gambler, or any number of other things some might consider taboo.

No point in talking to him about it unless I could iron down more details about the blackmailer. He puts enough value on his secret to pay seventy grand.

I sat in the marina's courtesy car and stared at the lake across the street. Thinking about people's secrets brought me back to Tristan. My friend had gotten in with drug dealers, and while they might want to kill him, it appeared that they hadn't yet. My mind flipped back and forth over whether he was dead or alive.

My gut felt that he wouldn't stay out of contact with his family for this long; however, there were secrets that he was keeping. Maybe he was tired of family life. I didn't know Tristan, the husband and father.

Considering his actions throughout his life, Tristan might have found the family man role too intense for him. He needed the attention, and while I didn't have a lot of parenting experience, it seems that toddlers require a lot of attention. I hated to consider that he would just quit on Kayla and Abbie, but it was possible.

Of course, he could easily be running from Moreno. Knowing that he owed the man that much money could have lit a fire under him. I hoped that if that was the case, he ran thinking that his disappearance would protect his family. It was stupid. He should have at least planned for the eventuality that Moreno would go after Kayla or Abbie just to get to him.

I wanted to find some of the people that Tristan was close to now. If, as Moreno suggested, Tristan stole the drugs for his own payday, then someone would have dealt with him. Finding someone to buy twenty-five thousand dollars' worth of drugs isn't as easy as posting on Craigslist. It's one of those who-you-know kinds of scenarios.

Before he started running drugs, Tristan was working in Lake Park. Kayla told me the name. Hometown Hardware. The people you spend the most time with tend to be co-workers. Tristan was one to get comfortable. He might even brag about how much he was making or how much he stole.

I decided to take a chance. Pointing the car toward the ocean, I drove toward Lake Park. Just like Lake Clarke Shores, Lake Park was a town bordered by several munici-palities.

The marina's car was equipped with an older GPS, something I was grateful for at the moment. The only time my general distaste for carrying a cell phone is tested is when I need directions. No one knows where anything is nowadays. And asking for directions leaves me getting furrowed brows and curious glares.

The trip was estimated at forty-one minutes. It took me forty-three. My foot is light, and I am never in a hurry-part of why I chose a sailboat over a trawler.

Hometown Hardware was situated on the corner of two major cross streets. It was a locally owned store, as noted on the sign on the building. The hardware store was at the end of a shopping center that housed a grocery store, a handful of small businesses, and a local chandlery. The chandlery looked like one of those junk stores that had collected parts off of boats for the last twenty years. They also were stocked with seriously over-priced new retail items they bought from the national chains. The industry standard is that anything with the word "marine" in its description automat-ically garners a higher price. The used parts, though, tended to be significantly cheaper. I made a mental note to return one day and spend some time digging through the aisles for a treasure or two.

The hardware store where Tristan had worked gave off the vibe of an independent store trying to stave off the economic volleys of big box stores. The sidewalk in front of the Hometown Hardware was lined with Adirondack chairs, grills, and a couple of lawnmowers. I walked through the automatic doors and felt the swoosh of a cool air-conditioned breeze rush over me. The white tiled floors were filled with aisles of various supplies. The first few seemed to be filled with lawn and pest equipment. Followed by paint and plumbing.

The singular cashier, a man with a pair of wire-framed glasses and thin white hair that was past retirement age, looked up as I entered.

"Welcome to Hometown Hardware," he spouted off cheerily. Whether he was or not, the gentleman looked knowledgeable. I was sure that he was asked for advice multiple times a day on everything from installing window screens to unclogging drains.

"Thank you," I said, "I'm looking for the manager."

"Oh," the old man sounded astonished and disappointed at the same time as if I had made an affront to his superior customer service. He lifted a phone receiver and said, "Let me get him for you."

I smiled at him, hoping to ease his worries that I was an upset customer. He spoke into the phone for a few seconds before hanging up.

"He'll be with you in just a minute," he told me.

"Thank you," I said gratefully.

Meandering around the front aisle, I looked at the different choices for my pest control needs. Although many might think that was an issue not relegated to boats, it was a constant battle to prevent roaches and ants from making their way aboard *Carina*.

"How are you?" a man wearing a shirt and tie appeared in the store. He was about ten years or so older than me. His rosy cheeks suggested he recently spent some time outside, something that was probably outside of his norm. "I'm Stephen. I understand you needed to talk to me."

"Yes, sir," I greeted him with an outstretched hand. "I'm hoping you can help me out. My name is Chase Gordon. I'm hoping to talk to you about a former employee of yours, Tristan Locke."

Stephen cocked his head slightly. "I'm not really at liberty to talk about employees. What is it you want to discuss?"

"Well," I started, "can I take you into my confidence?"

He turned his head slowly to the cashier, nodding slightly.

"Tristan has gone missing, and his wife is worried that something has happened to him."

Stephen's eyes widened. "That's terrible. I had no idea."

"Yes, she's distraught," I said in a hushed and urgent tone. "You know he has a little girl too."

The manager shook his head. "I'm sorry. I don't know how I could help. He hasn't worked here in quite a while."

"Look," I explained, "I'm not official or anything. Tristan and I were in the Marines together..."

"Oh," Stephen said with surprise. "Thank you for your service."

I resisted the urge to roll my eyes. While I greatly appreciate the implied sentiment behind people's gratitude, I don't like it.

"Thank you," I said. "Anyway, I know the kid. He might be staying with someone that his wife didn't know. You know what I mean." I hoped that he took that innuendo wherever he needed.

"I don't know about that," Stephen said. "He left right after I started. I didn't know him very well. I think he went to work for a local contractor."

I let my head drop intentionally. "That's what I'm afraid of. His wife thought the same thing, but he gets paid in cash. No way to know who he was working for."

"There's a lot of that these days," Stephen said. He didn't continue, and I was grateful. Few things grate under my skin more than diatribes about the perceived state of our society by people making no attempt to better it. Stephen struck me as just that type.

"Nonetheless," I said, "we are at an impasse of sorts. I'm just searching for straws."

Stephen pursed his lips and nodded along as if he was perplexed by this situation that we now shared. He, of course, didn't know how to react. His motivation to help me or Tristan was nearly, if not completely, non-existent, but one can't express that type of heartless lack of empathy about someone who might be in trouble. What would people think?

"You have any idea what the contractor's name is?"

Stephen glanced at the white-tiled floor. "I don't, but I think he was the one that was killed a few months back. I can't be sure."

My curiosity perked up. "Killed? How?"

"Heard a couple of guys broke into his house and killed him. Random bullshit we can't seem to get away from around here."

I studied his face. His brow was furrowed.

"Do you know anyone here that might have an idea where he might be?" I asked, shifting gears back to Tristan.

"Maybe he was friendly with someone that still works here. I'll take anything. I just want to make sure that this Marine is safe and back with his family."

I did think that my calling Tristan a Marine was a little heavy-handed, but if Stephen wanted to express his gratitude for our service, then maybe that would motivate him.

He shook his head. "I'm not sure exactly," he said. Eventually, he conceded, "I guess we could ask Tommy. He's been around longer than I have. I think that the two of them were friends. Maybe he knows something about him."

"Great," I said. "Is Tommy here?"

"No, he's not today."

"Stephen, I appreciate the help," I coddled him. "Do you mind having Tommy call me?"

The man nodded. "I can give him the message."

"I don't have a cell phone, but he can reach me at the Manta Club in West Palm Beach." I gave him the number to the bar.

"He is off the next couple of days," Stephen remarked.

"Oh," I said, disheartened. "I don't suppose you can give me his number."

He shook his head. "No, I can't," he said. "That would be a violation of our policy."

"Thank you anyway," I told him. "Hope he gets back to me."

Stephen shook my hand. "I'm sorry I couldn't help more," he said. "I do hope Tristan is okay."

I gave a nonchalant shrug.

"Do you think that he could have just run out on the wife?" Stephen asked with a curious tone.

"Maybe," I conceded, "but I just want to make sure he's safe."

"Seems like you are going above and beyond for him," he suggested.

My eyes narrowed a bit. "That's the thing about serving together. We watch each other's back, no matter what."

His face tightened a bit, and the store manager nodded and said, "I get that."

He didn't, though.

21

The sun was bouncing off the ripples on the surface. Light danced along the edge of the dock like fairies playing chase. My third cup of coffee for the morning was already half gone, and I was considering where I might get a fourth. The Corps trained me to go without sleep, but the feat was made easier with the influx of coffee. Strong, black coffee made it just that much easier.

I strolled along a sidewalk that trailed along the waterfront overlooking the Boynton Marina. After a busy night behind the bar last night, I found myself staring at the overhead in my berth, unable to sleep. A storm rolled through in the middle of the night, and the waves rocked *Carina* fiercely.

My sleeplessness was filled with a marching of ideas through my brain.

Tristan's house was searched, and given the amount of damage the vandals inflicted, my guess was that the object they were looking for wasn't found. Were they looking for stolen drugs? That could have been Moreno's men, but the destruction had a more intense feel. Moreno wanted to send a message, but in the grand scheme of his business, I bet that a twenty-five thousand dollar loss was minimal. His pride was wounded, and he'd make Tristan pay for that in person.

I also wondered about the phone number I found on Tristan's boat. I cursed the bad luck. The swim I took that morning to avoid Spiky and Muscles ruined any chances of reading it. How and if it fits into the puzzle flitted about my head for a bit. The lightning flashes through the portholes created a creep show effect in my cabin.

Revisiting *Kristol* seemed in order since my last trip was interrupted. After listening to the clanging of halyards in the wind for the next few hours, I decided to head over to Boynton Marina at first light.

Estaban Velázquez, or Scar as I was used to referring to him in my head, was sitting in a black Suburban in the parking lot. He must have drawn the short straw to be up so early. I didn't think Scar saw me yet, and I pulled around to a neighboring apartment building. He was situated so that he could watch the main dock. I'm sure Moreno's man was still looking for Tristan, and after the way we left things off the other night, I wasn't sure that he would offer me much courtesy. After a few seconds of thought, I decided that a less direct route might go unnoticed. Even if he had been relieved by one of Moreno's other hired hands, a stakeout like that was boring and routine. It's easy to lose focus staring at the same thing for hours.

I passed the slip where *C'est Vie* was berthed the other day. The slip was empty, harkening to possibilities that she was out bashing the waves or anchored in a small cove. Jealousy welled up in me. That call to the voyage was screaming at me already. I couldn't help but look out to the sea, although, in truth, all I could see was the barrier island that blocked the surf from pounding against the marina.

Kristol was still in her slip. She might have had a slight starboard list, and I thought I might want to check to ensure the bilge pump was working properly.

The salon door that I had picked the other day was ajar. It occurred to me that I disembarked *Kristol* into the water, and Moreno's men probably weren't considerate enough to lock up Tristan's boat. I climbed aboard. My feet splashed as they landed on the deck. The cockpit was holding a half-inch of water, and I took a quick look for the cause. The drain hole leading out the transom was clogged by a rag washed to the back during last night's storm.

The retained water receded quickly when I pulled the cloth from the hole. I tossed the greasy, wet towel onto one of the benches.

A rotten smell struck me as soon as I stepped through the salon door. Turning my head instinctively into the fresh air, I swallowed a lungful before moving inside. There was no help. The cabin was like a balloon filled with rotting air just trying to escape.

Tristan's boat had been searched just like his house. Maybe not as destructively. The salon was tossed, and all the compartments were opened and emptied. I wondered if they searched the boat first, and then Tristan's house. That might explain the level of damage that the house sustained as the searcher was growing more frustrated.

I began picking up the charts and papers that seemed to belong in the navigation table. There was no method to the search. They simply threw everything out of the way to find whatever it was. That would seem to indicate it was a specific thing they were looking for, and they knew exactly what it wasn't. Even small compartments and containers were opened and strewn about.

When I retrieved all the paper charts, I organized them and began flipping through them until I found the chart for the Texas coastline. The one that was missing a corner. I recalled it being a single-paged chart, as opposed to some that were in booklets.

I collapsed onto the settee with a bit of dejection. I had hoped that I could find the chart that had been under the now-torn paper when Tristan had jotted down the number. Maybe I could find the impression and make out the phone number. The search party had thrashed that idea by wrecking chaos throughout the cabin.

Picking up the cushions, I straightened the cabin up some. There was no way I was going to spend the hours it would take to clean everything up. I just wanted to be able to move around.

The Bertram's circuit board had been turned off, and I flipped the circuit breaker that let the batteries recharge from the shore power. The little green light for the bilge pump illuminated, and I heard the whir of the motor as it pumped the rainwater from last night into the ocean.

The refrigerator was opened, and the source of the bad air was found. Without power, the food that had only been moldy before had begun to spoil. Buzzing flies had congregated around the fridge. My hand pushed the door closed hoping to trap the odor inside. I picked up the toolbox that Tristan stored in the gimballed oven. The box was open and empty. The VHF radio was under the table. I found the handheld GPS chart plotter in a corner where it had been tossed without thought.

Turning it on, I watched as the little globe rotated while the device connected to the satellites. The screen was small, but it showed the coastline with a small arrow that pinpointed the location of the GPS in the marina. It was an older model, and it looked like it hadn't had a software update in a few years. Still, as a backup device, it would get a sailor where he needed to go.

There were two saved points in it. I looked at the coordinates. Both were to the south and within a half-day's journey on the Bertram. Maybe a bit longer for *Carina,* but I'd expend almost no fuel to get there.

They probably didn't mean anything. One looked like it was just west of the Gulf Stream. I'd have to double-check, but it looked like it was somewhere on Long Reef. I'd done some diving along there. The area was loaded with sea life, and usually, I could spear something for dinner.

The other point was farther south-just west of the Keys.

Probably just some good fishing spots, I told myself. Or, I considered, it could be a couple of good rendezvous points for someone picking up contraband.

Powering off the unit, I stuck it in the left pocket of my shorts. I wanted to look a little closer at those coordinates. If they were somehow connected to Moreno, that information might prove valuable at some point. On the other hand, if they were just one of Tristan's favorite spots to find some fish, then I would love a day on the water with a hook hanging off the side.

The forward cabin was tossed as well. The full-size mattress from the bed was turned up on its side, the hanging closet was left open. While the boat was a mess the first time I came aboard, this time, it looked like it needed a complete refit. That might be a stretch, but if it didn't get cleaned up soon, the end result might require a complete gutting of the interior.

I stepped out of the salon and into the cockpit. The

sliding door couldn't lock without a key, but I could at least secure the hatches and try to make sure no water got inside.

Turning to disembark, I stopped and stared at Scar. He stood about thirty feet down on the walkway, waiting. I climbed off the Bertram and looked down the dock at Velázquez. He seemed to be inviting me to approach him. He was wearing a brown jacket that I guessed hid whatever gun he had chosen to replace the Colt .45 I took from him the other night. His eyes were dark and bruised, and I didn't want to give him a chance to repay me for those black eyes.

"Mr. Velázquez," I greeted him as I came closer.

His lip sneered at me. My eyes darted around for a second. We didn't have any eyewitnesses about this morning, and I wasn't sure why fortune was frowning on me.

"Sorry about the nose," I remarked.

"I'll repay you for it, don't worry," he growled in a thick accent.

"I'll let you one day," I told him, "or at least, I'll let you try. As long as you understand that what I told your boss is true and in play. If something happens to me, I can promise that your boss will catch a bullet one day."

He glared at me.

"Don't worry," I assured him, "I made sure to describe your jacked-up face too."

Scar said, "That's if they find you."

I pointed at the cameras hanging on the corner of the covered docks. "Don't get filmed doing it then," I said. "And don't bet that there is a criteria for how dead I am or how I got that way."

He grunted. "Mr. Moreno has said that if you can provide Locke's location, you'll be spared any retribution."

"I can't help you there," I replied before I sidestepped around Scar.

He was still standing on the dock when I reached land. He started to walk back, and I tried to put myself on alert, in case he had one of Moreno's other goons lying in wait for me. Instead, I noticed a delivery van in the next parking lot. The driver was sitting in the running vehicle. I waved at him and, I suspected, Agent Kohl or one of his agents.

I was back on-board *Carina* twenty minutes later. The chart plotter I have is a bigger and more detailed one than Tristan's handheld. I pulled up the coordinates and found the first point. I was correct, it was at the far end of Long Reef. Roughly a hundred miles south and situated in the Biscayne National Park.

The second point was near Key Largo, the chart showed it on the edge of Molasses Reef. I stared at the screen with both points highlighted.

Finally, I got to my feet and jumped onto the dock. Climbing the steps to the Tilly, I plotted my time frame. I'd need three days, I figured.

Hunter was behind the bar, and I climbed onto the stool.

"Hey, Chase," he greeted me. "Get you something?"

"No, I was wondering if you could manage everything for a few days."

Hunter winced. "Over the whole weekend?" he asked.

I nodded. "Yeah. I'll make it up to you. I just need to run out a bit."

"Fine," he agreed, "but I want seven days off next week. In a row."

I smiled. "Thanks, man."

He tipped an imaginary hat to me as I jumped off the stool.

"You better tell Missy," he said. "She's been in quite a mood today."

I groaned a little and headed downstairs to her office.

22

The wind was coming out of the east, and the water was choppy enough that *Carina's* bow would climb on the wave and bash majestically into the trough. We were cruising at only about six knots. There wasn't any rush today.

Missy was lying on the cockpit bench, soaking up the rays of the sun. Her bikini top was hooked on the helm so that she could grab it if needed.

When I went downstairs to talk to her yesterday, I found that Hunter was right. She was in a mood. I'm guessing that whatever headway Michael tried to make with her after our talk had backfired. When I told her my plan, she reminded me that I offered to sail away with her.

I beat into a southerly wind for several hours before we were able to anchor in Biscayne Bay. Today was a short sail out to the coordinates that Tristan marked.

"What do you think is out here?" she asked.

I shrugged. "Probably nothing. Even if this is just a rendezvous point, then we aren't likely to be there at the right time to meet someone. It'll end up being a nice couple of days on the water."

She hummed with satisfaction. "I'm okay with that. I needed some sea and sun."

I glanced over at her bronze skin. She didn't miss out on too much of the sun, but that didn't seem to be what she really needed. There is something soothing about being on the water.

"It could just be a wreck that Tristan logged," I mused. "Long reef is loaded with them. Might be the best thing we find is some snapper or maybe a fat grouper."

"That's not a terrible thought," she remarked, "provided you have something to go with it."

"Don't worry," I assured her, "the galley is fully stocked."

The blue stretched out forever, and behind me, the Miami skyline was shrinking, but far from gone yet. The spot we were heading for was only four miles offshore.

"Are you planning to dive it?" she asked.

"Yeah, do you want to go?"

She shook her head. "No, I don't mind snorkeling, but I don't think I'd like being all the way under the water that long."

"It's pretty serene. There's nothing around you. Not quiet, mind you. The noises are just different under there."

"Will we be able to anchor this far out?" she asked. "I don't want to have to drive around in circles looking for you."

"We should be able to. Most of Long Reef is less than forty feet deep."

"Shouldn't you have a partner?" she asked. "A diving buddy?"

"Ideally, yes," I said, "but I should be able to manage anything that goes wrong."

"Cause you're a tough son of a bitch?"

"Cause I'm a tough son of a bitch," I repeated to her with a chuckle.

My hair whipped around in the breeze, and I sat back and watched the water dancing around us. I couldn't think of a better place to be than here. The water was a little rough. However, the wind was strong, the sails were full, and a beautiful topless woman was sunning herself beside me. If only my coffee cup wasn't empty. Those are first-world problems, I sighed. Life was perfect.

The little arrow on my chart plotter that represented *Carina* was closing in on the destination point. The autopilot kept the rudder aimed where I needed it to be. I reached over to release the tension on the sheet for the genoa sail. As the forward sail began to flap in the wind, I reeled the line that furled the sail back up into a tight roll.

Our speed dropped after the large genoa sail spilled its air. With only the mainsail up, we slowed to about three knots. Firing up the engine, I wanted to be able to maneuver in tightly to get as close to the coordinates as possible. I released the halyard that hoisted the mainsail and allowed the sail to drop. Even as it descends, the sail catches any wind. I sprang forward and pulled the rest of the main down to prevent that.

Even with the diesel motor running, the problem is that the sea doesn't always care how close you want to be. She's stronger than the motor. And she's always moving, and even in the time it takes to lower the anchor, she will have moved the boat quickly out here in the open water. In a protected bay, it's a lot easier. This was going to be tricky.

It was going to prove even trickier as I watched the depth jump from thirty-six feet to seventy-eight feet in a second. According to the chart, the point that I wanted to be at was eighty-two feet deep. Not impossible to anchor in that depth, but generally inadvisable.

I cursed under my breath as I turned the helm to come about.

"What's wrong?" Missy asked. "Why are you turning around?'

"I lied to you," I replied, "I can't anchor very easily here. I'm going to have to take the dinghy closer."

When the depth gauge read about twenty-five feet, I released the anchor windlass from the control in the cockpit. The fifty-pound Rocna anchor dropped off the bow into the sea. When it settled on the seafloor, I locked the windlass and put *Carina* in slow reverse. When I felt the anchor resist the motor's pull, I shifted the gears back to neutral.

"What do you need me to do?" Missy asked.

"I'm going to load up the gear into the dinghy," I explained, "and if you want to ride out, you can make sure the dinghy doesn't go too far from me."

"Guess I gotta put a top on," she sighed as she sat up and reached for her bikini top.

My scuba gear is in the starboard compartment, and I started pulling out what I needed. Last year I bought a compressor that can fill the air cylinders. That way, I don't have to go into port every time I need air. I do a lot of diving, and while the cost is a significant factor, the best diving spots are remote. Carrying more than two cylinders seems impractical, as did going back to the dock every day to refill them between dives.

Attaching the air regulator to the cylinder, I tested the flow of air. I hooked the cylinder to the inflatable buoyancy compensator device or BCD before putting the entire contraption into the dinghy. Around my waist, I cinched a weight belt. I tend to float, and any extra help getting to the bottom fast is always needed.

Grabbing my fins and mask, I tossed them into the dinghy before lowering the dinghy to the water's surface. I strapped my dive knife to my calf and grabbed my speargun. Might as well hope to snag some lunch.

"Ready?" I asked Missy.

She waited until I stepped into the dinghy so that I could offer her my hand for extra balance.

"It's easy to operate," I told her. "Should start on one pull."

With that, I barely pulled the rope, and the four horsepower outboard fired to life. I carried Tristan's handheld chart plotter so that I could get back to the coordinates. As we drew close, I dropped a fifteen-pound anchor over the side. The rope raced through my hands as it descended. I pulled two extra-long lines that I had on board. The one tied to the anchor was about a hundred feet long, and when I felt the rope stop as the anchor settled on the bottom, I tied the end off to the dinghy.

"I'm going to attach this rope to me, so I should stay within a small radius of the boat."

Missy nodded as I explained what I was about to do.

I continued, "If I have to untether myself, I might need you to bring the dinghy to me. You'll need to pull in the anchor and the extra rope. I will stay tethered, though, unless I have to. In that case, I'll give you three sharp pulls in a row. You should notice a change when I let go."

"Okay," she replied nervously.

I smiled as I slipped my arms inside the BCD and attached the clasps. Donning my mask, I rolled back into the water.

"Can you hand me my speargun?" I asked Missy.

I checked the time on my watch. "I won't be down more than twenty minutes."

The air released from my BCD, and I sank below the surface. About fifteen feet below the surface, I felt the pressure build in my ears. Over the years, I've done enough diving that I can adjust to it without thought. By the time I passed forty feet, I had another wave of pressure. This time I pinched my nose and blew out gently to relieve it.

The rest of the descent was slow and quiet. The stream of bubbles every few seconds as I exhaled was the only sound. I followed the anchor rode down since I was as close as possible to the coordinates when I dropped it.

The visibility was good, and at fifty feet, I could distinguish the bottom. With the sun out, the light was making its way down to the floor. The depth change that I noted on *Carina* was caused by a sudden drop-off, and the result was a cliff wall about seventy-five feet to the west of me.

I reached the bottom and checked my watch. The descent had taken about three minutes. If I didn't want to make a decompression stop during my ascent, I needed to keep my bottom time to about twenty minutes. I could stretch it to twenty-five, but I like to keep a good buffer for myself.

The seafloor was mostly sand with a few rocks and coral growths. This was too deep for most of the recreational divers exploring the reefs and wrecks in the Biscayne National Park area. Plus, it was on the farthest edge of the reef. There was still plenty of sea life, but without the extensive outcrops of coral and artificial reefs created by the slew of wrecks in the shallower waters of Biscayne, there was a lot less.

The fish that were meandering by were large and seemingly unaffected by my presence. A grouper swam up to me curiously watching me. Grouper makes a great sandwich, but many species are overfished. Not being an expert, I usually look for a Scamp Grouper. This one wasn't one of those. When I got back to *Carina*, I could look it up in a handy field guide I keep aboard. Until then, he could just tag along with me.

Visibility was incredible down here, and I could still clearly see the surface. The waves and movement of the water made it look like a distorted glass ceiling.

That also left me somewhat disheartened. There was nothing down here. I wasn't quite sure what I expected. If Tristan was tagging this coordinate for a rendezvous, there should be nothing down here.

Kicking my feet, I glided along the bottom. A pair of antennae stuck out of a small rock formation. My fins pushed me past until I felt the rope tug against my BCD. I'd reached the limit of my radius. Beyond my reach, the seabed looked similar. My time on the bottom had only reached eight minutes. I started on a circle, taking a western bearing. Using the guide rope as a radius, I swam around the bottom.

When I completed the route, I checked my time. I had been down for sixteen minutes. My grouper friend had bored of me and swam off after some small fish. Making my way back toward the rock formation I had passed earlier, I thought I might investigate those antennae.

Probing the crevice in the rock with the end of my spear-gun, I coaxed a decent size lobster from his hidey-hole. Snatching him by the tail, I stuck him in the mesh bag hooked to my BCD. With a couple of minutes to spare, I searched the rock hole with my spear point until I saw the tell-tale antennae come out of the opening. Swiftly, I grabbed him as well, adding him to my bag as well.

With my lunch securely fastened to my BCD, I checked

my time once again. Safely under my twenty-minute deadline, I kicked toward the surface. When I passed the fifty-foot point, I began looking upward for the dinghy. Inflating my BCD a bit, I gave my legs a break as I ascended slightly faster.

By the time my head broke the surface of the ocean, my BCD was fully inflated. The dinghy was about twenty feet from me, and I rolled to my back and pedaled my feet to propel me backward toward it.

"You're back!" Missy exclaimed as I grabbed the side of the boat.

Tossing the bag of lobsters into the dinghy, I said, "I brought you lunch."

She let out an excited squeal as I detached the inflated BCD and cylinder from my back. My fins kicked downward, pushing me up over the side of the boat. I sat up and pulled the rest of my gear aboard.

"Find anything?" Missy asked. "Besides the takeout?"

"Nothing," I admitted.

She poked at the bag and jumped back when the lobsters moved. "You do know I can't cook," she said.

I looked up at her with a grin. "No worries," I promised her. "I can do amazing things with lobster."

She beamed at me. "Good. Get me back to the boat, and I'll do amazing things too."

23

Moving *Carina* closer to shore, I felt a lot more comfortable with the anchor's holding. We were sitting in about twelve feet of crystal-clear water with a white, sandy bottom. Lowering the anchor slowly, I slipped the engine into reverse to pull the ground tackle deeper into the sand. When the boat was secure, I fired up the little propane grill attached to the railing of my cockpit. The two lobster tails fit nicely on the grate, and I seasoned them with some garlic butter seasoning.

While I was cooking lunch, Missy dove into the ocean. She was about fifty yards off the starboard side, snorkeling a small reef. I had restocked some of my provisions earlier in the week, and I found some instant mashed potatoes and a can of green beans. The can of beans fit on the grill, and all I needed for the mashed potatoes was some hot water.

The art of cooking aboard is tricky. When I'm out for an extended cruise, most of my food is easily stored-lots of canned foods, instant potatoes and noodles, and dried foods. Between spearfishing and casting a line, most of my protein comes from the sea. Fresh produce comes from local markets or bartering with locals. My refrigerator is tiny, and only things that absolutely have to be kept cold, like beer, get that special storage.

"Missy!" I shouted at the figure, kicking erratically along the surface. I might need to teach her the best method for swimming in fins so that the kicks didn't break the surface.

Her head popped up and looked about curiously, reminding me of some video I had once seen of a sea lion.

"Lunch!" My voice raised above the waves.

She responded with an understanding nod and began kicking awkwardly back to me. I took her mask and fins so that she could hoist herself up on the boarding ladder.

"There was a baby stingray out there," she exclaimed as her wet body raised out of the water. "That was so cool!"

"Awesome," I said, smiling at her enthusiasm.

"Do you ever get tired of that?" she asked.

"No," I answered. "I'll spend four to six hours a day in the water. At least most days when I'm at anchor."

"I just don't do it enough," she sighed as she settled onto the cockpit bench and donned her Prada sunglasses. "Lived here my whole life, and I can probably count the times I've been on the water on both hands."

"Ugh," I grunted before handing her a plate. The meat was bursting through the lobster tail from the cut I made along the top. A square of soft butter melted over the bright red shell.

"Wow," she said. "You should be cooking more often."

"Don't let it fool you," I confessed. "Lobster is easy. The rule is just don't overcook it."

"So is this really what your life is like out here?"

I shrugged. "Some. Usually, I don't have a schedule. I'll find an island with a nice protected cove and drop anchor for days. Sometimes weeks. There's a lot of time in the water followed by long naps in the afternoon."

"Does it get lonely?" she asked.

"I get a lot of alone time," I said, "but there are often lots of other boats around."

"Lots of girls in bikinis?" Her eyes flashed green with jealousy.

"Not that it matters," I stated, "but most of the girls in bikinis are with significant others. Not a lot of single women sailing alone. Sadly."

She rolled her eyes.

I watched her swallow a bite of lobster. Her eyes closed as she savored the morsel. She had pulled her hair into a ponytail, but four or five strands still fluttered around her face.

"Of course," I commented, "the offer still stands if you want to come along. We could do a month or two. Just to see if you like it."

"Who'd run the Tilly?" she questioned.

"Hire a general manager. Take on a partner. It's not like it's impossible."

She stared across the water, lost in thought for a moment. Finally, she breathed, "It would be nice."

"I can't promise lobster at every meal, but during bug season, I usually get one or two a day."

She leaned back as if she was considering the offer. "Why do you think your friend saved these coordinates?" she asked, veering the subject back to Tristan.

"It's a wild goose chase," I admitted. "He might have just found a couple of good fishing holes. The worst case is I spend a couple of days with you on the boat in paradise."

"That's your worst case?" she asked in jest.

"Yep, my life is pretty good."

"You still want to check the other spot?"

I nodded. "Might as well. It's only a few hours' sail south. We can, at the very least, squeeze in some time in the water."

Her pupils peeped over her glasses as she offered a salacious smile.

With *Carina's* holding secure, we zipped around for a few hours in the dinghy. Missy enjoyed exploring a couple of the wrecks, that over the years, had begun teeming with life. The *coup d'etat* was the *Mandalay*, a steel-hulled schooner that operated in the early sixties as a luxury cruise liner. The sailing vessel ran aground on New Year's Day in 1966.

"This is so cool," she gasped through her snorkel after a moray eel wriggled past us.

Missy was enthralled in the sea life among the rotting hulks of wood and metal.

"Come on," I urged her. "We need to get back."

Her eyes seemed to deflate. Seeing someone fall in love with the sea is an awe-inspiring thing. I grew up pretty far inland in Arkansas. The best we had around there was the Barnes River and a few lakes in the Ozarks. I was intent on finding my way to the salt and sand from the first day my feet were in the surf. I was maybe eight or nine. My dreams were cast as I watched crabs scamper toward the receding waves.

Putting my hand against her tight rear, I pushed her up into the dinghy. She rolled onto her back, and I heard her laughing. I pulled myself over the gunwale and onto the boat's deck.

"How soon do we have to set sail?" she asked.

"It should take us about three hours or so to get there. We'll have plenty of time before dark."

She glanced around and rasped, "We're all alone here."

I grinned at her giddiness before she pushed me back onto the deck of the dinghy and pulled her top off.

The dinghy seemed to buck and sway on anchor as Missy rocked back and forth. The waves bashed against the hull, drowning out her moans. When she rolled off me and onto her back, we were both staring at the white cloud wisps swirling overhead.

"That was something," she said with a giggle.

"Mmm-hmm," I agreed.

"This isn't comfortable," she stated.

The stringer of the boat was running up my back, but I wasn't about to agree with her or complain about it. A lesson I never had to learn was that if a woman was willing to have sex with you, never criticize or complain about any of it. Just go along and be happy because somewhere out there are millions of men not getting laid at that moment.

She pulled herself up and immediately fell back down beside me.

"There's someone there," she mumbled.

I lifted my head and peeked over the side of the dinghy. A twenty-five-foot sailboat had dropped anchor about fifty feet from us. Two kids, probably teenagers, were flaking the mainsail. The girl was tan and blond with a lithe body that she was flaunting for the mop-headed boy, whose freckles I could see from even this distance. A visible giggle came out of the girl as she glanced our way. She made a comment to her friend, who shared her amusement.

I laid back down. "Yep, we got company."

"This is embarrassing," Missy muttered.

I rolled onto my elbow. "Why?" I asked her. "You are a gorgeous lady. That little girl is jealous as shit. She should be worried that her little boyfriend will be thinking about you later because I promise you the kid is wishing he was me right now."

Her face swept in and kissed me hard. "You do know the right things to say," she said. "Now hand me my bathing suit and get me out of here."

I kissed her back and stood up, naked, and waved at the kids. Both of them looked away quickly, and I pulled up the anchor, started the motor, and drove toward *Carina.*

"Are you trying to give the kid a complex?" Missy joked as she sat up and found her bathing suit.

"You know," I said, "there's no need to get dressed. We'll be on the boat alone for a few hours. Might as well get rid of all the tan lines."

"Nice try," she retorted as she slipped her feet back into the thong.

"Darn it," I muttered with feigned disappointment.

Transferring the snorkel gear to *Carina* took only a few minutes. I hoisted the dinghy up on the davits and secured it.

Before I pulled up the anchor, Missy leaned over and kissed me. "Thank you for bringing me along."

I smiled up at her.

"This might have been the best day I've had in years."

"Glad I could be a part of that," I responded.

The boat vibrated as the motor on the anchor windlass whirred, and the stainless steel chain sounded like it was grinding through the gears as it automatically stowed itself in the chain locker.

Wrapping the main halyard around the winch next to me, I pulled the rope hand over hand, using the winch as a pulley to hoist the mainsail. The wind was ready to fill the sail. We were facing the wind so that when the main was fully raised, we wouldn't start racing along. I steered the helm until the boom swung to the port, and the bow pushed through the waves.

"Hand me that halyard," I told Missy. She gave me a blank look, and I pointed to the rope next to her.

She handed it to me. "Why don't you just call it a rope?" she asked.

"I don't know," I replied as I repeated the process I did when I raised the mainsail. This time I was unfurling the genoa sail on the bow of the boat. As the canvas caught the wind, the sail came unrolled in a flash. I cinched it tight on the winch and used the winch handle to flatten the sail.

I continued to explain when I had finished setting the sail. "When you're on a boat, they don't call them ropes. They're considered lines. The ones that raise the sails are called halyards. If you want to control the direction of the sails, they are called sheets. Don't ask me what genius decided to come up with the various names."

"That's a lot to remember," she said.

I shrugged. "I call things by the wrong name all the time."

With both sails up and the wind from the east, *Carina* rode the wind, clipping along at about twelve knots. The boat was heeling on its side, and I noticed Missy silently grip the side. The sensation of a sailboat riding on a tilt is somewhat disconcerting the first few times. I made some adjustments to the helm and sails, and the vessel righted itself, giving Missy a little comfort.

"Dolphins!" Missy exclaimed several minutes later. She pointed off the starboard side where two dolphins were swimming about fifty yards off. She smiled and leaned back on the bench, soaking in the ride around her.

With the auto-pilot set, we relaxed in the cockpit for the next few hours.

24

Missy was still asleep in the v-berth. Her breathing alternated from a soft rhythmic heaving to a light snore. She'd never admit that she snored, and I wouldn't want to disillusion her. Personally, I found such traits just enhance my attraction.

A steaming cup of coffee was resting on the cockpit table while I prepped my scuba gear. I was able to drop anchor close to the second coordinate that Tristan had saved. From here, the dinghy wasn't necessary, and it could stay hanging on the davits while I entered the water from the stern of *Carina*.

I sat back for a moment and sipped my coffee as I watched the sun rising slowly over the turquoise sea. The day seemed perfect, and a satisfied grin was on my face. A few puffy clouds drifted low over the water casting shadows across the waves. We were anchored on the edge of the color change. The white sands beneath us offered a sky-blue tint. Not far aft of the boat though, I could see the light blue make an abrupt change to the deep blue caused by the intense-drop off of the sea bottom. The depths would change from the fifteen-ish feet where we were currently hooked, to the four-hundred-plus feet deep of the Gulf Stream coursing along the eastern coast.

I expected the dive to be as uneventful as yesterday's. I don't like leaving a stone unturned, but I wasn't expecting much. In thirty to forty minutes, I could complete the dive and be back aboard before Missy woke up. Then we could take a leisurely sail north home.

Before I strapped into my BCD, I unhooked the main halyard from the sail and hooked it to the clip next to the boarding ladder. When my dive was over, I could use it to lift all of my scuba gear out of the water so that I didn't have to climb the awkwardly tiny boarding ladder with an extra hundred pounds strapped to my back.

I took another look at the handheld GPS to determine the current direction I needed to head. Stepping over the rail, I let myself fall back off the stern of the boat into the salty water. After a quick check of my gear, I descended beneath the surface following the anchor rode to the sandy bottom.

The seafloor was all sand, and the water was clear as a bell. I looked up to see *Carina's* keel and the dark brown bottom of her hull. A few barnacles had attached themselves to the bottom. I needed to scrape those off soon before they multiplied and began to hinder *Carina's* performance.

Even at eighteen feet down, I could determine where the sun was, and I kicked my feet to swim east. Ahead of me, the sand seemed to stop, and an abyss opened up. This was the cause of the sudden change in water color I viewed from the cockpit. The chasm was really the edge of a cliff, and my head peered over the ledge.

The bottom of the drop was visible, but I couldn't determine how far down it was. There is difficulty determining distance underwater, especially in such clear conditions. It seems like a contradiction. Clear water should be easy to judge. It just wasn't for me. Growing up in Arkansas, even the clearest water only had five to ten feet of visibility. My mind can't always account for a hundred feet or more. When the bottom is all sand, it seems to be impossible. There is no contrast for the eye to pick up on.

The same problem was plaguing me here. The only clue that gave me any indication that it was significantly deeper was an unusual sight. A mooring ball floated a few body lengths below me. The once-white buoy, now covered with green and yellow algae, swayed in the current, attached to the bottom by a cable.

It was out of place and didn't make sense. The placement of the buoy was purposeful but far too deep to be useful as an actual mooring. The cable tethering the ball to the sea bottom was taut reaffirming my initial thought that it was placed here intentionally.

The bubbles rolled out of my regulator and raced to the surface. I kicked my fins and took the plunge over the edge. The sensation of slowly settling toward the bottom in a creeping free fall is surreal.

Drifting slowly downward, I passed the mooring ball. Small cichlids were circling the ball and nibbling on greenish strands of slime. The buoy was secured to the bottom by what appeared to be an engine. I hoped whatever idiot thought that was a good idea at least had the where-with-all to remove the toxic fluids.

Leveling off a foot above the seafloor, I checked my depth. The gauge read fifty-eight feet. The bottom was all sand with a few rocks scattered about the floor. A large snapper hung against the cliff wall staying in the shadows.

The rusted hulk of an engine was sitting in an alcove next to the cliff. Rock encircled most of it and rose thirty feet toward the surface. Toward the east, another rock wall rose from the floor. I swam toward the wall. I realized that I was at the bottom of a hole, like a small canyon. I circled the gap along the rock walls. The sea life was not as abundant as some reefs, but there were still small fish darting around the rock facing.

The question of the submerged mooring ball bounced about my head. Why was it here? It must have been a marking of some sort. I swam around the engine anchoring the ball in place. The motor was covered with the early layers of rust, but the metal structure was still sound. Another fifty or sixty years might leave some severe scars to it. So far, the rust was minimal. It had probably only been submerged six months to a year.

By my watch, I had been down for twenty-six minutes. I wasn't limited by the depth today, but I hadn't found anything either. My gut was telling me that Tristan was using this as a marker of some sort. It wouldn't have taken a lot of effort to drop the engine from the davits on his Bertram. Guiding it into the alcove might have been tricky, or maybe he just got lucky. The hunk of metal would sink straight down. Perhaps, it bounced a few times off the rock wall. He just had to be situated on the surface.

It would make a good pick-up point. If something were sunk at these coordinates, they could only be retrieved by a diver. It was impossible to put up any surveillance here, and even if something was found here, there was a degree of deniability. It was off the beaten path and meant the odds of a meandering boater or diver even finding something were slim.

On the other hand, it could be a fluke. I could spend my

entire dive speculating on why the damned thing was down here only to find no answers. There wasn't anything else of interest within a hundred feet of the motor.

If I could sigh underwater, I would have.

Pressing the button on my BCD, I inflated it and began ascending toward the surface. The walls of the little alcove seemed to be sliding down as I rose in the water. A moray eel, most likely startled by the bubbles I was exhaling, zigzagged over my head as it fled the hole where it had been hiding.

As I passed the eel's rock shelter, I released the button on my BCD and spread my fins to slow my ascent. Something caught my eye, and I had to release some air to sink back down to look.

The crevasse in the wall was about a foot and a half wide. I unclipped the small dive light from my vest and shone it into the hole. A pink plastic box was shoved in the back of the opening. Twisting the box, I was able to extract it from the hole. The box had the remainders of stickers that had a floral design. The edges of the remaining ones were flaking up and shredding slowly.

I peered back into the hole for anything else. It appeared to be empty.

I still had plenty of air and time, so I descended again to the seafloor. From the bottom, I commenced a thorough search for more openings as I started back to the surface. By the time I cleared the edge of the cliff, I had only seen the one hole. Had I not been extremely lucky, then I would have missed it completely.

Orienting myself, I kicked westward toward the anchor chain I saw straining ahead of me. I surfaced next to *Carina* and spat the regulator out of my mouth.

"Hey, are you a mermaid?" Missy said, sticking her head over the side of the boat.

"If only," I answered. I handed the pink box up to her. "Here, can you take this?"

She reached over and took the box. "You went shopping," she joked.

"It's just a tacky t-shirt." I unclipped my BCD and attached the main halyard that I had left for me.

"Holy shit!" Missy exclaimed.

"What is it?" I called out.

"Did you open this box?" she asked.

"No."

"You need to come see this," she told me.

I tossed my fins onto the swim platform and pushed myself up.

Missy sat on the cockpit bench, holding the opened pink box. In her right hand, she had a necklace laced through her fingers. Diamonds sparkled brilliantly in the sun.

"Uh…" I stammered.

"Did you just find this?" she asked.

"Yeah, stuffed inside a hole and guarded by an eel."

I climbed into the cockpit and took a closer look at it. The strands appeared to be silver, tarnished green. The necklace was filled with lots of diamonds of various sizes. Some were quite large.

"Are they real?" I asked Missy.

"Oh, these are very real," she confirmed. "Trust the Jewish girl in me to know that. This has to be expensive. Those are two and three-carat diamonds in there. That's just the big ones."

My butt fell back onto the bench. I stared at the glittering jewels for a full minute and said nothing. I was speechless.

"Do you think this was Tristan's?" she asked.

"I don't know," I finally answered. "I was expecting a cache of drugs. Was there anything else in the box?"

She shook her head.

I leaned forward and put my forearms on my knees as I stared at the necklace. "Does the Jewish girl in you know how much this is worth?"

She shrugged. "I'm no expert. I'd guess a lot. There are hundreds of little diamonds in there, along with some big honkers. This wasn't something you bought at the mall. This was custom and handmade."

"Someone is definitely missing it then," I said.

"Yeah, someone is missing this."

I looked up over the blue water, thinking.

"Those home invasions," Missy suggested.

"My thoughts exactly."

"You think your friend was the one doing those?"

I didn't want to consider that, but the fact is, Tristan was capable of that.

"If you had a drug dealer hounding you for twenty-five grand," I said, "something like that might seem like an escape plan."

"Wasn't one of those homeowners killed?"

I nodded.

"That means..."

"That Tristan is likely a murderer, too."

"What are you going to do?"

"We need to get back. I need to find out who is missing this necklace."

I started moving to pull in my dive gear so that we could pull up anchor. My mind was already doing the calculations. Even if the wind wasn't cooperative, the diesel engine could get us back to West Palm Beach by tonight.

Missy placed the diamond necklace back into the pink box and sealed it up.

"Put that below so we don't lose it."

She took the box below as I raised the anchor.

25

"I'm going to be happy this is someplace safer than onboard the boat," I remarked.

Missy took the necklace from me and placed it inside the safe in her office.

"What are you going to do now?" she asked. Her cheeks were pink from the sun, and her hair had some frizz from the salt air.

"These recent home invasions," I commented. "This kind of jewelry was stolen. From someone high-end."

"You think this might have something to do with the robberies," she suggested.

"Maybe," I said, dropping into the chair across from her desk. "I don't have a lot of other ideas right now."

"It's possible Tristan didn't hide that box."

"Possible. But it's a big coincidence. He saved those coordinates for a reason. Do you mind if I use your computer?"

"Yeah, go ahead. I'm going to shower and dress. Don't want the entire staff to see me all wind-blown and salty."

I smiled at her. "I think you make sea hair and no-make-up look crazy sexy," I said. "I'm glad you came along."

She sat on my lap and pulled her face up against me, and kissed me. "Me too," she said. "That was the most fun I've had in a while. I see why you want to get out there again."

"The offer still stands," I told her with a lascivious smile. "We could spend months out there. No husband, no work, no clothes."

She kissed me again without saying a word before turning and walking to her private bathroom.

I wasn't foolish enough to think that she and I were anything permanent. Missy might enjoy a few days of cruising, but she wanted certain amenities that didn't automatically come with my lifestyle. I lived most months on a few hundred dollars; she would want fancy restaurants and expensive wine. I'm happy with cheap rum and whatever I pull from the ocean. The sea and sun were something she wanted to experience in small portions. To me, it was my life. I would shrivel up and die without it. She needed stability, and I was already feeling like I had stayed in port too long.

I was a novelty, and I had to remember that. There is nothing wrong with being a novelty.

But it was nice to have someone to share the adventure. I stared at the bathroom door, feeling a wave of melancholy.

Pushing the glum moment away, I moved behind Missy's desk. Opening her internet browser, I searched *home invasions in Palm Beach County*. Several news stories came up. They dated back two years but seemed to increase over the last six months. I added *robberies* to the search terms and quadrupled the results. Most of the hits I got were in the local crime blotter website that tracked everything from jaywalking to murder for Palm County.

There were too many to write down, and the details

were minimal. There were fewer murders and assaults, so I cross-referenced them with robberies and found the two that Peterson told me about a few days ago.

The first was a break-in. The details were sketchy. The seventy-eight-year-old owner of the home, listed as Carl Woodman, interrupted the burglary. He was discovered later that evening by his wife and daughter. He had been beaten to death.

The second invasion ended in an assault. The victim was a sixty-seven-year-old man; his name wasn't listed. He was transported to the hospital.

None of the entries I read made mention of what was taken. I stared at the screen for a minute.

Picking up Missy's desk phone, I dialed Jay's number.

"Delp," he answered.

"Jay, it's Chase."

"Hey, man," he responded. "You hear anything about Tristan yet?"

"No," I said, "and honestly, it's gotten a little strange."

"Strange?" he asked. "Like, how?"

I considered his question. "Let me keep it vague so that you don't feel like you have to react like a cop."

"I can ignore that reaction," he assured me.

"Let me start with a question. In a home burglary, do the police have a list of stolen goods?"

"Yeah, it's huge," he said. "What are you looking for?"

"Recent burglaries in Palm County. High-end jewelry, especially."

"Shit," Delp said in his thick Mississippi accent, giving the word two extra syllables. "That kid stepped in it, hasn't he?"

"I'm not sure yet," I answered, "but it sure seems like a typical Tristan move."

"How's his wife and kid holding up?"

"She's up at her mother's. A couple of Julio Moreno's guys went to her house, trying to bully her."

"You didn't do anything stupid after that?" he asked as if he knew my answer.

"I explained very nicely to Julio Moreno if something happened to me or Kayla and Abbie, one day someone I know would put a crosshair on him and drop him. I think he got the point. He hasn't been around too much since then."

"You think Tristan's dead?" Jay asked.

"Until yesterday, I did. Now it might be that Tristan has gone too far and knows he can't come back."

I could hear Jay's mind whirring. "If it gets sticky, you know to call me."

"You know it," I assured him. "Just see what you find on these lists. I'm taking a wild guess, but this might all have to do with a string of home invasions here. If I can get a tangible link, maybe it will lead me somewhere."

Jay groaned. "How bad are we talking? Home invasions can get dicey."

"There have been some homeowners assaulted, and one died," I said. "Remember, this is all supposition. I don't want you too involved yet."

"My jurisdiction ends on Highway 98," he reminded me.

That wasn't the truth. I knew Jay, and he'd balance his loyalty to Tristan and me with his duty. I didn't want to force him to make too many ethically-questionable choices.

The shower was still running in Missy's bathroom. I was going to need to take one too. Maybe find a clean shirt and a razor. For a second, I considered joining her in the shower but decided to head to the marina shower instead.

It was almost noon, and I cut through the Manta Club.

Taylor was behind the bar. The lunch crowd was sparse, and Bobby and Kristy were both leaning against the rail.

"Chase!" Bobby howled at me as I came through the doors. "You working today?"

"I don't know," I admitted. "I got back earlier than I planned. I'll probably see if Hunter wants the night off."

"Cool, I'm working a double," Bobby said. "I love hanging with you."

I smiled. Bobby was a bit energetic and far more talkative than I preferred, but he was a good barback. I never ran out of beer when he was on shift.

"Hey Taylor," I called over the bar, "can you put in a tuna sandwich for me? Rare. To go."

"Yeah," Taylor spun around to the computer and typed in my order.

Wilson Peterson was sitting alone on the backside of the bar. I ambled around and sat two seats down from him.

"Hope I'm not too ripe," I said, "just got back from a few days down in Biscayne Bay."

Peterson chuckled, "Naw, I've smelled worse in the city council chamber. Old Harrison Bowe came in once with fish blood all over his shirt."

"Lovely," I commented, not sure who Harrison Bowe was.

"Biscayne Bay, huh?" Peterson mused. "How was it?"

"Weather was good. I had the wind in my hand, both ways."

"Do any fishing?" he asked. Peterson had no real interest in fishing, but he was a politician. Fishing was a safe topic around here. Along with crabbing, gator sightings, and Florida State football.

"Just a couple of nice sized lobsters." I looked over at him and asked, "Have you had any other calls?"

He shook his head. "No, and I appreciate your help."

"No, Wilson, I was happy to do it. You were more than generous."

He gave a curt nod that indicated that the topic was finished. I turned my attention to a tennis match on the television. Taylor gave me a cold Miller Lite. It wasn't my drink of choice, but as a bartender, I never look at the label of a free drink.

He finished the last two bites of his burger. "I have a lunch meeting over at the Hyatt," he complained between chews. "It always seems that I never get a chance to eat at these things."

"So, you're eating lunch before your lunch?"

"The price of public service," he joked. "Always be sure to eat before any function. Otherwise, I end up with a cold plate while the succubi glad-hand me. Besides they always dry out the chicken at the Hyatt."

"I had a similar motto in the desert. Often it involved sleeping whenever the opportunity was there because, at any time, we might be on the go for three days straight."

Peterson gave a little sigh. "Chase, you might be cut out for politics."

He slid his card across the bar. When he paid, he said, "I have to get going, but I have something in the car for you, Chase. Why don't you come grab it?"

Curious, I walked through the lobby with Peterson. My disheveled sailor look clashed with his starched Brooks Brothers suit.

"I do appreciate your discretion in this," Peterson remarked. "This has kept me up."

"Of course," I assured him as we approached the Mercedes that the valet had left on the curb.

He opened the back seat and pulled a box out. Opening it, I found a bottle of Pappy Van Winkle Bourbon.

"Wilson, this is too nice."

"I figured you for a bourbon drinker. This is a bit of gratitude, is all."

"Wilson, you already gave me too much for what I did."

He waved me off with a "Nonsense."

I cradled the box of expensive bourbon. "Thank you."

Peterson clapped me on the shoulder and got into his Mercedes. "Well, I have a date with some dried chicken."

Pappy Van Winkle was the creme of the bourbon crop, and I did enjoy a good bourbon. Although, I never classified myself as a bourbon drinker. I wouldn't tell the mayor that, though.

He drove out of the Tilly's circle drive and onto the street. My eye caught sight of a Jeep parked against the opposite curb with two kayak holders on the roof. When Peterson turned onto the street, the taillights on the Jeep lighted up as the engine started.

I took off into a run and dashed across the circle, dodging an older Cadillac that was pulling into the valet. I reached the sidewalk in time to see the license plate on the Jeep. It was the same Jeep from the surveillance video at the dentist's office. I repeated the tag number three times aloud to commit it to memory.

Peterson's problems weren't over yet.

When I got back to the Manta, my sandwich was sitting on the end of the bar in a Styrofoam container. I groaned a bit at the packaging, but it seemed inevitable sometimes. I handed Taylor a twenty-dollar bill and picked up the phone.

"Delp," Jay answered again.

"It's me."

"I should get used to the area code," he commented.

"Can you run a plate for me?"

"Yeah."

I gave him the number. The clicking of keys was audible.

"The car is registered to a Sean Gilliam. He lives in Haverhill."

I jotted down the address on a bev nap and thanked Jay.

"He has a pending charge for possession with intent."

"Delightful. Anything else?"

"No, he's only twenty. I'm guessing he was small-time and got his ass in a wringer."

"Thanks, Jay."

"You think he has something to do with Tristan?"

"No," I said, "This is something else."

"You are a busy little bee, Chase."

I hung up with him, took my sandwich, and headed back to *Carina*.

26

A fter a long, hot shower washed the last few days of salt from me, I sat in the salon of Carina, staring at the bottle of bourbon Peterson gave me. The foam container on the counter held the last bite of bread from my tuna sandwich. The faint aroma of fish still lingered in the boat, but I was growing accustomed to it.

The automatic air freshener would squirt out a timed blast of fresh linen spray. That was a trick I learned the first summer I was living aboard. The small space took no time to become rank. Every time I left the boat and closed the hatches, the inside would develop a less-than-attractive musk to it.

Between the moisture and the smell that builds up on an enclosed boat, it sometimes felt like a losing battle.

Knowing who the blackmailer was left me wondering how to proceed. Whatever Sean Gilliam had on Peterson; the mayor didn't want me to track him down. On the other hand, I had a feeling that there were going to be more problems for Peterson. Gilliam was following him now, and that could escalate. Eventually, Gilliam would make another demand or take a different tack.

He's working right now under the assumption that he's completely anonymous. Maybe Peterson already knows who he is.

The best way to head him off, either way, is to make sure he knows that he's no longer an enigma.

I climbed out on deck. The air was shifting. The drop in pressure was noticeable from the tingle on my skin. The same information was available, and in far greater detail on the battery-powered weather station, I keep on my navigation table. Were I on the water, I'd be working to determine how big and where the storm was. In the slip, I just double-check the dock lines.

Haverhill was one of the few little cities I knew. There was a great little Jamaican jerk place where I like to get some quality jerk pork and festival bread.

Of course, Gilliam didn't live at the jerk joint, so I still needed the GPS to find his house.

It wasn't a house. Gilliam lived in a small apartment building. More like a quadplex. There was no sign of the Jeep, but I did see two older plastic kayaks chained to the side of the building.

I left the Toyota about half a block away and walked up to the building. His unit was on the second floor, and I rang the bell.

Shuffling noises came from inside, and after a second, the door opened. A dark-skinned girl opened the door. Big copper eyes looked at me, and I had a hard time not noticing that she was only wearing a tank top. She was young. Nineteen at best, if I were a betting man.

The copper eyes stared at me as she tried to decipher who or what I was.

"Can I help you?" she asked.

My eyes darted over her shoulder to take in the apartment behind her. The only thing visible was the den and part of the kitchen. Both looked like a tornado had whipped through. I counted two bongs on a coffee table.

"I'm looking for Sean," I said. "Is he around?"

I wanted to sound like Gilliam and I were already well acquainted. Maybe I could pass for his dealer. Although given my build, I might come across more like his dealer's version of Scar. My goal was to sound more amiable than that.

"He's not here," she replied.

"Damn," I said dejectedly. "I was hoping to catch him. Do you know when he'll be back?"

"Should be later this afternoon."

"Thank you," I tried to make myself seem charming. Usually, that doesn't work for me.

She pushed the door closed, and I returned to the car. The afternoon waned on, and I waited. That jerk place was sounding pretty good. The sky was growing darker. Something I already predicted. That was good because the temperature was dropping, and the breeze was kicking up. Orange blossoms and flowers surfed on the wind, and I planned to keep my window down as long as possible.

A few minutes after five, the Jeep pulled up. The storm was crawling in from the east, and the sky had gone black and green. The air was moving slower, a good indication that the bottom was about to drop out. Gilliam was getting out of the car. The kid looked like he was still in high school. He had blond hair and a pale complexion, he was skinny, like a track star. He might outrun me, but if I got a hold of him, he'd be toast.

I got out of the car and double-timed it up the sidewalk. Gilliam was almost to the steps when I came up behind him.

"Sean," I said sharply.

The kid turned around with a look of surprise. I debated how to handle him since he was just a kid. Granted, he was committing a felony, but still just a kid. No need to hurt him, but a little fear does provide a lot more cooperation than injury.

"Who are you?" he uttered as I reached forward and grabbed the front of the t-shirt with a Devil Wears Prada logo emblazoned on the front.

"What the hell?" he hollered. I shoved him against the wall, stunning him for a second.

Dragging Gilliam by his shirt, I pulled him under the stairs out of sight of the street. His eyes widened in fear, and I scowled at him.

"Let's have a little talk," I hissed at him.

"What do you want?"

"I want whatever you have on Wilson Peterson."

"Peterson?" His reaction was dumbfounded. Then he recovered his senses. "What are you talking about?"

"Look, kid," I growled at him. "I found you very easy. You were an amateur. You have a simple choice. You can pony up the video and whatever else you have now, or I can drag your unconscious ass up these stairs and force your girl up there to give it to me."

"No," he begged, "don't hurt her."

I raised my eyebrows as if to tell him to do what I wanted.

"Do you know what's on the video?" he asked.

"I don't care what's on it," I spat the words out. "I want it. Every copy you have of it."

He nodded quickly. He said, "He's not a good man."

"Who is?" I questioned. Gilliam was likely right. I knew that I didn't want to know what was on the video. I could speculate all day long, but if I didn't know, then I could handle the situation.

"He'll come after me and Leah."

"What makes you think he won't now? You've taken seventy-thousand dollars from him. He isn't going to continue taking that. The cops could swoop in and arrest you. The whole thing would be swept under the rug."

He sighed. "It's upstairs."

"The money?"

"That's mine," he said with shock.

"No, it's not," I reminded him. "I can go back to dragging you up the stairs and finding it myself."

He shook his head quickly.

"Good, let me explain how it's going to work," I bellowed with a threatening tone. "We are going upstairs. You're going to give me everything you have on Wilson Peterson and all the money that you've bilked him for. Then you are going to forget everything about him. You don't try to blackmail him again. If you do, I'm going to find you again, and we won't have a nice conversation."

His eyes deflated.

"This seems a little personal for you," I noted. "Stop that shit. Making it personal will only get you in deeper trouble."

Gilliam stared at me. "You just don't know," he mumbled.

"Come on," I urged. "Let's get this over with."

He walked up the stairs with my hand guiding him along. Gilliam didn't seem like the overtly brave sort. However, he might be the overtly stupid sort, so I was prepared for him to make a move.

He opened the door, and the dark-skinned girl popped her head up over the back of the couch.

"Hey!" she exclaimed. She was still wearing only the thin tank top.

She looked at me. "He was here earlier," she told Sean.

"Shut up, Leah," he ordered her.

The girl didn't obey. "What's he want?" she asked as if Gilliam never said anything.

"I said, 'Shut up'."

A flash of fear crossed Leah's face as the gravity of the situation sank in. She held her tongue now.

"Why don't you sit down?" I suggested.

She did sit down.

"Where is it?" I demanded.

Gilliam walked over to a desk with a brand-new computer. It was some type of gaming computer with red neon glowing off the corners, no doubt a recent purchase from the extortion money. He handed me a USB drive.

"Delete it off the computer too."

He sat at the computer and moved the mouse. I glanced over my shoulder at Leah, who watched from the couch.

She obviously couldn't stand it any longer. "Is he taking the video?"

Looking at her, I stated, "I already explained the situation to Sean here. This ends today."

"No!" she howled, tears bubbling up in the corner of her eyes. "He can't."

I watched the girl sobbing on the couch. Sean dragged a file to the recycle bin on the computer's desktop. When he emptied the computer's trash, I gave him a nod.

"The money, now."

"No," the girl whined through her tears.

Gilliam looked from me to her. "Just take the video, and we won't ever bother him again."

I shook my head. "The two of you committed multiple felonies here. Even if I decided not to force you to give it to me, it would only take one call to have both of you arrested for an assortment of crimes. Grand theft, extortion, and probably a handful of other things. Or I can take the money, and Peterson never has to know."

"He'll know," Leah muttered.

I ignored her and stared at Gilliam impatiently. I was starting to feel some compassion for the two kids. I didn't want to imagine what might be on the flash drive.

The kid finally relented and vanished into the bedroom. I didn't like having either of them out of my sight at all, but I hadn't prepared for him to walk out. It goes without saying, I don't have much practice at this type of thing.

"Don't move!" I snapped at Leah before following Gilliam.

When I came through the door, he was digging through a drawer. With two long strides, I crossed the room and caught his hand as he pulled a Smith & Wesson .38 out of the drawer.

"Dammit," he cursed as I wrenched the gun from his grip.

"It's unloaded," I said, surprised. "You dumbass, don't ever pull an unloaded gun on someone. You'll get yourself killed."

"I..." he started.

"Shut up and get the money," I told him. I whispered under my breath, "Pull an unloaded gun."

Gilliam opened the closet door and pulled out a backpack. He tossed the pack on the bed; I unzipped it to see stacks of hundred-dollar bills.

Pulling a stack out of the bag, I fanned the bills on my thumb like it was a deck of cards. I tossed it onto the bed.

"That's yours," I said, "as long as you are never heard from again. Understand?"

He nodded.

"If you left any prints on the boat you stole, you have more trouble coming for you. I don't want to hear from you, though, even if you get picked up for that. Otherwise, I'll make damned certain that Leah goes down as an accomplice with you."

"I wiped it all down," he promised.

"Not my concern," I explained, "as long as I never hear your name again."

"Okay."

"If anyone goes after Peterson again, I'll be coming for you two first. Got it?"

"Yeah," he responded.

"I don't know what is on here," I said, holding up the USB, "but let it go. You'll live a longer life that way."

He nodded.

"You better explain it to her, too," I said.

"I will." His tone was filled with humility.

I tossed the bag over my shoulder, threw the empty .38 on the bed, and left the room. Leah was sitting on the couch with tears streaming down her face. Gilliam was right behind me as I walked past her. He moved around and sat on the couch with her.

I walked out into the sunlight feeling like I hadn't done a lot of good today.

27

The first time I noticed the older Trailblazer was a few blocks from Gilliam's house. Some subconscious part of my mind saw it and alerted me. The little maroon SUV had already crossed my vision, I just wasn't sure when it happened. The broken passenger mirror was the telltale sign that my brain picked up and set off the mental alarms.

Since I was carrying a backpack filled with stacks of hundred-dollar bills, I was more than a little uneasy. This could be a set-up. Maybe Gilliam had a partner beside Leah. That didn't track, though. There was no chance that he knew I was coming. Even if he did, there wasn't enough time for him to rally the troops to be in place to pick me up when I left Gilliam's home.

At this point, the possibilities were endless. The DEA, Moreno, or someone associated with Gilliam. I had been kicking over rocks all over the last few days. Unfortunately, under stones is where the creepy and dangerous things live.

Ditching them was possible. No matter who it was in the

driver's seat, there were lots of reasons sitting in the seat next to me to lose them.

On the other hand, my curiosity was getting in the way. Finding Tristan was becoming a murky affair. Everything I found out just made matters worse. At first, I thought I was protecting Tristan from Moreno and Kohl. Now, he might have been involved in a string of burglaries and murder. If he was involved in that, then there was no way to protect him. But there just weren't any answers that satisfied me yet.

I took a right at the next light. The Trailblazer was three cars behind me when it turned right as well. Time to do something.

A shopping center was coming up on the left, and I scanned through the businesses; a Starbucks, a dollar store, and a gym.

I parked between the dollar store and the gym. The Trailblazer was smart enough to go past the first driveway that I used and turn in the second. They parked at the back of the parking lot near the Starbucks. The front of the truck pointed toward me.

Grabbing the backpack, I slung it over my shoulder and walked into the dollar store. I bought a bottle of water, a cheap padlock, and a black backpack, similar to the one on my shoulder. It was a far cry, but it would have to do. I took the bottle of water out of the plastic bag before stuffing the rest of my purchases into the money-filled bag hanging off my shoulder.

The Trailblazer hadn't moved, and from where I stood, I only counted one head in the front seat. Holding the bottle of water, I walked into the gym.

A thick, over-muscled black man stood behind the counter. He lifted his head as the door swung open.

"Welcome," he said when the front door chimed to announce my entrance.

"Hi there," I said, "I'm new to the area. I have been looking for a gym to join."

"Oh," he replied, "let me help you out then."

"Can you tell me about your services?"

He began to rattle off the different things this particular chain offered. It was the standard fare. A variety of workout machines from treadmills to stationary cycles. They had some sub-par classes for the uninitiated, as well as a tanning area.

"No pool?" I asked with some feigned disappointment in my voice.

"None of our locations have a pool."

"Oh," I said, "I like to finish my workouts with a swim. What about a hot tub or sauna?"

He shook his head slowly. "How about I give you a three-day membership?" he offered. "You can try everything out and see if it fits your needs."

With a reluctant nod, I agreed. "Yeah, that would be nice."

He took a card with the gym logo on it out of a drawer, scrawling the date and his signature on it. "This will expire in three days. After that, you'll need to sign up for one of our memberships."

Taking the card, I asked, "Is there a locker room?"

"Yes," he said, "I can give you a full tour."

"No," I said, "that's fine. I can handle it. Just point me to the locker room."

"Absolutely," he sounded relieved to not have to rattle off the same spiel he spouted every day. "Just straight down that hall there. The men's locker room is the last door on the right."

"Thank you," I replied as I walked to the locker room.

It must have been too early for the crowd. Only four people were working out. Three women on treadmills and one older man working on the free weights. A long row of televisions hung from the ceiling from the front of the building to the back. Every four or five seemed to repeat between the various twenty-four-hour news channels and two cooking shows. Nothing like working hard to burn off calories while watching someone teach you how to make a peach pie with real lard. I wasn't sure what the motivation was at that point.

The locker room had two walls lined with lockers that had been placarded with inspirational logos and the gym's corporate slogans. A thirty-two-inch television hung on the back wall showing a couple of talking heads on ESPN discussing some one-off sporting event. I didn't pay it much attention.

I chose a locker in the middle of the wall. Something that would be in clear sight of anyone in the room. I removed the new backpack I had just purchased along with the lock and stripped it of any tags. Next, I put the bag filled with money in locker number twenty-seven. I padlocked it and pocketed the key.

The new bag looked deflated, and I began filling it with paper towels from the dispenser. When it looked about the same as the other, I checked my watch. I'd only been inside the gym for twenty minutes.

When I exited the locker room, the new bag was slung over my back. The Trailblazer was still visible in the lot. There was still a silhouette of a head watching the gym.

I found a weight machine facing the window. A few reps wouldn't break me out in a sweat, but I might not be noticed. Lots of people go to the gym and don't put in a lot of effort.

I spent about fifteen minutes at that station, trying to be invisible. I decided that I had been inside long enough, and I exited the building. The driver in the Trailblazer was anticipating me. The truck shifted forward slightly before I was even behind the wheel of the marina's courtesy car. He was right behind me as I pulled out of the driveway.

With the money somewhat safely stashed away, it was time to figure out who was following me. Making random turns, I zigzagged my way back toward West Palm. I didn't want to go back to the Tilly, but I decided to pull into the Publix parking lot. I parked close to the west entrance of the store and walked inside in my most casual I'm-just-shopping stride. From the corner of my eye, I watched the Trailblazer park on the next row over.

When I entered the store, I cut to the right and walked the length of the store to the east entrance, where I came out, hopefully, unnoticed by my tail. I walked up the row of cars until I could flank the Trailblazer. I moved along the parked cars, trying to use the larger trucks and SUVs to block my approach.

When I made it to the row where the maroon SUV was parked, I crept along slowly, keeping the rear of the Trailblazer in front of me. There were a few moments when the driver might be able to see me if he were watching his back, but I was gambling that instead, he was watching the door for me to come out.

By the time I reached the Trailblazer, I was crouched down behind the tailgate. Moving swiftly, I rose and closed the gap from the rear of the truck to the driver's door in two quick steps. The door was locked, and the driver was gone.

I glanced around, surprised to find my quarry gone.

A figure came around the front of the Ford coupe parked next to the Trailblazer.

"What the..." A greasy-looking white kid hollered at me as he pulled a Glock out of his shorts. I pushed off the Trailblazer and rolled on my back over the hood of the coupe as the nine millimeter popped twice.

My right hand and knees hit the sweltering asphalt. The balls of my feet were already shoving me into a cowering sprint before the kid could get a bead on me. I wasn't listening for gunshots anymore. Just moving my feet. Worrying about being hit would have to come later.

A mother with two small children was huddling behind the minivan on my right.

"Go!" I shouted and pointed for them to move. The mother was shielding the kids and mouthing words to them, they didn't budge.

"Shit!" I howled, and I turned away from them and started running upright across the parking lot away from the defenseless family.

I heard another shot as I slid behind a Dodge truck. Behind the cover of the truck, my head popped up to evaluate my situation. The gunman, probably less of a kid than I first thought, looked to be in his late twenties or early thirties. He tossed a black bag into the Trailblazer. My black bag.

The Trailblazer's tires squealed as it jerked backward out of the parking spot. I caught sight of the license plate and memorized it before the SUV sped off. He clipped a Nissan Maxima as he cut the corner toward the street.

I rushed over to the family, still cowering.

"Are you alright?" I asked.

The mother, shaking and sobbing, looked up at me.

"It's over. Are you all okay?"

She pushed the kids away to look at them. The kids were both under five. Two girls wearing little cotton sundresses.

Neither seemed overly fazed by the action. The mother fell back on her butt and cried, she pulled both of the girls into her arms as she bawled.

One of the little girls looked up at me. "Mama, he's hurt."

The mother turned her head up to me. Her cheeks, wet and flushed.

"You're bleeding," she told me.

I looked down to see my shirt was covered in blood. Lifting the bottom of the shirt showed a wound on my side where one of the rounds grazed me.

"It's just a flesh wound," I stated, but I slipped down to the ground.

A crowd was forming from the front of the grocery store. A security guard approached with his hand on his weapon.

"What happened?" he demanded.

"This man started shooting at him," the mother declared.

"I think I interrupted a robbery," I said, looking toward the Tilly's Toyota and the broken driver's window.

"The police are on their way," the guard assured me. "Is anyone hurt?"

"He's been shot," one of the girls replied.

I lifted my arm to show my blood-stained shirt. The first responder was a single West Palm Beach Police car. The officer immediately approached the security guard, who seemed to give him a brief description of the events.

When the officer finally approached us, he asked, "What happened?"

The first little girl who noticed my blood said, "The man got shot."

"He saved us," the mother exclaimed.

The officer took a slow turn of his head to me. I just sat there, bleeding slightly.

28

Despite my protestations, the EMT wouldn't back down on taking me to the emergency room. The police officers on the scene insisted as well, and they began to grow suspicious when I wanted to refuse treatment. To avoid any suspicions, I finally gave in and let the ambulance carry me to the hospital.

While the bullet only caused a flesh wound, it turned out to be more than a graze. The round left a clear entry and exit wound that the paramedic felt needed a few stitches. The attendee finally goaded me to let him administer a local anesthetic before making any stitches. I was lying on the bed in the open ER area after he had finished the suturing. Agent Kohl walked in with another man that had the look of an underpaid government employee.

"Mr. Gordon," Kohl asked, "how are you feeling?"

"I'm fine," I assured him.

"You look fine," he commented after a glance at my stitched side.

"What are you doing here?" I asked coldly.

"I flagged your name in case someone shot you, or you

shot someone," he stated flatly. "Seems my instincts were correct."

"You could have brought flowers," I sneered.

My side was feeling tight. There wasn't any pain after the doctor hit the area with the local anesthetic. Now I was just feeling the stress of the stitches.

"This is Detective Charles," Kohl introduced. "He's here about the shooting."

"You just tagged along because you were worried about me."

"You are a person of interest in a federal case," he pointed out. "I'm here to make sure you haven't shit all over three years of investigative work."

"I hate to disappoint you," I said, "but this wasn't Moreno's guys."

Kohl furrowed his brow. "Are you sure?"

"Pretty sure," I told him. "I've run the gambit with Moreno's guys. This was a white kid that looked like he should be popping pills between catching a wave. I don't think he fits the job description for working on Moreno's crew."

The detective glared at me. He noted, "He shot you, though. You must have made an impression somehow."

"Maybe Moreno should be recruiting the surfer demographic," Kohl joked.

"I caught the kid stealing my backpack out of the car," I said. "I thought he was just a meth-head or something trying to get a quick fix. I didn't anticipate he had a gun."

"From what I've seen of you," Kohl stated, "that doesn't track."

"We all drop our guard sometimes," I remarked.

"I didn't think Marines were allowed to do that."

"Well, I'm retired."

"The mother," the detective started but stopped to look at his notebook for her name, "Ms. Kelton said you were drawing his fire away from the kids."

"I wasn't thinking. Just reacting."

Kohl stared at me. Then he asked, "Are you sure that this wasn't Moreno? What was in the bag?"

"Gym clothes," I said. "This guy's gonna be disappointed."

"You gave the officer on duty the plate number," Kohl mused.

I nodded. "I saw it when he was peeling away."

The detective watched me. "After you were wounded?"

Kohl raised his hand to stop the detective's train of questioning.

"The car was stolen," Kohl stated, "so it doesn't lead us anywhere."

"Where was it stolen from?"

"From up in Jupiter."

Not having any idea where Jupiter was, I just listened.

"If this isn't Moreno," Kohl said, "then I'm no longer needed here."

"So nice of you to visit, Van," I retorted with a touch of snark.

He looked at Charles and said, "My guess is that whatever he says isn't the entire truth, and he doesn't know when to get out of the way."

"That's hurtful," I panned.

He ignored me and walked out of the ER.

Detective Charles focused on me. "What else can you tell me about the shooter?"

"I only had a second before he started shooting. He was white. His hair was longish. Maybe shoulder length and stringy. It looked like he hadn't washed it."

"Any facial hair?"

I shook my head. "Did the security cameras get anything?"

Raising an eyebrow, he said, "In fact, it showed you enter the store and exit out the other entrance and approach the suspect's vehicle."

"That's true," I said. "I noticed him following me. After my recent run-in with Julio Moreno's guys, I wanted to make sure that I surprised them and not the other way around."

"Seemed that didn't help," he pointed out to me in a condescending tone.

"I'm not perfect. I wasn't expecting him to just want to rob me."

"Why wouldn't you alert security at the store? Maybe call us?" Charles asked.

I shrugged. "I thought I had it handled."

"What would you have done if he hadn't shot you first?" His question was pointed.

"I just wanted to know why he was following me. I was unarmed," I explained. "With no desire to do anything but find out who he was."

He squinted at me, trying to decipher if Kohl was right about me, only telling half-truths. I assumed that the detective had already made some snap judgments about me.

With his notebook in hand, Charles said, "I'm going to need a phone number for you."

I offered an apologetic look. "I don't have a phone," I explained.

A confused look crossed his face. "You don't have a phone?"

"I get that a lot."

"Everyone has a phone," he responded.

"I live on a boat and spend more time cruising in the

Bahamas than on the mainland. Plus, after many years of the U.S. government keeping me at its beck and call, I like the idea of being out of contact."

He shook his head, incredulously. "Everyone has a phone," he repeated under his breath. "How can I get in touch with you?"

"You can leave a message for me at the Tilly Inn. I bartend some nights at the Manta Club."

He jotted down the number as I rattled it off to him.

"I don't have anything else," the detective said. "I'll let you know if we recover your belongings."

"I won't hold my breath," I said, adding, "The kid might when he finds my sweaty clothes."

He looked at me skeptically, and I imagined that even if Kohl hadn't besmirched my honesty, then the good detective would question it.

"Thank you, Detective," I said as he left.

I was left alone for another fifteen minutes or so before a nurse came through. She was in her late fifties with red hair that came from a box and glowed nearly neon. She reminded me of a lady from my childhood. I couldn't remember her name, but she sat two rows in front of my mother every Sunday and sang three octaves off-key during every hymn.

"Mr. Gordon, do you have a ride home?" the boxed redhead asked.

"No, I'll take a cab."

"You need someone to take you." She was making a note on my chart as if it was some incurable condition to not have a ride.

"If you are offering, I have to warn you that I was shot and might not be at my full virility."

Her eyes scolded me.

"I was shot," I pointed out as an excuse for my sarcasm.

"That is why you need someone to take you home."

"I don't have anyone. A cab will be fine."

The dowdy red-haired nurse left with a frustrated countenance. I waited. By now, I was pretty sure I should have just stayed in the parking lot. I could have been back at the marina with a stiff rum cocktail to alleviate the pain as I licked my wounds.

The next nurse was much younger. Short black hair with dark skin and brown eyes that might have inspired Van Morrison if she was born forty years sooner.

"Mr. Gordon," she said, proffering a clipboard, "if I can get your signature, we can get you out of here."

Her name badge read Anna, and I gave her a smile as I took the paperwork and signed it. "Am I done?" I asked.

"That's all. You're free to go."

"Can I use a phone? I need to call a cab."

She motioned for me to follow her. The phone at the nurse's station was next to the red-haired nurse that eyeballed me as I called for a cab.

"Mr. Gordon, there's someone in the waiting room for you," Red said with some scorn and a hint of satisfaction.

I hung up the phone and walked out the doors leading to the waiting room. Missy sat in a corner away from the rest of the crowd. She was wearing a black suit, her regular attire when she planned to walk the lobby and greet guests.

"What are you doing here?" I asked, sliding into the seat next to her.

"The police called about the car," she responded. "I dropped Randy off to drive it back."

"I'm sorry about that."

She waved me off. "Are you alright?" she asked, staring at the blood-stained shirt I was wearing.

"It's just a scratch. Like six stitches total."

She shook her head in disbelief. "Six stitches," she muttered. "Would you like a ride back to the marina?"

"Yes, you'll make the nurse's day. She was frantic that I didn't have a ride. I thought she might offer to take me home with her."

"You can still go with her," she quipped. "If you want."

I smiled, "No, it's nice to see you instead. Do you mind if we make a stop?"

Missy drove me to the gym. I was nervous that the greasy kid that shot me might have figured out my simple ruse. Once he found a backpack full of paper towels, he definitely would. At that point, though, he was running out of time with the stolen Trailblazer. Unless he was stupid, which I wasn't discounting yet, he needed to ditch it and get a new ride.

As luck would have it, the backpack was still in the locker. There was a different attendant at the check-in desk, but my temporary membership card got me in the door with no questions asked.

I garnered a questioning glance when I left the gym two minutes later. The attendant didn't say anything, and if he questioned whether I was carrying a bag or not on my way into the building, he didn't have a chance to ask it.

"Is this about the necklace?" Missy asked.

I shook my head with some doubt. "I really don't know," I admitted. "I can't see how anyone would have known we got the necklace from its hidey-hole in the Keys, but I am also pretty certain it wasn't Moreno's guys either."

"Maybe," Missy suggested, "it's time to let Tristan go. Talk to the wife."

I considered it while I was waiting to be stitched up. Tristan put himself into a rather deep hole. He dug multiple ones simultaneously, and there is no way to know which one has swallowed him up. Kayla and Abbie should stay with her family and let this whole thing blow over. If Tristan came back, then things would need to be sorted out. If he didn't ever show up, then it was likely that he was dead.

On the other hand, things were happening. There was still the possibility that the guy in the Trailblazer was working with Gilliam in blackmailing Peterson. My gut said that wasn't the case. Gilliam and Leah hatched that plan, and if I dug at them, I'd very likely find a concrete connection to Peterson. At this point, I wasn't willing to do that.

"I have a couple of things I'm looking into," I told her, "but if that doesn't pan out, I think I'll have run out of roads to look down."

"What are you doing next?" she asked.

"Tonight's agenda is going to involve collapsing in my berth and sleeping till morning. Then I'll figure out what to do next."

29

"I'm going to grab a drink at the Manta," I told Missy when we pulled into the lot. "Want one?"

She shook her head. "No, we're supposed to have dinner at the in-laws."

I couldn't contain the cringe on my face.

"They aren't that bad," she lied, mostly to herself. "Besides, Paige is going so that will be a nice buffer."

The marina's complimentary car sat in its regular parking space. Clear plastic covered the broken window. Randy had covered the edge of the plastic with several strips of silver duct tape.

"I'll pay for the window," I told her. "I'm sorry about that."

"We have insurance. You just cover the deductible," she replied as I opened the door.

She put her hand on my leg and leaned over and kissed my cheek before I got out. "Please be careful," she pleaded.

"I'll try. I'm just going to wash down these antibiotics with some rum before I call it a night."

She pulled away and left me in the parking lot, watching

the red taillights turn north and blend into the traffic. When the lights were indistinguishable from the others on the road, I gave up my preposterous vigilance and ventured into the bar. I felt like I needed to call Peterson too. This bag of money was something of an albatross around my neck. I wanted to get clear of the whole Peterson debacle without compromising any moral choices I might be forced to make.

The Manta Club was busy. The din of laughter and conversations drowned out the overhead music that, if I strained to listen to sounded like John Mellencamp. Kristy whizzed past me with a tray of drinks. She broke character and gave me a coy smile. I dodged a pair of gentlemen talking with wide sweeps of their hands and stepped behind the bar. Hunter glanced up at me while pulling a draft.

Picking up the phone, I dialed Peterson's number. He didn't answer. His voice mail message told me that he was unavailable, and I left a brief message that I needed to talk to him.

The albatross was still there, and I had to decide what to do with it until I got it back to the mayor. Taking the bag to my boat seemed like a poor idea. There were already too many people interested in my comings and goings to be sure that it would be safe there. After some careful thought, I went to the public bathroom downstairs and found it empty. It was usually vacant. For some reason, it seemed out of the way enough that guests never used it; instead, they opted to cross the lobby to the one by the front desk. Stepping up on the toilet, I lifted the ceiling tile above the stall. The stitches in my side pulled. I ignored them and slipped the bag into the hole before replacing the tile.

When I finished, I returned to the Manta for that drink that I deserved after a hard day of being shot. I sidled up and sat at the bar, waiting on Hunter to make his way to me for my order.

"Hey," Hunter remarked when he got around to me. "I heard you got shot today. Is that true?" He studied me, looking confused that I was sitting upright.

"Word gets around."

"Really," he was shocked. "I can't believe you got shot."

"It was a graze. Barely broke the skin."

"Randy came by after he got the car. I wasn't sure if he was shitting me or not. You doing okay?"

I pointed at the hole in my shirt, caked in dried brown blood. "It was just a flesh wound. The stitches were a bigger pain than the bullet hole."

"Still, that's crazy," he said. "Were you ever shot when you were in the Marines?"

"Once in the leg."

"Damn," he whistled. "Does it hurt?"

"The leg? Not anymore. The stitches throbs a little right now."

"Need a drink?" he asked, then he restated it as "You need a drink."

"Yeah," I agreed. "Give me a rum and Coke."

He stepped off to make my drink. He returned a minute later with the glass and two slips of paper.

"You have a couple of messages," he said, handing me the paper.

I nodded my thanks and read them. The first was a number and the name "Tommy." Perhaps it was the Tommy from Hometown Hardware. I was a little surprised to even hear from him. Maybe Stephen came through.

The second was from Kayla. I froze as I read the note under her name that said, "Tristan texted to meet at the house."

"Hunter," I called, "when did this one call?"

He looked over at the message. "Is that the girl? It was early. Maybe two or so."

"Shit!" I cursed. "Can you hand me the phone?"

Hunter tossed the cordless receiver to me as he continued making a margarita. Kayla's number rang twice and went to voice mail.

"Kayla, it's Chase. I'm on my way to your house. If you haven't gotten there yet, wait until you hear from me."

I hung up the phone and looked at Hunter. "Did she say anything else?" I asked him.

Hunter shook his head and shrugged simultaneously. "Just that she was supposed to meet what's-his-name."

"Tristan," I filled in the blank under my breath.

Jumping up, I said, "I gotta go."

"Is everything okay?" he asked with a look of deep concern on his face as if he was at fault for delivering the message so late.

"It's just a bad feeling I have," I answered.

My untouched drink sat on the bar as I hurried out the door. The other set of keys for the Toyota was still in my pocket. Randy had most of the broken glass out of the driver's seat.

Heading toward Loxahatchee, I wondered if it was true that Tristan had reached out to Kayla. That would be a relief, but my gut wasn't convinced. I didn't like the fortuity of the whole thing. The phone call from Kayla was just a few minutes after the kid in the parking lot shot me. The greasy bastard in the Trailblazer might have realized that the bag was a decoy and decided to go a different route. He was just trying for a smash and grab. That meant that he wasn't looking for anything big. Something small enough that it could fit in a backpack. Like a diamond necklace.

Maybe it was just timing or pure luck. If Tristan heard that I was looking for him, he could have decided to resurface now. Perhaps it was just a coincidence that it was less than an hour after I was shot and robbed.

As I said, I don't like coincidences. Not because I don't believe in them, but they aren't dependable. They should never be trusted. Better to prove it's good fortune than find out later it wasn't.

The roads were dark as I headed west along the golf course that lined the northern side of the street. As I got closer to the Locke's house, the few streetlights were becoming even farther apart until I was on their street. The street was dark, and the darkness was only broken by patches of light coming from windows of homes where people were dulling their minds with whatever police procedural or reality show was beaming in from the satellites far above the earth.

An older Ford minivan was parked in the driveway of Tristan's house. My headlights illuminated the dark house when I pulled in behind it. The plywood that I used to cover the front door was missing. The door frame was an eerie maw for a house full of shadows.

Leaving the lights on so I could see, I got out slowly. The sound of crickets and cicadas sang through the dark. Tiny spots of light flashed around the yard as fireflies talked back and forth.

The air was still and hot. A typical inland Florida night. I swiped away the buzzing of a mosquito near my ear.

The minivan was empty, but from the booster seat in the back, I guessed it was Kayla's.

"Kayla," I said aloud. If anyone else was around, they already knew I was here. There was little need for stealth at this point.

The only answer was the insect cacophony that reverberated through the night.

I walked through the front door and found the light switch. The house looked the same. The plywood barricade was lying on the floor, but the rest of the house still looked trashed.

Turning lights on as I passed through the kitchen and hallway, I found an empty house. I stopped suddenly.

The door to the bathroom was busted as if it had been kicked in. The doorknob was ripped from the cheap hollow door. Two feet stuck out of the doorway.

I knelt in the darkened bathroom over Kayla's prone figure. Her head was caked in blood, but she was breathing. Someone had hit her on the head, but she was breathing.

"Kayla," I asked. "Can you hear me?"

She groaned.

"Kayla."

Her eyes fluttered.

I searched around for her phone in the dark. When I found it, I was dismayed to find the screen smashed.

Another groan from Kayla.

"Abbie!" she howled.

"Kayla," I tried to comfort her. "It's Chase."

"Chase." Her voice was frantic. "Where's Abbie?"

"I don't know," I answered.

"He took her," she cried.

"Who?" I asked. "Tristan?"

She shook her head barely, wincing in pain.

"No, some guy," she whispered. Her hand grabbed mine as she tried to pull herself up.

"Take it easy," I said. "You got whacked pretty hard."

She turned her eyes to me. "He's got Abbie."

"Okay, let's get you up slowly, though."

She put her arm around me, and I lifted her to the edge of the bathtub so she could rest.

"Sit for a second," I begged her.

She nodded slowly.

"Can you remember what happened?"

"I got a text from Tristan," she started.

"Did you talk to him?" I asked. "Or just a text?"

"Just a text."

I nodded for her to continue.

"I drove down right away. The house..." Her words trailed off. "He was in Abbie's room. He told me he wanted to know where Tristan hid the necklace."

She started to cry as the shock hit her. "I tried to lock us in here," she stammered. "He kicked the door down."

"It's okay, Kayla," I put my arms around her. "Did he say anything else?"

"I don't remember," she bawled. "The door broke, and I don't know."

"We have to get you to the hospital."

"I have to find Abbie," she demanded.

"We will," I promised her, "but you have to get checked out."

"I don't know what he was talking about," she murmured to herself.

"I think I do." I helped her to her feet. "We'll get her back, I promise. Tell me about the guy."

"He was skinny. White guy. Maybe around my age."

"Did he say anything about calling you?"

She shook her head. "I guess he has my number."

"Yeah," I sighed as I showed her the broken phone.

"How are we going to get her back?"

"I think he and I already met today, so he knows who I

am. But if he texted from Tristan's phone, then we can assume he has it."

I walked her slowly out to the car and got her buckled up.

"I'll come back and secure the house for you."

"No," she said flatly. "I just want my daughter back."

I nodded and shut the door. Kayla's head bobbed a little as if the effort to hold it straight was too much.

As I pulled out of the driveway, she listed over toward my leg. She was crying as I sped down the road.

"I hate him," she mumbled through her tears. I assumed she was talking about Tristan.

"I'll get her back," I promised again because I didn't know what else to say.

30

The lights of the Manta Club were still on when I finally made it back to the Tilly. I peered through the closed glass doors to see Hunter closing up the bar. He was cleaning the service area as I came in.

I spent the last few hours consoling Kayla as we waited in the hospital's waiting room. When the emergency room doctor finally saw her, he insisted that she stay for observation.

"The police will come by," I told her before I left. "I'd suggest you tell them everything. They might be able to help."

She nodded silently. Her eyes were red and swollen.

"I'm going to try to reach out to him on Tristan's phone," I said. "I'll work something out."

The nurses decided that I had been there long enough and shooed me out. Hoping to still find a drink, I headed back to the inn.

Hunter saw me standing at the locked door and let me in.

"You're back late," he commented.

"Yeah," was all I could muster.

"Everything alright?" he asked. "You look a little dismayed."

"It's been a night," I mumbled. I sat at the bar.

"Is it the girl that called?" he surmised.

I nodded. "She was attacked, and her daughter kidnapped."

"Oh shit," he said. "You need anything?"

I waved off his offer. "I have to make a call," I said. "You going to be a minute?"

"I'm almost done but take your time."

On my way through the front door, I grabbed the valet's cell phone. I'd tell Missy I had it in the morning, but right now, I wanted to start the ball rolling.

"The girl better be safe," I typed. "I have what you want. Let's trade."

I wanted to be vague but make the appropriate demands. Knowing that Abbie was safe was the most important thing.

Hunter set a glass of whiskey in front of me.

"I already dumped the ice," he said, "but you look like you need something."

"Thanks," I replied before I slugged back the liquor. The slow burn of whiskey coursed through my abdomen. "I'll get out of your way."

"You need me to cover tomorrow?" he asked.

"You've been on all week," I said apologetically.

"Yeah, well," he said sheepishly, "it sounds like you have your hands full."

"I'll make it up to you," I promised.

He gave me an agreeing nod.

Leaving him in the bar, I walked toward the marina. The sky was clear, except a few clouds that drifted in front of the stars. The difference in the air from here versus Tristan's house was astounding. The ocean breeze made the night almost cool and pleasant.

When I climbed into the cockpit, I sat back on the starboard cushion and called Jay.

"Delp," he answered sleepily.

"Sorry I woke you," I said.

"Chase," he sounded surprised. "What's up?"

"I think it's time I fill you in completely. Things have escalated out of control."

"Yeah, hold on," he replied. I could hear him moving around, maybe getting up out of bed. He asked, "What's going on?"

I began filling him in with all the details that I had purposefully left out for his own sake.

When I finished, he asked, "Is Kayla alright?"

"Yeah, it was a bad concussion."

"I'll book the next flight down," he said. "I'll see what's going out in the morning."

"I want to find this guy before I set any meeting with him. He was alone when he shot me earlier, but he might not be working alone."

"Are you sure it's the same guy?" Jay asked.

"Not totally positive, but what are the odds?"

"You think Tristan and this guy were burglarizing houses?"

"It was just a theory, but he told Kayla he wanted the necklace. That starts to tie it all up."

Jay said, "I ran through the lists of stolen goods for you. There was one that reported a stolen diamond necklace appraised at forty-five thousand."

"That has to be it," I said.

He gave me the address of the house. "The victim is

listed as Sharon Goddard. Her husband, Harold, was killed during the burglary. Bludgeoned with a marble statue."

"Any chance that you have a phone number?" I asked. "I want to talk to her tonight, and I don't think she will be receptive to a stranger at this time of night."

"Yeah, it's in here." He gave me the phone number.

"Thanks, Jay," I said.

"There's a flight at 7:50. I'll be there by noon."

I hung up with him. Sharon Goddard's number was in my hand. I paused before I began dialing. It was almost midnight. The woman had endured something horrific only a few weeks ago. I was about to dredge it up for her.

An image of little Abbie Locke eating chicken tenders in the Manta flashed through my head. The girl was the only thing that mattered right now.

The phone rang three times before a woman answered.

"Hello," the voice sounded raspy.

"Mrs. Goddard?"

"Yes?" Her tone was less groggy and began to veer toward either concern or annoyance.

"I'm sorry about the late hour," I said. "I'm pressed for time, and I was hoping to talk to you about the burglary."

"Who is this?"

"My name is Chase Gordon. I'm going to get to the point. I don't mean to be insensitive or disturb you this late, except that it's very important."

"Well, get to it, Mr. Gordon," the woman stated matter-of-factly.

"A little girl was kidnapped today, and I believe that the man that took her was the same one that broke into your house."

Sharon Goddard was silent for a moment. Eventually, she asked, "Who exactly are you?"

"The little girl is the daughter of my friend. I am not involved with the police, but I'm sure that they are also looking for the girl."

"What's the girl's name?" she asked. Maybe it was a test, or perhaps she needed to humanize the problem.

"Abbie," I answered. "She's three years old."

"How is this connected to me?" she asked.

"I know it's late, ma'am, but would you have time to see me tonight?"

"It is rather late," she scolded.

"I know, but I'm a little desperate."

"I suppose that if you have my phone number, then you must have my address as well."

"Yes, ma'am."

"I'll put some coffee on," she said.

"Thank you." I hung up as I was climbing onto the dock.

The drive to Sharon Goddard's home was very quick at this time of night. Her house looked like a marble castle resting on the bluff overlooking the ocean. The front window was illuminated by a chandelier that from the front sidewalk appeared to be ten feet in diameter with hundreds, if not more, crystals refracting and reflecting the light.

The door opened before I could knock. A brown-haired man in a Florida State shirt and black sweatpants stood in the light.

"Are you Mr. Gordon?" he asked with some caution.

"Yes, is Mrs. Goddard in? She's expecting me."

"She is. I'm her son. She called me and asked me to come over."

He didn't invite me in, and I waited for a few seconds.

"Harry," a woman's voice called from another room, "bring him to the kitchen!"

Harry gestured for me to enter. He eyed me carefully,

and I didn't blame him. His father had been murdered in this house less than a month ago.

He led me through a small well-displayed museum of Japanese art and trinkets that pretended to double as a sitting room. The kitchen was larger than *Carina*. It was almost bigger than the Manta Club. A stainless-steel refrigerator and oven reflected the soft light. The walls were lined with alabaster cabinets.

A handsome woman stood from the dark oak table. She rose to my height, her blue eyes stared into mine as she appraised me.

"Mr. Gordon," she said flatly.

"Chase. Thank you for seeing me so late."

"I admit I was somewhat cautious," she spoke sternly.

"Understandable," I affirmed.

"Would you like some coffee?" Mrs. Goddard motioned for me to sit.

"I never turn down a cup."

"Harry."

Her son poured some coffee into a delicate little porcelain cup. He gave me a questioning look.

"Black," I responded to the unasked question.

He handed me the ornate cup.

I began to talk. "Some of what I'm going to tell you is my own conjecture. The girl I told you about is the daughter of a friend who served with me in Afghanistan. His wife came to me last week because he has been missing for weeks. Unfortunately, I think he may have been killed, although I can't prove it. What I do know is that earlier today, a man took his daughter. His demand to the girl's mother was that she 'return the necklace.' Here is where I get into theoretical, and I'll try to not bore you. I think that the necklace in question is the one that was stolen from you."

"Why would your friend's wife have my mother's necklace?" Harry questioned with a sneer of disdain.

My head turned to Mrs. Goddard. "I think that my friend was also involved in the burglary."

"It was a murder!" Harry hissed at me.

"Yes," I admitted.

"I hope your friend is dead then. His daughter be damned."

"Harry," his mother admonished.

"I am sorry for your loss."

Mrs. Goddard stated, "It's not the girl's fault."

I nodded.

"There were two men," she began. "We were going to be out of town, but I was feeling under the weather. I had retired to my room, and Harold was downstairs.

"I heard a noise," she continued. "A man came into the room. He was surprised to see me there. He just stared at me for a bit. Then we heard..."

Her voice caught in her throat as she fought against the emotions. "I think he was shocked to hear Harold cry out. He told me to hide in the linen closet. He promised he wouldn't let the other man hurt me. He said to be quiet."

She paused and took a sip of her coffee. Mentally gathering herself together, she said, "He told the other man that there was no one upstairs. It felt like forever before I didn't hear them anymore. I came out and found Harold in the den."

Harry put his arm around his mother.

"Did you see the man downstairs?" I asked.

She shook her head.

"Could you identify the man that put you in the closet?"

"If I saw him," she answered.

"Can you describe him?"

She took another sip of coffee. "He was blond with blue eyes. He was a boy."

"Was there anything else about him?"

She studied me carefully. "He had the same tattoo that you have?"

She was pointing at the unit tattoo that we all got before we went to Afghanistan.

"What are you going to do about the girl?" Harry asked.

"I have to find the man first," I replied, "but I have to get her back."

"It was your friend," she spoke with determination.

"I think so," I admitted. "I'm sorry about that."

"We cannot be our brother's keepers," she informed me. "He did save my life, though."

"Mother," Harry interjected, "that doesn't excuse his involvement."

"Harry, I never said it did. There is more to this than just your father's murder."

"If my friend is alive," I vowed, "he'll see the justice he deserves."

Sharon Goddard gave me an approving gesture. "It seems," she said pointedly, "that the young girl's safety is of the utmost concern. Please let me know if I can help at all."

The austere woman stood up, signaling my time with her was ending.

I rose to my feet. "Thank you, Mrs. Goddard, for your time."

With a curt nod, she ordered, "I expect to hear the outcome of this."

"Yes, ma'am."

31

"Chase," Missy called from the companionway.

My head was still buried in the pillows near the bow of the v-berth, where I had collapsed last night. Lifting it, I tried to guess the time. Maybe half-past six, I thought.

My right foot hung off the bed and extended through the door to the front cabin. Missy touched my bare foot.

"Chase," she said again. "A detective is looking for you at the inn."

Groaning from the twitch of pain in my side, I pushed myself up and turned so that I was sitting on the edge of the v-berth facing aft. Missy was looking at me. She ran the palm of her hand gently over my stitches. Her eyes crawled up my chest to my face.

"Does it hurt?" she asked.

"Not so much," I explained. "The stitches pull some."

Her fingers stroked my cheek. Two days without shaving had left some stubble that probably felt like sandpaper. She smiled at me.

"He's waiting in the lobby," she said.

"Let him wait," I mumbled.

"Is this about the shooting?" she asked.

"I doubt it," I answered. "Kayla was attacked yesterday, and her daughter was kidnapped."

"The little girl from the bar?"

I nodded. "He told Kayla that he wanted the necklace."

"The one in my safe?"

"I can only assume." I stepped past her and grabbed a pair of shorts. "Right now, no one knows that we have the necklace. It was stolen during one of the recent home invasions. Tristan was one of the burglars, along with the guy that shot me and kidnapped Abbie."

"It was the same guy?"

"Pretty sure," I pulled a clean shirt with a Guy Harvey painting screen printed on it.

"Why did he shoot you?"

"I plan to ask him that, but I guess he thinks I have the necklace."

"Which you do."

"But he can't know that." I slid my feet into a pair of canvas deck shoes. "Thanks, Missy."

She caught my hand. "You need to be careful."

I kissed her.

Detective Charles was waiting in one of the wingback chairs next to the grand piano that was currently playing automatically. Something classical, but my music expertise only begins around the late sixties.

"Mr. Gordon," he said, standing, "you seem to be in a lot of trouble."

I sat down in the other chair without a word.

"You took Mrs. Locke to the emergency room last night."

"I did."

"How did you come across her?" he asked.

"I found her at her house."

"Why were you there, Gordon?"

"I was looking for her," I explained.

"How are the two of you acquainted?"

Rolling my eyes, I replied, "Her husband and I served together."

"Her husband, Tristan Locke?"

I nodded.

"This is the one that Kohl said had been employed by Julio Moreno?"

"That's Kohl's suspicion," I stated.

"Where is he?"

"I don't know."

"So, you went to your friend's house to see his wife."

I wasn't sure if he was asking or telling. So I didn't answer.

"Mrs. Locke said that she was attacked before her daughter was kidnapped."

"That's what she told me," I confirmed.

"Her description of her attacker seemed to be very similar to the suspect who shot you yesterday."

Again there wasn't a defined question.

He sighed at my silence. "What do you make of that?" he asked.

I shook my head. "I wouldn't know. I never saw the guy before he shot me."

"Mrs. Locke's home looks like it was searched. Does this have anything to do with Julio Moreno?"

"Look, Detective Charles, I honestly don't know. The man yesterday didn't fit the demographic that Moreno has working for him."

"Mrs. Locke said that the man wanted a necklace. Does that mean anything to you?"

"I did a little research," I offered. "A valuable necklace was stolen during a home invasion a few weeks ago."

Charles narrowed his eyes. "The Goddard house?" he asked.

"It might not be the same necklace, but it's my only guess."

He stared at me for a second before shifting his eyes back to his notebook. His face was perplexed. Unraveling threads that he hadn't seen left him speechless.

"Is there anything else?" I asked.

He shook his head. "No, that's all I have right now. Stay around in case I have more questions."

I crossed my legs as the detective walked out of the lobby. A few seconds later, Missy dropped into the detective's seat.

"He didn't arrest you," she commented.

"No, he didn't. But the day's still young." I looked at her. There are so many ways I see her, from naked and sweaty to this professional hotelier. The green dress she was wearing cast an emerald glow.

"Has anyone told you that you look beautiful today?"

"Not yet," she answered.

"I would say everyone has dropped the ball because... damn, you look good."

Her eyes twinkled.

"What are you doing today about the girl?" she asked.

"One of the other guys from my unit is coming in today. I'm hoping that we can get in contact with the guy that has Abbie and make a swap for the jewels."

"You didn't tell the detective about the necklace then?"

"If we have to make a trade, I don't want anyone interfering. I'm not sure what the cops would do, but they might take an approach that will endanger the girl."

"Your friend," she questioned. "Is he like you?"

"I'm not sure what that means," I said. "He's a bad ass, though."

She pursed her lips.

"Can you set a room aside for him?" I asked.

"Yeah, what's his name?"

She took his name to the front desk, and I walked over to the coffee stand to pour me a cup.

"He's good to go," she said, handing me a key card. "1127."

"I'm going to check on Kayla," I told Missy. I showed her the phone I took from the concierge desk last night. "I have the valet's phone. I used it to text what I hope is the kidnapper."

"I'll call if anyone comes looking," she replied.

For a moment, I wanted to kiss her, but restraint prevailed. Our eyes lingered on each other for a second. The sigh remained in my chest, and I turned to leave.

Kayla was dressed when I got to the hospital.

"My mom is on her way down." Her somber voice echoed softly in defeat.

"The detective came by to see me this morning."

She nodded. "He told me that they would be bringing in the FBI because it's a kidnapping."

"I sent a text to Tristan's phone, hoping that the kidnapper will get it."

"What are you going to do if he answers?"

I sighed and sat in the seat facing the bed. She turned and let her feet hang off the hospital bed, her cheeks were puffy and red. I wondered how much rest she got last night.

"I'm going to set up a swap," I explained.

"Did you tell the detective?"

"Not yet," I stated. "It would be premature. This might

not even work. He may not even have Tristan's phone anymore."

Her gaze narrowed on me, and she furrowed her brow. Her voice croaked as she asked, "Do you think Tristan's dead?"

My stomach flipped with a wave of nausea. I swallowed back some bile, feeling the effects from my throat to my stomach.

"I think he must be," I finally said. "He was into some bad things, but I don't believe he would have abandoned you. Not like this."

She shook her head. "He was a good man," she iterated.

"He was," I assured her. "He only started out trying to take care of you and Abbie. Things just spiraled out of control, and his attempts to stop it just made matters worse."

"The drugs?" she questioned.

"That seemed like easy money. I'm pretty sure he was picking up drugs off the coast and smuggling them in for a Miami drug dealer. That was going fine until the Coast Guard boarded him. He dumped the drugs to avoid being arrested, but the drug dealer still wanted his product."

She blinked as she listened to me.

"Miami was still looking for him, so I don't think they killed him. He got involved in something else. Something that could get him some money to pay off the dealer and protect both you and Abbie. That's what went awry."

"What did he do?"

"He was burglarizing houses. A man was murdered, and that seemed to be the line that Tristan didn't want to cross. He didn't kill the man, but he did save the man's wife."

"Oh," she uttered, tears welling in her eyes.

"I talked to the woman last night. She described Tristan to me, right down to the tattoo on his arm. She said that when his partner murdered her husband, that Tristan was surprised. That must not have been the plan. He hid her in a closet, knowing she could identify him."

"You think his partner found out and killed him?"

"I think that Tristan kept a valuable necklace, intending to probably pay off the Miami connection, and the partner killed him for it. He was tearing your house apart looking for it. He shot me thinking maybe I found it. His last straw was coming after you in case you knew about the necklace."

"I don't have it," she said. "What's he going to do to Abbie?"

"Nothing," I said. "I told him that I had it. If he wants it, he has to keep Abbie safe."

"You told him?"

"In the text to Tristan's phone."

"What if he doesn't have his phone?"

I sighed. It was a strong possibility, but I wanted to keep her hopes up. "Doesn't matter," I said, "she's his only ticket to getting the necklace."

Tears formed in her eyes again.

I put my hand on her knee and tried to comfort her. "Did Tristan ever talk about Jay?"

She wiped her knuckles across her cheek. "From your unit?"

"Yeah, him. He's going to be landing here in an hour or so. The two of us are going to get Abbie back, and nothing is going to stop us."

She nodded.

"I am sure that the police will be back in touch with you," I said. "I already told Detective Charles that Tristan was involved in the burglary. They may be able to find his partner through official channels."

I added, "If he contacts you about Abbie, tell him we have what he wants."

"Do we?"

"We want him to think so," I replied. "Maybe we can make him see reason. Just tell him that I'll make the swap."

"Should I call the detective?" she asked.

"Yes," I answered. "I'll do what I can, but honestly, I'm more of a pointy stick. The cops have a lot more experience in this area."

I was struggling with the police's involvement. The Corps had ensured my skill set involved a wide range of things. Finding kidnappers wasn't one of those.

Why didn't I mention I had the necklace in my possession, you ask. Human nature being a predictably undependable sort of thing; I couldn't tell how anyone would react if I revealed the necklace. Mrs. Goddard, or more likely, her son, Harry, might demand the jewels back immediately. Maybe the insurance company would want possession of them. Even the police might lock them in an evidence locker. All the while, those diamonds might be the only real negotiation tactic to get Abbie back.

I don't mind playing with others, but in this case, showing all my cards didn't seem prudent yet.

Leaving Kayla to wait on her mother, I decided to wait at the Tilly for Jay to meet me there. I pressed the down button on the elevator as the phone in my pocket chirped.

"No cops," the text message said. "I'll contact you to meet."

32

"Flash," I heard the voice behind me exclaim.

Twisting on the barstool, I saw Jay standing at the entrance of the Manta. He was holding a canvas duffel bag and smiling behind a pair of aviator glasses.

"You look like a cop," I quipped. "Want my license and registration?"

"I'd be surprised if you hadn't had it taken away already."

"Flash?" Missy asked with an eyebrow lifted slightly.

"It was my call sign," I admitted.

"Oh," she chuckled, "Gordon, right? You guys aren't that creative."

I hopped to my feet and wrapped my arms around Jay in a bear hug. Jay planted a kiss on my cheek.

"You look good," he howled as I pulled away from him.

"Jay, this is Missy. She owns the hotel."

"Ma'am," Jay extended his hand and deepened his Mississippi drawl. "Thanks for keeping this asshole off the street with work."

"I wish I could keep him here more," Missy said. "He has an aversion to staying put too long."

Jay gave her a congenial smile, and he looked at me warily. "What's the plan?"

"Don't worry. Missy knows what's going on."

He said with relief, "Good, what have you heard?"

"I got a text about an hour ago. He sent me a picture of Abbie to prove he had her."

"Did you call the police?" he asked.

My head drooped a little. "No, I didn't. The police don't know that I have the necklace he wants."

Jay nodded along. "Afraid that it will be taken out of commission?"

Missy perked up, having heard me say the same thing just before Jay arrived.

"Yeah, I figure it would be better to know I had the bargaining chip in case it was the only option."

Jay took the seat next to mine. "Has he set a meet?"

"Not yet," I told him. "I wanted your opinion on this."

"It's going to depend on him. How much control does he want to have? He needs to think he has all the power until we get the girl back. Does he know you?"

"Kinda," I said. "I think he's the guy that shot me."

Jay seemed to be thinking. "Then let's keep him watching you. Let's figure this out. Do you have any gear?"

I smiled. "Follow me."

The marina has a small section of storage units that the liveaboards can rent to keep items too large for a boat. Unit 4C was one of the smaller ones. It could store a small grill or maybe a power washer. Or, in my case, it held a small armory stored in a large airtight cooler.

"I'm so glad to know that if Cuba invades West Palm Beach then the Tilly Marina will be well protected," Missy said when she saw the stacks of guns as I opened the cache.

Jay reached in and removed a M45 and checked the action. The familiar clink echoed in the storage unit.

"Did you take all your service weapons?" he joked as he slid the handgun back into its holster.

"No, these were all aftermarket purchases," I assured him. "I bought these at an estate sale for an old colonel over in Sarasota. Barely scratched the surface of his collection. His widow was making a small fortune off his guns."

He grabbed a box of .45 ammunition and loaded the magazine. "Ooh, give me that M240," he said, pointing to the belt-fed machine gun on top.

"That might be overkill," I pointed out, handing him a M40 Sniper Rifle. "Why don't you take the rifle instead? If we need that many rounds, then we already failed this mission."

He sighed, "Fine." He took the M40 rifle from me. "But when this is done, we need to go to the range with that gorgeous lady."

"I've never heard a man talk about guns like that. Boats and cars, but not guns."

"You never met a real man, huh?" Jay said, cutting his eyes at me.

"Seems that was the complaint on all three of your divorce papers," I snipped.

"How far can you shoot with that?" Missy asked Jay as she watched him shoulder the M40 and peer down the sights.

Jay answered, "I can hit a stationary target every time from at least half a mile. If they're moving, I need to be about three hundred yards out."

"Wow," she whistled.

"You should get him to take you shooting with us," Jay said. "Nothing like six hundred rounds a minute pounding through that beast to get your blood flowing. Better than sex."

"Again, that was the complaint your ex-wives said. You shot out your ammo within a minute."

"Ahh," he pointed at me with a grin.

Missy twinkled and grinned at Jay. "I'll be sure to make him do that sometime. I mean, take me shooting. I have to go do some work. Be careful, guys."

"Thanks, Missy," I said. She smiled at me as she walked away.

After pulling a canvas sea bag from the box, Jay slipped the M40 Sniper Rifle into an Army green tote. He stuffed a box of cartridges into the bag.

"You and her got a thing, huh?" he asked casually as he pulled the strap around the sea bag to close it.

"She's married."

"But..."

"It's a pretty low-key thing. She's not leaving him, and she's even more married to the hotel."

"Yeah, that doesn't fit your Viking lifestyle, does it?"

"Viking?" I retorted, "They stayed too far north for me."

"When we get the girl back..." he started. His eyes turned wistful, and he commented, "Seems like this guy might have taken out Tristan."

I nodded. "Maybe, but it would mean he got the drop on Tristan."

"He got the drop on you," Jay said, pointing at my side. "The fact is that we have to assume that Tristan is dead and that he had a part in it."

"Unless Tristan is behind the whole thing."

"You think he'd kidnap his own kid and knock his wife around?"

I considered the question. That side of Tristan was one that I wasn't willing to see.

"I loved that kid, but he never listened," I muttered. "He should have come to us before this happened."

"That doesn't matter," Jay said, "He probably killed him. And now, kidnapping his daughter. There needs to be some justice dolloped out, don't you think?"

I remained silent.

"Can we grab some grub at your bar?" he asked after a moment.

I slammed the storage locker shut and motioned my head for him to follow me.

Michael was seated at the bar when we came back through. An empty martini glass sat in front of him, three olive spears were collected on the napkin beside him. He glared at me and examined Jay, trying to surmise him.

"That one of your SEAL friends?" he asked, and I felt Jay bristle.

"Shut the hell up, Michael," I admonished him.

He sneered at me as we grabbed two seats on the other side of the bar.

Hunter came over and dropped off two bev naps. "He just downed three martinis since you guys left."

Jay looked a bit confused. "What? Is he an angry drunk or something?"

Hunter chuckled quietly. "More like 'an angry all the time' type. The man hate-drinks as if the martini told him he had a small prick."

"Maybe he does," Jay suggested, and Hunter howled in laughter.

"That's usually something Chase would say," Hunter joked.

"That's Missy's husband," I leaned over and said.

"Ahh," Jay spoke with sudden comprehension. "So, it is a small penis thing."

"Give us two tuna sandwiches," I told Hunter in an attempt to steer the topic away from Missy's husband.

When he left to order our food, Jay asked, "I'm guessing the husband knows all about you."

"The whole sordid thing is a shit storm. I should know better."

"Shouldn't we all," he muttered.

Jay was in the midst of his third divorce. He married his first wife when they were both eighteen. It was one month before Jay shipped off for Parris Island. She filed for divorce before he got out of basic. The second, Lara, he married while we were stationed in Mobile, Alabama. She lasted two years. I only met the third at the wedding. At this point, I think Jay had given up on marriage. Jay told me that there were some things he was extremely good at doing; being married wasn't one of them.

Hunter placed two bottles of Coors Light in front of us.

"Where's this necklace?" Jay asked.

"Locked in a safe in Missy's office."

"I don't like that we are forced to sit here waiting to hear from him," Jay commented. "He should want to get this over with. What are the chances that he's watching you?"

"It's possible, but I spotted him pretty quickly the other day. Unless his surveillance skills have greatly improved, I think he would be noticeable."

I looked up as Wilson Peterson strolled past Michael, who was now joined with Missy in a heated but under-the-breath discussion. Peterson gave me a wave and flagged his phone at me in an unspoken response to my message.

"Give me a sec," I said to Jay as I stood up.

Approaching Peterson, I asked vaguely, "Have you heard anything new?"

Peterson smiled amiably and replied, "Not a word."

"Good," I exhaled. "I need to talk to you about something, and it needs to be a discreet conversation."

He furrowed his brow.

"I'm tied up at the moment, but I'll call you later."

With a confused look, the mayor nodded. "Okay, Chase. Is everything okay?"

"No, it's all good," I said when I saw his concern. "I'm not planning to shake you down if that's what you think."

He grinned sheepishly as if my suggestion never crossed his mind.

"You sleeping with his wife too," Jay asked when I sat back down to find our sandwiches had arrived.

"That's the mayor of West Palm."

"Don't you get around," Jay joked. "So, are you sleeping with his wife too?"

"How's the divorce going?" I jabbed at him.

"That's a little cold."

My pocket buzzed, and I pulled the phone out.

"Tonight at eleven. DuPuis Corbett Campsite."

Jay read the text when I flashed him the screen. "Where is that?" he asked.

Shaking my head, I admitted, "I don't know."

"Don't you live here?" he asked, dumbfounded as Hunter passed by to check on us.

"Chase?" Hunter laughed. "He only lives here. He doesn't go anywhere if it's more than walking distance from the Tilly."

I shrugged. "I'm a creature of habit, but this week has skewed my average."

"Do you know what the DuPuis Corbett Campsite is?" Jay asked Hunter.

"That's the DuPuis State Park. Lots of hiking trails between Okeechobee and the beach," Hunter said. "Chase wouldn't know because it doesn't involve boats."

"That's fair," I conceded.

"I bet there's a brochure or something at the concierge desk," Hunter pointed out.

A two-minute trip to the concierge earned me a brochure of the Dupuis Management Area, that offered hiking and equestrian trails with several primitive campsites.

"I'm betting it's this one," I said to Jay, pointing to the most remote campsite on the map. The little tent icon sat on the edge of the border of the DuPuis Management Area and the Corbett Wildlife Management Area.

"Smart," Jay commented. "It looks like the only way to get there is on foot. If we involve the police, then it might be obvious. He could disappear into those woods."

"What are you thinking?" I asked, watching the strategy working through his head.

"This is easily seven or eight miles of hiking from the road. You'll have to take the long way, but right here," he pointed to an intersection of roads on the map, "is only a mile or so as the crow flies."

"And a large canal," I pointed at the canal dredged from Lake Okeechobee. "Down here, if there's more than six inches of water, there's gonna be gators."

"Beats the sand," he said.

Hard to argue with that.

33

A constant low hum of nocturnal bugs communicating back and forth filled the dark around me. The only light among the tall pine trees was coming from half a moon shining in the southeast sky. It was enough that I was able to see the outline of the trail in front of me. I chose to park in an area five miles away from the trailhead that leads to the campsite. Taking the extra five miles on foot would, I hoped, prevent anyone from waiting to ambush me near the start of the trail.

A five-mile march was a piece of cake, and it would take me just short of an hour at most to cover it. Keeping 50 feet off the road at night made my approach invisible. When I reached the trailhead, I held my position for half an hour. No one came or went. Most hikers wouldn't be out after dark. They were all crowded around a campfire, letting the smoke drive the mosquitoes away.

Not me, I thought, as I lost count of the bites I was feeling. I was making my way with only a partial moon along the trail that would eventually lead to the Atlantic.

My eyes had adjusted to the dark, and while I couldn't

make out details, the sandy trail was almost illuminated by the lunar light. My pace was fast, but careful. The odds there could be a trap waiting to be sprung on me was still high enough to keep me wary. My steps were quiet, and very few would even see me pass in the dark.

The diamond necklace felt increasingly heavier in my pocket with each step. My hands felt for it every few seconds to comfort the paranoia it would somehow work its way loose from my pocket and become lost in these woods. The M45 in my waistband added a level of relief, knowing if someone decided to attempt to take the jewels, I would not hesitate to stop such an attempt in a second.

Jay had a two-hour head start on me. He spent a few minutes studying the map before he decided to have me drop him off on a dirt road only a mile or so from the campsite. By the time I made it to the entrance of the DuPuis Management Area, Jay had time to make his way to the campsite and burrow into a blind.

Unfortunately, we were going in under radio silence. Mainly because I didn't have any radios. There was no way to confirm Jay was in position. I just had to trust him and know Jay was there.

All of that was a given. There were only two or three other people on this earth who I warranted that kind of faith. All of them were Marines.

The luminescent arrows on the hands of my watch showed it was ten minutes to ten. Judging from the steps I was mentally tracking, the campsite should have been within a mile from my location. Give or take. It's a hard science judging distance in the dark.

My final approach would be the most dangerous. It would be an amateurish mistake on the kidnapper's part, but lying in wait for me near the finish would seem to be an easy move. Especially if he thought I was going to act like most people traversing an unknown forest at night. Most would be walking by flashlight. It would be like waiting for a lighthouse to come past. Hard to miss.

Predictability would get you killed. This kid already surprised me, and I had no intention of letting him do it again.

My plan was to get off the path as I neared the campsite and flank the kidnapper. The site was close enough that I decided it was time. Having studied the map before I stepped foot in the woods, I could use the moon and tiny compass attached to my wristwatch. It was a handy addition I used when I was diving; one I never expected to use in the woods.

The pine needles on the forest floor kept my shallow footsteps from making a sound. I felt like my feet were treading on carpet.

The trees still seemed to sing with the cacophony of an entomological orchestra. While the mosquitoes were steadily harvesting my blood, they were of lesser concern to me than other things. I could smell water, which as I pointed out to Jay, meant there were alligators. I have seen my fair share, and they are far more fascinating than frightening. However, in the dark, even a four-foot one might startle me. I didn't want to have to explain why I gave away my position while shooting an alligator.

The trees ahead began to show glimmers of light. I turned north to skirt the campsite. There were voices. Male and inaudible from where I was.

Using the trunks of the tall pine trees, I cloaked my approach. Even if the two men at the campsite were looking directly my way, I didn't think they would see me in the shadows.

These guys were definitely amateurs. They had a couple of flashlights with enough lumens to light up a ball field, and they were focused on the trail as it entered the campsite. Even from where I was standing with the M45 I had, I could easily drop them both before they knew what happened. That wasn't going to happen. Abbie was still a variable, and her safety was paramount.

I recognized the greasy kid that shot me immediately. The other man was older than me, and he seemed to be the one in charge. He made a few motions that were obvious orders, and the kid complied.

They had a tent set up behind them. I prayed Abbie was in the tent. If not, then...well, I didn't want to think of that.

Before I made a move, I wanted to set eyes on Abbie. Now, I was uncomfortable. If she was in the tent, I wouldn't be able to confirm she was safe when I made my approach.

I knew I had the advantage of Jay covering me. These guys didn't know that. Even with that, there was no point in leaving anything to chance. Once they knew the necklace was here, Abbie and I would become expendable. Better to ensure we didn't become that way.

Pulling the diamond necklace from my pocket, I took the Swiss Army knife I carried and stabbed the blade into the pine tree I was behind. The pendant hung gently on the knife. The diamonds caught the bits of lunar light and reflected them like stars.

"Hope I remember which tree," I muttered to myself.

I walked slowly to the edge of the woods. The kidnappers still had their backs to me. My feet moved slowly as I came up behind them. I considered checking the tent, but I worried I was taking too many chances. Better to roll the dice and take my turn.

My hand gripped the M45 and slipped it from my waistband.

"Where's the girl?" I asked sharply.

The greasy kid jerked in surprise and turned.

"Dammit," the older one swore.

"That's him," the greaser said.

I repeated, "Where's the girl?"

"Where's the necklace?" the kid asked.

"It's in the woods," I replied, "and if you even think about going for it, I'll drop you both."

The older one stated, "No need to worry. The girl is in the tent."

"Get her," I ordered.

The older man gave the kid a nod, and the kid moved toward the tent. The man twitched a little, and I knew he was carrying too. He wasn't going to pull, I figured. He'd let the kid do it while he was holding Abbie. He would assume my attention was drawn away and my concern for Abbie would stop me from shooting.

The strategy might not be a bad move for most people. Except I had years of training hammered into me. I was a dead shot, and I knew Jay had the guy's head in his crosshairs.

"Where's the diamonds?" the man asked.

"They are stashed in the woods. No more than fifty feet from you right now. As soon as you let the girl go, I'll point them out to you."

The kid reappeared with a very sleepy-looking Abbie. He was holding a Glock nine millimeter. The girl seemed to be trying to focus.

"Abbie, can you see me?" I asked.

She looked in my direction and nodded.

"Do you remember me?" I asked. "I'm Chase. I gave you some ice cream last week."

She nodded again. I glanced between the kid and the older guy, neither was making a move yet. They still didn't have the necklace, and they weren't about to lose it too soon.

"Are you hurt, Abbie?" I asked.

She shook her head.

"Good. I'm going to take you home to your mommy."

"Enough." The kid tightened his grip on Abbie. "Where's the necklace?"

"I'm just guessing," I said, "you're the one who killed Harold Goddard, right?"

"The necklace," he hissed sharply.

"Stay calm," the man warned him.

"What about Tristan?" I asked.

"Look, Mr. Gordon," the man said, "we just want the necklace, and everyone can get back to their lives."

"Tell me about Tristan," I prodded. "Which one of you killed him?"

The kid shifted his eyes to the man.

"Mistakes were made," the man admitted. "Let's get past this for now. We don't want anyone to get hurt."

"I think I figured the bones out," I said. "Tristan was down for some easy money, but murder was a line he didn't want to cross. He had debts though, and the necklace was more than enough to buy his way out of those. Of course, that didn't sit well with you two, did it?"

"Seriously," the kid snapped, "shut up."

The M45 was still trained on the older man. His eyes were wider, and he was starting to think he had underestimated the situation.

"Let the girl go," I urged. "She can start walking toward the trail."

"The necklace," the man replied sternly. "He'll let her go when I have it in my hands."

I smiled. Not a congenial one. I've been told I have an angry smile. While I've never seen it, I have heard it described as "scary."

"When he gets his greasy hands off her, I'll tell you."

The kid put the gun closer to Abbie's head.

"You truly are a shitheel," I growled at the kid. "You seem to only be able to kill old men and little girls."

The kid's eyes flared.

"He's baiting you," the man warned.

I shrugged. "Did you know Tristan well?" I asked the man.

He didn't answer.

"Guess not. He might have told you about us. Maybe you'd have thought twice about killing him."

"Us?" the man questioned.

I raised three fingers in the air. Then I did a silent countdown. Three. Two. One.

The man dropped to the ground as the slug from Jay's barrel tore through his kneecap.

The kid let go of Abbie and spun toward the woods. I shot him in the shoulder as soon as he turned the Glock away from Abbie. I rushed forward and swept her up in my arms before kicking the kid's gun away from him.

The man howled in pain, and I grabbed a .38 semi-automatic from his belt.

Abbie buried her head into my shoulder and had both of her hands over her ears. I carried her away from the two men writhing in the dirt.

"Hello, sweetie," I whispered to her when she looked up.

"Where's my mommy?" she begged.

"I'll take you to her," I promised. "She's worried about you."

Jay emerged from the trees. His face was dirty, and pieces of pine needles extruded from his hair. Abbie shook in my arms.

"Don't worry," I told her. "He's my friend. His name is Jay."

She straightened up in my arms to look at him.

"I don't like it here," she said.

"We'll get out of here," I told her. "I need to talk to Jay first."

34

A fter a short discussion where we considered, only for a moment, dropping the two of them into one of the canals bordering the wildlife management area, Jay strongly suggested we call the Palm Beach County Sheriff. Jay pointed out we might have a harder time explaining how Abbie was safely returned without dealing with law enforcement. Jay made the call while I split the two kidnappers up. Using some straps I cut from the tent, I tied both up. The older man, who turned out to be Tommy Evans according to his driver's license, wasn't going to be running anywhere. Neither of their escapes was of great concern for me. They wouldn't make a few feet with their injuries. I wanted to keep them separated, though. No point letting them make any plans or corroborating their stories.

I was guessing that Evans was likely the Tommy from Hometown Hardware, but at this point, he was refusing to talk to me, except to complain that I shot him in the knee and he'd never be able to walk again.

The kid didn't have any identification. He wasn't talking either, and really, I didn't care anymore. Abbie was safe, and

I still had a bit of a grudge against the kid for shooting me in the first place.

"They're sending a chopper," Jay told me when he hung up. "It's going to take a while for them to get here." He walked over and stood between me and Evans, who was still moaning about his knee.

"These guys picked a remote enough spot for a swap."

"Might be the only thing halfway smart they did," he said, staring at Tommy Evans. "Too bad they didn't think about the hundreds of acres of coverage surrounding them."

"How much trouble is this going to be?" I asked, holding onto Abbie's hand. The girl yawned and fidgeted around my feet.

"It's going to be hairy," he admitted, "but I hope my badge will smooth over some of it."

"I want to go home," she whined.

I squatted on my hindquarters beside her. "I'm going to get you to your mommy. It's going to be a few minutes, though."

The first deputies took almost an hour to reach us. Three side-by-side ATVs hummed through the trees. The light bars atop the roof lit up the campsite like it was the middle of the day. The buzz of the wildlife had been masked by the din of gas-powered motor noise. Overhead, the helicopter circled us a few times as they were waiting for confirmation the scene was secure enough to land.

Before the sheriff deputies got close, we had already placed the rifle and my M45 on the ground. Jay held onto his M45 and held his badge aloft until the first deputies came into the clearing.

"I'm a police officer," Jay shouted, waving his badge in the air as he tossed his pistol to the ground. Two deputies flanked us with their service weapons drawn.

Abbie stirred as I lowered myself to my knees. She had fallen asleep on my shoulder after we talked to her mother on the phone. During the hour we waited for the sheriff's department to arrive, I called Kayla to give her the good news.

"Kayla," I said into the phone. "I have Abbie."

"She's with you?" she exclaimed, relieved.

"Yes, she's safe," I assured her. "All she wants right now is her mommy."

Her tears were audible through the phone. "Oh, thank you, Chase," she muttered. "Thank you, thank you."

"I think she wants to talk to you," I said as I handed the phone to Abbie.

"Mommy," the girl said.

The girl talked to Kayla for several minutes before she handed the phone back to me. I couldn't make out what Kayla was saying, but I watched as the little round face nodded into the phone.

"Thank you so much, Chase," she blubbered when I got back on the line. "I don't know what I would have done."

"It's the least I can do. We may be a while, but I'll call you when I know where we end up. I expect the cops are going to want someone to talk to Abbie."

"I'll be right here," she promised before we disconnected. "Please don't let her out of your sight."

"I won't let go of her," I promised Kayla.

The nearest deputy attempted to take Abbie from my arms. I resisted, saying, "She stays with me until her mother gets here."

"We need to check her out," the older deputy told me. "Let me just give her a quick look."

"Let him," Jay told me. "Just stay with her."

The deputy and I exchanged glances, and he nodded his

approval to Jay's suggestion. I followed him to one of the side-by-sides and gently laid the sleeping girl on the seat. My back was against the ATV as the officer, whose name-plate read Jepson, looked her over.

"We have some paramedics on the way. She looks okay, but I'll have them check her out," he assured me.

From the ATV, I could hear as Jay began explaining everything that occurred to the other detective. A decision was made that he should do most of the talking. His badge might smooth out any legal indiscretions committed today. Every four to five minutes, Abbie would shift positions restlessly.

After he finished his initial statement to Deputy Jepson's partner, Jay walked over and stood next to me. He stared at Abbie's face.

"She looks like Tristan," he stated quietly.

I nodded. We both spent a few seconds quietly memorializing our brother.

Breaking the silence, Jay said, "They are taking the two of them out on the chopper for medical attention. The feds have a guy coming out since the management area falls under federal land."

"We certainly know how to complicate things," I commented in a hushed tone.

"The deputy offered to take her out in the chopper to meet her mother at the hospital. I explained that wasn't possible," he said.

While we stood by the ATV waiting, the deputy Jay had been talking to approached us and covered her with his jacket. "Try to keep the mosquitoes off her," he commented. "Don't want to get her back to her mother covered in bites."

"Thank you," I said.

"I'm Detective Jackson," he introduced himself when

we stepped away from the sleeping girl, leaving Jay to guard over her. Jackson was much older, nearing retirement, with thinning hair and a developing gut. He squinted through a pair of bifocals. "I want to get your story on all this."

"It's long," I started. Beginning with the day Kayla walked into the Manta Club, I filled in all the details for him.

When I finished, he asked, "You kept the necklace instead of turning it over to the West Palm PD?"

"I wasn't sure what it was. It was at the bottom of the ocean. I didn't know for sure it was a part of this for sure until Abbie was kidnapped. I didn't want to risk her life for a shiny piece of jewelry."

"But, you knew it was stolen when you spoke with the Goddards."

"Things started happening too fast then. Abbie was kidnapped, and I wasn't ready to give it back until I knew it couldn't save her."

"And when you got the demands for trading the diamonds for the girl, the two of you opted not to report it?"

"I did call the police," I said, "he's over there."

"He's out of his jurisdiction," Jackson squawked.

"We made a judgment call," I answered. "Jay could get in unseen to provide cover. This didn't need an entire SWAT team swarming the woods. I was concerned for Abbie's safety."

"I have to ask a question," he said. "Why didn't you two just kill them?"

I lifted an eyebrow out of curiosity.

He explained, "You were certain that Locke was involved in some bad shit. These guys probably killed him too. I thought you special forces guys might have a vendetta."

"I don't know," I said. "If we had, we could have saved a lot of time."

Jackson nodded. "And paperwork. If you fed them to the gators, I would be able to get off my shift on time and be in bed."

"For the sake of the girl and her mom," I told the detective, "this whole affair needed to end, and killing two men in front of a three-year-old girl wasn't going to help that."

"You still shot them in front of her," he stated.

"Yeah, but we didn't kill them," I pointed out. "That has to count for something."

Jackson glanced over at Jay, who was leaning against the ATV watching Abbie.

"He's a hell of a shot to hit the man's kneecap." His tone was full of admiration.

"The man's a natural," I commented.

"I knew some snipers in the Army," Jackson replied. "They were all a little off."

"Jay's a bit different," I told him. "He doesn't enjoy it. Never did. He didn't get the rush of power that some guys feel. Our whole unit was like that. We could kill, but we weren't killers. Maybe that's why we didn't kill them. There wasn't a need to. Vengeance wasn't going to bring back Tristan. If it was the only way to save Abbie, that would be different."

"Some deputies are on their way to retrieve Mrs. Locke. We'll bring her to the girl. You and Detective Delp are going to be held for more questioning. Don't plan to leave anytime soon."

I nodded an understanding. He walked away to talk to a pair of deputies preparing to accompany the injured men on the helicopter.

"What do you think?" I asked Jay.

"It's going to be a long couple of days," he said. "If the feds are involved, then there's going to be some territorial pulling back and forth. We get to be the bone these dogs fight over."

"Awesome," I mumbled under my breath.

"When it's all said and done, though," he said, "they won't level any charges against us. Too much hassle. The media would have a field day over two war heroes who risked their lives to save a child. Media nightmare. I'll probably get in some trouble back home, but we'll see. My captain was in the Corps years before us, so he understands."

"Sorry to drag you into it," I said.

"Eh," he waved me off. "Don't offend me. You know the game."

I motioned toward Detective Jackson. "He asked me why we didn't kill them."

Jay just shrugged. That seemed like enough of an answer.

35

H unter was more than happy when I was finally able to get back behind the bar. I felt like I owed him a few days off. He said something about heading to the beach when I said I could work.

Over the last twenty-four hours, I had been questioned and moved. After being questioned by Detective Jackson in the woods, Jay and I were held for questioning by two agents of the F.B.I. and a short, angry U.S. Fish & Wildlife Officer who refused to relinquish his chance to interfere.

Kayla showed up an hour after Detective Jackson said he sent for her. A deputy drove her in on another side-by-side ATV. She grabbed the sleeping girl up in her arms and kissed her until Abbie woke up. After five minutes or more of the mother and daughter reunion, she finally let go of Abbie and hugged Jay and me around our necks. The reunion didn't last long before the Locke girls were taken from the campsite, and we were left talking to the cops there. We endured the hours of interrogation both at the scene and later when we were transported to the sheriff's station. When the questions seemed to be repeating themselves for the fifth time, we were finally released around ten the next morning.

We hadn't heard a word from Kayla since then. The police may have her and Abbie tied up, or perhaps, the woman just took her daughter and ran back to her mother's house. I hoped the latter was the case. I'd check in with her in a few days if she didn't reach out.

When the detectives finally released us, Jay made a point to remind Detective Charles it was my actions that retrieved the stolen necklace, and the insurance company should consider the fact.

"Will it even matter?" I asked him in the car.

"The insurance companies are often happy to pay a finder's fee as opposed to the whole amount."

"It would only seem fair if we split it."

He shook his head. "I'm a cop. They don't tend to look too fondly on cops getting rewards for doing their jobs."

"If there is anything," I decided, "Let's just give it to Kayla. She could use the leg up."

Still somewhat dazed, I was jerked back to reality when I heard my name. Kristy stood at the server station, waiting for me to finish a couple of Walk-Me-Downs for a pair of young kids. They were legal, but only barely, Kristy told me. Not a surprise.

"I heard you were on the news this morning," she said as I handed her the two blue concoctions.

"I'm not surprised," I answered. Two news crews attempted to get a statement from me when we left the precinct this morning. I hadn't seen the coverage, but Missy already popped in to tell me there was some footage of me leaving the police department. Luckily, my name hadn't been mentioned.

With any luck, the news cycle would forget about me as soon as the next big thing happened.

"I want to hear what happened," she cooed at me. "We could grab a drink after work."

I smiled at her and stuck two paper straws in the blue cocktails without answering.

She returned my smile, and I guessed it took shooting someone to register as interesting to her.

I filled a bowl with the bar mix we serve. It was mostly a variety of peanuts and cereal bits. The mixture often made up my dinner if I was too busy to stop and eat a proper meal. I've thrived on handfuls of it chased by olives or maraschino cherries.

The full bowl of mix replaced Miller Lite's empty bowl on the backside of the bar. He was nursing the one beer and munching his way through the bar mix. Some days I'd be annoyed, but today I took it in stride.

Instead of being annoyed, I moved over to talk to Bombay Sapphire and tonic. She was a statuesque brunette in a neatly pressed jacket and blouse. I was guessing lawyer on the bartender's occupational roulette table.

"How's the drink?" I asked.

She glanced up from her phone, surprised she wasn't alone. She took a look at the few cubes of ice and mangled lime.

"I guess I'll have another."

When I returned to her, I found Jay sitting next to her. He was staying a few days in case the feds wanted to ask more questions. He was more than willing to take advantage of the few days off.

"Jay," I greeted him. "Beer?"

"Yeah, something on draft."

He started talking with Bombay Sapphire, and after I

dropped a Twisted Trunk Finn McCool in front of him, I left him to the presumed lawyer. Given his persistence, Jay would end up having dinner with her, or worse yet, she might end up being Mrs. Bombay Sapphire Delp.

When I saw Wilson Peterson walk in, I flagged him down.

"You dining alone?" I asked.

"Yeah, just a drink," he said, pulling a stool away from the bar.

"Before you sit down, come with me." Even I heard the ominous tone, but I didn't correct it.

Peterson's face contorted in confusion, but he obeyed and followed me out of the Manta and down the stairs.

"You're taking me to the bathroom?" he asked, with hints of curiosity and caution.

"Yeah," I replied.

Peterson watched me climb onto the toilet and pull the black backpack from the ceiling.

"Chase, what the hell is going on?" he insisted.

"I found your blackmailers," I told him, handing the bag to him.

"I told you not to." His voice was stern.

"I can keep it," I suggested, opening the bag.

He stared at the stacks of bills. "How did you do it?" he asked.

"It wasn't hard," I said. "In fact, I would guess you knew who they were."

"I..." he stammered.

"The video is on a flash drive in the bag," I told him. "I'm sure they won't bother you again."

"Did you watch it?" His voice trembled.

"I didn't watch it," I assured him. "I like you, Wilson, and I don't want to not like you."

His head bobbed like a toddler caught writing on the wall. He looked relieved.

"That being said," I continued. "I left them a little cash, besides what they may have spent, and a promise you wouldn't pursue them in any way."

He listened intently.

"Is that good?" I asked him.

"Yeah," he breathed quickly. He opened the bag and stared at the bundles of hundred-dollar bills. He pulled one out and handed it to me.

Staring at ten-thousand dollars in banded bills that could slip in my pocket made my mouth salivate. With the money I made off him so far and this wad of cash, I could spend a year or more away from land.

"This isn't a bribe," I told him. "Or any type of extortion."

"No it's not," he assured me. "You helped me out. Consider this payment for a service."

My hand gently wrapped around the stack of bills.

"I need to take this someplace," he said, holding up the bag.

"Yeah, I wouldn't feel too comfortable with it in my possession," I said, thinking about the other day when the kid was following me around.

Peterson scurried out of the restroom, leaving me alone and feeling a little dirtier than when I entered. I stuffed the cash into my pocket. It would wait until I could lock it up on *Carina* with the other seven grand Peterson gave me.

Jay and Bombay Sapphire were much closer and more intimate. She was ignoring her phone completely now.. I made another gin cocktail for her. The two were so engaged, she never registered me giving her another drink.

I passed around the bar to see Julio Moreno and Scar

sitting on the other side of the bar. I didn't see them come in, and I stiffened for a second.

"*Señor* Gordon," Moreno greeted me. "I would like a glass of Cabernet Sauvignon, please."

I glanced at Scar. "He's driving," Moreno explained.

He wasn't specific about what Cabernet he wanted, so I picked the highest-end Cab we had in the bar. He wasn't a boxed wine kind of guy, I was certain of that. I returned to the two men with the wine.

"Is there anything else I can get for you, Mr. Moreno?"

"I never suspected that you were a bartender," he commented. "Do you make a good *mojito*?"

"Damned good."

"I saw you on the news today," he said. "The little girl that was kidnapped? She was *Señor* Locke's *niña*?"

I didn't respond at first. I weighed how to handle the man. Eventually, I said, "Tristan's dead. Those two guys killed him."

Moreno nodded. "A shame," he said.

"I'm sorry about your money."

"It is the danger of doing business," Moreno contemplated. "Sometimes, there is a loss."

"I hope that his family won't be having any problems in the future." My tone was solemn with less than subtle hints of warning.

"No," he replied, "I don't foresee that happening. A man's mistakes should not fall on his children."

He sipped the wine. His face indicated he found it acceptable. "However, *Señor* Gordon," he said, "I have a proposition for you."

"I'm not looking for any new propositions," I said wistfully.

"Hear me out," he insisted. "You have shown you are

quite capable. Someone with your talents could make a great deal of money with me. I need someone dependable like you."

I smiled. "No, thank you."

"It would be much more money than you make mixing *mojitos*."

"I have no doubt," I said, "but if I screw up a drink here, the owner doesn't threaten to kill me if I don't pay for it."

"It's not like that," Moreno tried to explain.

"No, Mr. Moreno, it's pretty close. I like my life the way it is now. No need to complicate matters."

He shrugged. "If you ever find yourself in a different frame of mind, then you know where you can find me."

"Since we are on such good terms now," I joked, "I might come down to try the... What was it called? *Boliche*?"

He grinned and looked to Scar, whose face had been stone during the entire conversation. "He would like it, don't you think?"

Scar's head made one quick bob. I thought the henchman looked relieved I turned down Moreno's offer.

"*Señor* Gordon, you will be my guest," he said. "Anytime."

Moreno drank his wine in two large gulps. "We will be leaving, *Señor* Gordon."

"You might as well call me Chase," I told him.

"Chase," he repeated. He looked at Scar and said, "Pay the check, Esteban."

"No," I decided, "that glass is on me."

Moreno tilted his head in acknowledgment before standing. Scar tossed a folded bill onto the bar as they walked out of the exit facing the marina. I picked up the hundred-dollar bill from the bar. I had come to some unspoken agreement with Moreno. As long as there was no bad blood between us, I thought I could sleep better.

Two more tables came in while I was talking to Moreno, and Kristy was waiting on me to make drinks. I was midway through mixing a Moscow Mule when Missy stepped into the bar to survey the crowd. She gave the room a broad sweep with her eyes, but they settled on me. We exchanged half-smiles, and I turned to tray up the Mules and toss a half wedge of lime in each mug.

Want a little more Chase?
Get another chapter here that takes Chase back to a fateful night in Afghanistan.

PICK UP THE BOOK TWO IN THE CHASE GORDON SERIES

Dark Cay

Dark Cay

PRE-ORDER LONG SHOT
THE NEXT EXCITING CHASE GORDON BOOK

WANT A LITTLE MORE CHASE?

Subscribe to my Patreon for a new Chase Gordon short fiction every month.

OTHER BOOKS BY DOUGLAS PRATT

The Chase Gordon Tropical Thriller Series

Diamond Reef
Dark Cay
Deep Gold
Runaway Tide
Devil Water
White Coral
Shark Pass
Gator Alley
Havana Sunrise
Gulf Dreams
Red Light at Night
Green Flash
Dead Slow
Long Shot

OTHER BOOKS BY DOUGLAS PRATT

A Corsair Novel
La Playa de Los Muertos
Midnight Dance
Guerrilla Gold
Blood Trade

The Jay Delp Mystery Series
The Woman Under the Bridge
The Girl on the East Beach
The Body in the Bayou

OTHER BOOKS BY DOUGLAS PRATT

Max Sawyer Thriller Series
Blood Remembered

Baptism of Blood

Blood Stained

Crimson Blood

Blood River

Blood and Roses

Rikki Talens Adventure
Crossbones

Lost Cause

Lady Luck

Greene Wolfe Thriller (with Nicholas Harvey)

Missing in the Keys

Missing in Zanzibar

Missing in Hawaii

ABOUT THE AUTHOR

Douglas Pratt was born and raised in Memphis, Tennessee, Douglas is a graduate of the University of Memphis with a degree in Journalism, who now resides in Mason, Tennessee, or anywhere his sailboat takes him.

Visit the author's webpage at
http://www.douglas-pratt.com/

Printed in Dunstable, United Kingdom

70254961R00174